PITCH BLACK

ALSO BY ALEX GRAY

Never Somewhere Else

A Small Weeping

Shadows of Sounds

The Riverman

PITCH BLACK

Alex Gray

SPHERE

First published in Great Britain in 2008 by Sphere

A CIP catalogue record for this book
is available from the British Library.

ISBN 978-1-84744-068-6

Typeset in Caslon by M Rules
Printed and bound in Great Britain by
Clays Ltd, St Ives plc

Sphere
An imprint of
Little, Brown Book Group
100 Victoria Embankment
London EC4Y 0DY

An Hachette Livre UK Company

www.littlebrown.co.uk

This novel is dedicated to Donnie, with love.

We cannot change yesterday.
We can only make the most of today,
and look forward with hope toward tomorrow.

Inscription at the entrance to St Margaret's Chapel,
HMI Cornton Vale Prison, Stirling

Inspiring bold John Barleycorn!
What dangers thou canst make us scorn!
Wi' tippenny, we fear nae evil;
Wi' usquebae, we'll face the devil!

From 'Tam O' Shanter' by Robert Burns

KELVIN FOOTBALL CLUB

PERSONNEL

Kelvin FC Chairman: Patrick (Big Pat) Kennedy

Directors: Barbara Kennedy, Colin Sharpe, Jeffrey Mellis, Frank Devine

Kelvin FC Manager: Ron Clark

Assistant Manager: Neil Skinner

Coach: Alan (Ally) Stevenson

Club Doctor: Dr Willie Brown

Physiotherapist: Mary McCarty

Groundsman: Albert Little

Kitman: Jim Christie

Administrative Officer: Marie McPhail

Apprentice: Willie Penny

PLAYERS

Goalkeepers: Gordon (Gudgie) Carmichael; Craig Mitchell

Strikers: Leo Giannitrapani; Austin Woods; John McKinnery; Barry (Baz) Thomson

Mid-fielders: John Fleming; Simon Gaffney; Andy Sweeney (Captain); Hugh McGrory; Mark McCausland; Brian Finnegan; Donnie Douglas; Wolfgang Friedl; Jason White; Nicko Faulkner

Defenders: Ian Rammage; Rory Lynch; Kenny McSporran; Joe Henderson; Axel Rientjes; Davie Clark

(NB: Not all of these appear in the action of the novel.)

PROLOGUE

When the car rounded the corner of the road, she gasped. Up until now the cliffs on either side had masked the skyline so she was shocked by the streak of orange like a gash across the horizon in front of her, bleeding from the blackness. It took all her concentration to keep the vehicle from veering towards the sheer wall of rock on her left. A quick glance showed how near she'd come to clipping the kerb and she shuddered as the wheel turned under her grip. The slimy walls glowed with sudden reflected light; she'd been close enough to see tiny plant fronds uncurling from the cracks that ran up and down the cliff side.

It was better to slow down a little, let the fright of that panicked swerve subside before she dared take another look.

A huge sigh rose from her chest and she felt the tears prick under the sore places of her eyelids, which she'd rubbed constantly during the drive north. The reassuring hum of the engine and the straight road ahead gave her courage to turn her head a fraction.

Now she could make out dim hills, darker shapes against the ink-blue sky with its burgeoning shafts of dawnlight a beacon of hope.

Mornings had never felt like this before.

Here was a new day beginning and with it the excitement of a

1

million possibilities. It was like the first day of creation, newly-minted, given to her as a gift. All the other mornings of her life seemed to have begun with despair.

Her fingers were numb from gripping the steering wheel so tightly and she flexed first one hand then the other, slowing the car down so she could take peeks at the sky and the water. There was no artificial light here, just cat's eyes reflecting the full beam as she tried to keep to her side of the narrow road. Few vehicles had been travelling south on the opposite lane and her car seemed the only one taking this night-time route away from the city, so she gave a start when the lorry's shape appeared in the rear-view mirror. It rumbled behind her and she slowed down to let it pass. There was a swish of tyres and then the flanks of the lorry passed her by like a looming grey shadow. She watched it move away from her, then it cut back into the left lane after a decent interval. The sudden flash of the lorry's hazard warning lights thanked her for allowing it to overtake. She opened her eyes wide in surprise; when last had she been shown such courtesy? That it should be here in this lonely place and from an unseen stranger was surely a good omen. She must be on the right road.

Now the sky was lightening even more and pale grey clouds merged into the yellow patches above the horizon's rim.

A bird flew past, slowly winging its way inland, making her suddenly aware that there was life outside this cocoon of engine noise and road and gears. Just up ahead there was a black and white pole indicating a parking place, and she drove in and stopped.

She gave a half-turn to the ignition and rolled the window down, letting in a rush of cold air, then breathed deeply, closing her eyes for a moment against the gusts of wind. It was quiet but not silent. The first sound she heard was the lapping of water against the edge of the shore, like a living creature trying to break free from the deep masses that threatened to hold it back. She listened, mesmerised, then heard another sound, a peeping bird somewhere out of sight in the bushes, then an answering call further ahead. Straining her eyes did not help; the birds were invisible in this early light. The cool air chilled her skin and set her sneezing. A quick rummage in her jacket pocket found only used and still-sodden paper hankies so she sniffled instead, then rolled the window back up. There had been no time to look for her driving gloves before the journey so she tucked her fingers up into her sleeves to warm them, the way she'd done as a child.

A memory of her mother suddenly came back to her. It had been one of the days when she'd been brought home from school. The day had started out badly at home with a sore throat and difficulty eating her porridge, then became worse when no one had taken her seriously and she'd been forced out, to make the cold walk down to the bus stop. The shivers had begun as she'd sat wedged between a man in a big overcoat and a woman with sharp elbows; the only seats left on the bus were the bench seats facing the exit. Each time the doors of the bus had sighed open she'd been exposed to the cold air and had felt trickles of sweat against her flesh.

Later her mother had fetched her home with cuddles that she knew were born of remorse. She'd tucked her hands into Mum's coat pockets then, sitting on her knee as the bus trundled back out of the city.

Now Mum was long gone and her own children were simply memories of what might have been.

On the brightening horizon she could make out the colours on the distant hills, tweedy browns and greens with darker patches that told of clefts where waterfalls might run. She glanced at the fuel gauge. It was nearly empty. It was not a road she knew well but there must be a filling station at the next village. A signpost not far back had indicated it was only sixteen miles away. *Then what?* a little voice asked. She had no answer, just the knowledge that she had taken the only way she could. A bed and breakfast place, probably, once she had travelled further north. And it would be wise to take out more money from a cash machine if she could find one. After that she'd have to think about the long-term future. But not yet, not just yet.

Turning on the ignition, she released the handbrake and let the car roll back on to the road. The fresh air had woken up something inside her, a feeling that had become lost through all those months and years. How long had she been recoiling from that voice and those hands? Trying to avoid the blows and the weight of fear that had smothered so much of the woman she used to be. Now she felt like a girl again, a young, wild thing, free of any responsibilities with the whole world still to savour.

It was not yet tomorrow so there were still some hours before she needed to make her plans. So far, escape had been sufficient. What was behind her could be dealt with in time. His body would still be lying where she had let it fall. The blood would have congealed by now, and rigor would have stiffened his limbs. She had left no traces to tell a story, of that she was certain; nor were there any friends or family to come around enquiring about her. Perhaps there would be a call from the club in a few days, or maybe the smell of a decomposing body would alert a passing stranger. And if *she* should be found? If tomorrow brought questions and blame, then what would she do?

4

There was no easy answer. It was something she would think about later. Once the sun was high in the sky and the road had taken her into the wilderness. She yawned suddenly then felt her chest relax, her hands lighter on the steering wheel as the road disappeared under the twin beams. Shadows all around still shrouded the world.

Everything would be fine. It was not yet tomorrow, after all.

CHAPTER 1

The man trained his binoculars on the bird, his heart soaring with the sea eagle as its white tail feathers came into view, huge wings hardly moving, floating upon unseen currents of air. He watched the eagle fly into the distant haze until it was a mere speck, and then let his glasses fall with a sigh of pleasure. What a sight to see on their last day!

They'd decided to picnic in the Great Glen, making the most of the fine weather that had blessed their three-week holiday in Mull, and Lorimer had been scanning the skies hopefully all afternoon. Now he had that sighting and it was a treasured memory he could take back with him to the city.

'How many pairs are nesting this year? Did that fellow say?' Maggie asked him, her hand resting lightly on her husband's arm. Her gaze still followed that dot on the clouds, imagining the bird seeking some prey to take to its growing chicks.

'Gordon? He reckoned they had five pairs out at Torloisk this year. But nobody said anything about sea eagles over this way. Golden eagles, yes, but not these boys,' Lorimer replied, looking down at Maggie's earnest expression with a smile. 'Anyway, how about some food? I'm starving.'

Maggie wrenched her gaze away, thoughts of eagles fading as she looked down at their unopened hamper. It had been a good idea bringing it with them on holiday, especially to a self-catering cottage. Mary Grant had left the basics to start them off, but the old lady knew they'd want to stock up with local produce and so had left a list of suppliers from Craignure to Tobermory and beyond. It had been fun buying eggs and fresh vegetables from farms that were off the beaten track, finding other places of interest like the ancient stone broch while they were at it. Secretly Maggie suspected that was exactly what the old lady had in mind when she'd left the names and locations of out-of-the-way farms and crofts. But the main town on the island, Tobermory, had been the real treasure trove for picnics. Now Maggie unwrapped some rolls and handed one to her husband.

Lorimer leaned back against the grassy hillock and sighed. 'What a day. Imagine seeing that before we go home!'

Maggie, her mouth full of spicy chicken, nodded in agreement. It had been the perfect last day. Even the midges had left them alone for some reason: maybe it was that small wind stirring the bog cotton and bringing a scent of myrtle wafting towards them.

'Happy?'

She swallowed and smiled, nodding again. It had been a wonderful holiday, just the two of them exploring Mull together from their base at the cottage. They'd been content to live without the intrusion of radio, television or even newspapers; a real escape from the world outside. Even the West Coast weather had been kind, with almost no rain save an occasional nightly shower that had sprinkled the grass and kept it green. Tomorrow they'd pack up and catch the ferry from Fishnish then drive the long way round, making the most of their journey home. But for now they could bask in the sweetness of the Mull air, banishing any thoughts of returning to work.

Lorimer lay back against the soft, rabbit-cropped grass and

closed his eyes. It had taken the Detective Chief Inspector days to unwind, to forget that last, protracted murder case and now he was perfectly at peace with his world and his wife. In a matter of minutes his head tilted sideways and he began to snore softly.

Looking down at him, Maggie felt a tenderness that she had almost forgotten. How she loved this man! Yet there was an ache, a longing that sometimes surfaced. She thought again of that sea eagle carrying food to its chicks. That would never be her lot in life, she told herself. As a school teacher, Maggie had plenty of contact with kids and she was glad to leave *some* of them at the three-thirty bell. But there were others she'd have taken home in a minute, satisfying an empty space that she sometimes acknowledged to herself.

Maggie let her gaze wander over the hills and the ribbon of single-track road winding below them. They were so lucky to have had such a time here. What was she doing becoming wistful at what she couldn't have, when she should be grateful for all that life had given to her, she scolded herself. Then she looked back at her sleeping husband. He'd been such fun to be with these last three weeks. It was a shame it was coming to an end, but maybe there wouldn't be too much going on back in the world of Strathclyde Police. Or was that too much to hope for? After all, crime never seemed to take a holiday.

The cottage door closed with its now-familiar creak and Lorimer turned the key in the lock. Putting it carefully behind a lichen-covered stone where Mary Grant would find it, he picked up the final bag and strode towards the car where Maggie was busy sorting things into the boot. He took a last look at the whitewashed cottage and beyond: the gardens ran all the way down to the boat shed then petered out in clumps of reeds and small pools down by the shoreline. He and Maggie had scrambled over thrift-strewn rocks, stopping sometimes to look for seals out in the curving bay or listen to the seabirds' raucous delight as they dived for fish. Once, Maggie had whistled at a lone black head, coaxing it to swim nearer to shore, and it had, curious to find the source of her music. They'd been rewarded with a woofing bark then the seal had turned over lazily and disappeared beneath the dark blue water.

Lorimer took a last look at the Morvern hills basking in the sunshine across the Sound of Mull, a patchwork of yellows and greens that Maggie had tried to capture in watercolours. These three weeks had rejuvenated him, made him forget any evil that stalked the city streets. Under canopies of late night skies he had held Maggie close and gazed in wonder at the myriad stars and planets scattered across the heavens. Was there some hand at work in all of that? he'd wondered. On such nights it was not hard to believe in an almighty creator. They'd basked in the silence of the place, though by day it was full of birdsong, mainly the different species of warblers whose ubiquitous dun colouring made them nigh on impossible to identify without binoculars. And sheep, he reminded himself with a grin as a lone black face skittered along the cottage road, a panic-stricken *baah* emanating from deep within its throat. He was feeling fitter and leaner; every day they'd walked or climbed, every night he'd slept soundly, no anxious dreams disturbing his rest.

As they rounded the corner away from the bay, Lorimer heard Maggie give a small sigh. Taking her hand in his, he squeezed it gently.

'Maybe we could come back here next year?' he suggested and smiled as she grinned in pleasure at the thought.

*

A queue of traffic was waiting by the pier when they arrived. The ferry was usually right on schedule, they'd been warned, and space on this small craft was restricted.

'What's up?' Maggie nudged her husband and nodded towards a uniformed officer who was walking slowly down the line of cars, noting something on his clipboard.

'Maybe he's looking for that rainbow trout you guddled from the burn!' Lorimer joked. Maggie had tried catching fish with her bare hands after they had spent one interesting night staring out at the bay as silent poachers laid their illegal splash-nets at the mouth of the burn. They'd watched, entranced, at the pantomime being played out under a full, silvery moon. Mary Grant had hinted at such goings-on, telling how the local policeman always had a good sea trout for his dinner: a sort of reward for turning a blind eye. The fishing rights to the bay were quietly ignored by many of the locals, she'd told them. 'Better they get them than the seals!' she'd insisted.

Curious in spite of himself, Lorimer opened the car door and walked towards the policeman.

'What's up?' he asked, recognising the man as PC Gordon Urquhart, one of the team from the Royal Society for the Protection of Birds' Eagle Watch. They had been privileged to stay in a hide with the man for a whole morning, watching as an adult bird fed its growing chicks.

'Ach, there's been a report of some egg snatchers in the area. We've got their registration details but we have to check all cars coming on and off the island,' he explained. 'Not quite in your league, Chief Inspector,' the man grinned, recognising Lorimer.

Lorimer was about to reply but the familiar sound of Gordon's two-way radio made the policeman step away from him. He watched the other man's expression deepen; this was surely some business that far outweighed egg thieves?

As the island cop turned back in Lorimer's direction he was met with a pair questioning blue eyes.

'We've got some real trouble on our hands now!' he groaned. 'Got to pick up a woman coming off the next ferry,' he explained.

'Not an egg stealer, then?'

'No,' Gordon replied then stared at Lorimer as if seeing him properly for the first time. 'More in your line, sir.' He turned away and nodded at the car ferry making its way from Loch Aline.

'Looks like she's killed her husband.'

There was a dull thud as the metal hull of the boat made contact with the pier. Lorimer saw the ferrymen heave in the massive ropes, securing them to bollards on shore, then watched as one by one the cars made their tentative way down the metal ramp and on to the island. Urquhart stepped up to each one and smiled at the driver, his clipboard at the ready. Lorimer scanned every vehicle to see which one belonged to the murder suspect. He didn't have long to wait. A second officer appeared from the crowds and ushered a woman out of a dark green Ford then took her place at the driver's seat while Urquhart led her away.

As they passed him, the DCI caught a glimpse of shoulder-length blonde hair and a pale, haunted face. Perhaps it was his intent stare that drew her gaze but for a second the woman looked up and met his eyes before she disappeared into the waiting police car. But in that single glance he could see such suffering that he stepped back into the shadows. What was the story behind this face? He'd probably never know.

Lorimer turned to see Maggie waving frantically at him to come back to the car.

'Just in time!' Maggie scolded, as the line of cars moved off towards the ferry. 'What kept you anyway?'

'Oh, nothing,' Lorimer said. His curiosity was still unsatisfied but something stopped him confiding this incident to Maggie. It was unfair to burden his wife with anything that smacked of work, he told himself; if it was a murder case she'd see it in the papers soon enough.

Janis Faulkner sat staring at the floor. The cup of tea they had brought for her had long gone cold. Her stomach growled, reminding her that she hadn't eaten anything for hours, but the very thought of food made her feel sick. All these questions about Nicko! *When had she last seen her husband? What was she doing up here on Mull? Did she have a solicitor?* Only this last question had drawn any response from the woman and that was an open-mouthed 'Oh!' of surprise as if the enormity of her situation had only just dawned upon her. Now she sat slumped over the formica-topped table in Craignure Police Station, her eyes fixed on something that only she could see.

The woman shivered despite the stuffiness of the room. It had been madness to think she could find a way to escape. Every port in Scotland must have been on the lookout for her car once they'd found Nicko's body, even here on this island where she'd thought to find some kind of sanctuary. What could she say? How could she tell them what had really happened? And, anyway, who was going to believe her?

CHAPTER 2

FOOTBALL STAR FOUND DEAD

Police are today making inquiries into the sudden death of Nicko Faulkner, the new Kelvin mid-fielder, after Faulkner was found stabbed to death in his home in Glasgow early yesterday morning. The footballer, who had recently signed a contract with Kelvin FC, had been in the city during the last few weeks for pre-season training. Kelvin's new boss, Ron Clark, said, 'It is a terrible blow for the club as well as to Nicko's fans. Our condolences go to his loved ones.' Nicko was a well known player at Sunderland before his transfer to Kelvin. His had been a rags to riches tale: with no family to support him, Nicko had to struggle on his own as a youth footballer, but his skills soon earned him the respect of the English league clubs. He will probably be best remembered for his performance for England in the 2006 World Cup that earned him an England cap. Several Kelvin FC scarves and bunches of flowers were left today outside the club's gate as a mark of respect.

A woman is said to be helping police with their inquiries.

Tom Cairns, *Gazette*

Lorimer folded the Sunday paper. So that was one part of the story. He looked thoughtful. Perhaps the other part was waiting for him down at police headquarters. As the phone rang out, some sixth sense told Lorimer that this last day of his holiday was going to be cut short.

'Lorimer?' He listened as the familiar nasal twang of his boss set his teeth on edge. The superintendent was telling him exactly what he didn't want to hear; his presence was required at the Division. Yesterday would have been preferable, Mitchison grumbled, but now would just have to suffice. Officers were being deployed at the anti-war riots that had broken out in Edinburgh and Glasgow. And now he had this case on his hands. As his grip on the phone tightened, Lorimer wished the man would just tell him to shift his backside and get over there. It would have been easier than having to listen to his polished vowels and thinly disguised contempt. He hung up, biting his lip. Maggie wouldn't be too pleased. But as he thought about his swift return to the job, Lorimer realised that there was a quickening inside him that was not annoyance at all, but rather anticipation. Just what was he going to find out about Nicko Faulkner's murder?

'See you later!' His voice echoed along the sunlit hallway as Maggie heard her husband leave. With a sigh she contemplated the rest of the day; it stretched ahead like an empty canvas for her to colour as she chose. Well, she thought wryly, there was always another load of washing to put out on the line. The warm July weather still held and she had already pegged out their holiday bed linen. Maybe it would be dry for ironing by now? There was plenty to fill the hours till Bill returned home, whenever that might be. The prospect of a half-finished paperback and a lazy lie on the sun lounger was a more tempting prospect, she thought to herself as she grinned and sauntered out into the back garden.

Maggie felt the sheets; they were dry, right enough. She unpegged and folded them, and dumped them into the laundry basket. Just as she bent over to pick it up, a flash of something orange moved in the shrubbery. Maggie froze. Was it a fox? The garden, unkempt at the best of times, had become wildly over-grown in their absence. Could the creature, whatever it was, be lurking in some den of its own making? She remained motionless, eyes fixed on the spot where she'd seen the animal. Had it been her overactive imagination? Had the weeks of training binoculars on island wildlife made her think that every movement in the long grass was a wild animal?

The strain of holding the basket full of washing proved too much and Maggie let it sink into the uncut lawn with a groan. At that moment the animal shot out from under a trailing buddleia and bolted straight into the house.

It was a ginger cat. With a sigh of relief that was tinged with annoyance, Maggie followed the intruder indoors. Goodness knows what mess it might make. She dumped the laundry on to the nearest worktop. There was no sign of the cat.

'Here, puss. Here pussy pussy,' she called softly. Then, as if bidden by her voice, the animal emerged from behind the dining-room door.

It padded lightly towards her, regarding her with what Maggie could only later describe as a smile on its ginger face. The cat came right up, rubbing its head against her legs. The feel of its soft fur on her skin made her crouch down, instinctively returning the gesture by scratching behind the creature's ears. A low growl of pleasure emanated from the cat's throat, then it began to purr.

'Hey, where did you come from, fellow?' she asked, smoothing the animal's coat. It moved away with a little cry as Maggie's fingers touched a lump on its back. 'Someone hurt you, pet?' Maggie whispered. The cat returned to her side as she spoke, eyeing her thoughtfully. 'Would a wee drink of milk make you feel better?' She stood up slowly, half expecting the cat to bolt out of the kitchen but instead it followed her to the fridge where it sat, gazing longingly.

Maggie watched, bemused, as the cat lapped daintily from the saucer then looked up expectantly when the dish was clean.

'You are hungry, aren't you?' Maggie said. The animal gave a clear meow, as if it understood what she meant. Green eyes followed her to the larder and watched as she pulled a tin of tuna from the top shelf.

'Fancy this, then?'

The cat kept a small distance while Maggie filled the saucer but as soon as she stepped aside, its head was over the food, eating hungrily.

Again the dish was wiped clean so Maggie refilled it and waited until the cat had finished the whole tin. He stretched, sat down in a spot of sunlight and began to lick his amber fur as if this was something he performed every day in the Lorimers' kitchen.

Watching him, Maggie wondered. Had he been coming into the garden in their absence? Was he a stray? And what on earth had happened to his poor sore back? Maggie knew most of the neighbouring moggies by sight but this fellow was a stranger to her. Maybe the local vet could help? But as it was Sunday that would have to wait until tomorrow. Meanwhile, she'd stick to her plan and fetch out the sun lounger and her paperback.

There was something infinitely sensual about lying under the parasol, a sleeping cat nestled into the crook of her arm. It was a sensation she could happily live with. Perhaps the cat was a stray and needed a good home, a little voice suggested. Maggie smiled. She wouldn't mind. And besides, there was little she could do until tomorrow. Surely Bill wouldn't begrudge her the cat's company for one night? It probably belonged to someone nearby, anyway, and would make its own way home before the day was over. The thought of the animal wandering off again troubled her and she knew with a pang that some indefinable bond had been created between them. In the space of a few hours Maggie Lorimer had fallen under a spell and was now bewitched by the little creature. Her hand stroked the soft ginger fur and the cat stretched in its sleep, one languid paw coming to rest on Maggie's arm.

CHAPTER 3

The dust motes swirled round, captured in the one beam of light that filtered through a gap in the blinds. Behind him an insect buzzed drowsily against the window, seeking to escape from the confines of the room. Listening to its feeble struggles, Lorimer felt some empathy for the tiny creature. At that moment he would have given a great deal to walk out into the warm air of the city streets. Before him on the videoscreen were pictures of the deceased, not happy snaps at all. The scene-of-crime photographer had managed to convey each and every aspect of the man's death, from the bread knife sticking out of his chest cavity to the open-mouthed grimace portraying that final scream of agony. Close-ups of blood spatters surrounded the main pictures, adding graphically to the image.

'It was hot,' Mitchison commented, somewhat unnecessarily, releasing the stills and letting the film pan in on the body. The black patches around the wound showed a moving mass of flies. Lorimer could almost smell the scent of corruption and was glad for once that he had not been first on the scene. But now Mitchison's peremptory call had stolen the final day of Lorimer's break and he had to be brought up to speed if he were to take charge of this case.

'We've got the woman in custody and she'll appear in court in the morning,' the superintendent began, 'but there are some problems.'

Lorimer raised his eyebrows.

'She says she didn't do it, of course, despite the fact she drove all the way up to the Hebrides . . .' Mitchison's drawl tailed off.

'So, the problems are . . . ?'

'We need to have some forensic evidence to connect her to the crime. There's been nothing on her person and we couldn't find anything else in the house. Either she was extremely forensically aware and managed to remove any traces of blood from the scene, or she's telling us the truth.'

Lorimer, fixing his gaze on the images of a man who had bled to death, wondered what had provoked the attack. 'What's your own opinion, sir?'

Mitchison frowned. 'She certainly had the means to do it. There was a huge rack of knives on one of those magnetic strips. It was one of these that was the murder weapon. No prints, I'm afraid. No residual traces, either. And the door was locked. There was no sign of a forced entry.'

'Just circumstantial evidence, then?'

Mitchison nodded and screwed up his eyes in the half-light, then blinked. He'd probably been working through the night, Lorimer realised.

Method, means and opportunity, a familiar voice intoned in Lorimer's head. It had been old George's mantra. A wave of nostalgia for his former boss washed over him just then. Weary or not, George would never have delegated a case like this. He'd have ferreted away at it, looking for something more than the obvious. Though a runaway wife was a fairly obvious place to begin, Lorimer had to admit to himself. The method was straight-forward enough and, despite his level of athleticism, the victim might

22

have been taken by complete surprise. His expression alone was testament to that theory. She'd had the means easily to hand. And the opportunity? Who could say? Knife attacks were usually random affairs undertaken in a moment of frenzy.

'What d'you reckon, then? A domestic gone wrong?'

The super made a face. 'Janis Faulkner's saying nothing. No plea for mitigating circumstances. Just a persistent refusal to admit she'd had anything to do with her husband's death.'

'Anything else suspicious?'

Mitchison paused for a moment then looked past Lorimer. 'What would I call it? A strange absence of grief, I suppose.'

Lorimer gave a non-committal shrug. You couldn't charge the woman for failing to mourn her dead husband, but still ... His thoughts wandered for a moment to the sight of Janis Faulkner's face as she'd glanced up at him on Fishnish pier. Had she been showing remorse? That haunted look had stayed with him since he'd seen her yesterday.

'What do we know about her own movements before she scarpered?'

'Says she was down at the gym. We've checked and her signing in and out times tally with her story. But as for simply setting off afterwards and not returning home first, well that was fairly unlikely, don't you think? A few rounds on an exercise bike then she suddenly decides to leave her husband. It doesn't make sense.'

'So she'll be charged?'

'Yes, first thing tomorrow. There's not another shred of evidence to show anyone else was in the house. I don't care what Janis Faulkner claims; she did it, all right.'

Lorimer looked at his boss. The vehemence in Mitchison's tone surprised him. Or was it simply that he was afraid Lorimer would see things in a different light, take away his prime suspect and cause problems? There was a past between these two senior officers that had never been adequately resolved. Mitchison had been promoted to superintendent when everyone's expectations had been on Lorimer stepping into his old boss's shoes, but it was their different attitudes to police work that had been the real cause of friction between them. Mitchison did everything by the rule book, creating masses of paperwork for everyone, while his DCI preferred a more hands-on approach. Lorimer remained silent. He was being officially designated as SIO and unless something new emerged, Janis Faulkner's guilt or otherwise remained a matter for the jury.

'Her solicitor is bound to ask for bail to be granted, pending a full investigation. We'll see what happens in court tomorrow, but I have my doubts.' Mitchison passed over the case file. 'Don't expect you'll have too much bother with this one.'

Famous last words, Lorimer told himself as Mitchison left the room. Whether it was that quirk of fate placing him at the scene of her arrest on Mull or the victim's high profile, the DCI had a strong feeling that this case was going to be anything but straightforward.

The woman had been brought back from Mull and placed in the police cells for one more night until she could be brought to court and officially charged with Nicko Faulkner's murder. Lorimer waited outside as the duty officer unlocked the cell and stood aside. The first thing he noticed was the smell. It wafted towards him, a mixture of stale sweat and something more pungent that he recognised as menstrual blood. He'd smelt it before from women banged up over long weekends without any facilities to shower or change their clothes. Janis Faulkner was sitting in a corner of the

24

bunk, feet together, head down and clutching her stomach. A movement as the cell door was opening made him realise she had looked up for a split second but now her expression was hidden under that curtain of damp hair.

'Anyone thought to give her some paracetamol?' he asked the uniformed officer.

'Hasn't asked for it,' the man shrugged. 'What's she want it for anyway?'

'Just go and get some,' Lorimer told him, 'and a drink of cold water.' He let the man close the cell door behind them and stood waiting for the woman to look his way.

'Feeling bad?' he asked, as if she were an old acquaintance and not a stranger who was also his prisoner. He heard the sigh first, then Janis raised her head and looked at him. There was a brightness in her eyes that spoke of unshed tears. Her little nod and a flicker of recognition were all Lorimer needed to know he'd begun to win her confidence.

The door clanged open and the uniform strode in, proffering a tumbler of water and a strip of foil containing two painkillers. Both men watched as she unwrapped them, her fingers shaking as she clutched the glass and tilted back her head, then swallowed.

'Thanks,' she said, her voice hoarse. But it was to Lorimer that she spoke, to Lorimer that she handed back the empty tumbler.

'You'll have been told that we have to keep you here till tomorrow?' he asked quietly, a hint of apology in his voice. She nodded again, but her head had drooped once more and Lorimer sensed she was withdrawing into herself, just as Mitchison had described. 'You can talk to me if you want to,' he told her. There was no response at all this time and as the minutes ticked past he realised that there was little point in trying any longer.

25

As he turned to leave, the silence inside that cell was redolent of misery.

'Hi, anybody home?' Lorimer shut the door behind him. As if in answer, a questioning meow came from somewhere near his feet and he looked down to see a ginger cat regarding him with interest.

'Maggie! There's a cat in the—'

'I know, I know. It's okay. He's just staying over for a bit.' Maggie was there, smiling at him from the kitchen doorway, one eyebrow arched in amusement.

'*He*? Who does he belong to?' Lorimer was already hunkering down to the cat's own level. A tentative outstretched hand was met with a furry rubbing against his fingers and the beginnings of a purr. As he began to stroke the soft pelt, the cat reared up slightly, butting its head on Lorimer's knee.

'Friendly enough, I'll say that for him. Where did it come from?'

'Ah.' Maggie came into the room and perched sideways on a chair, swinging her bare tanned legs. 'Now that's a good question, Chief Inspector,' she began pertly. 'Don't actually know yet. He just appeared in the garden and he's been with me all afternoon.'

'It must belong to somebody, surely? I mean, look at the coat, it's in good condition.'

'He was really hungry, though. You should've seen the way he wolfed down a whole tin of tuna. Must have been starving, eh, boy?' Maggie slipped off the chair and knelt down beside them. At the sound of her voice the cat turned its attentions from Lorimer and began rubbing the side of its face on Maggie's ankles.

'Well, seems he knows which side his bread's buttered on,' Lorimer muttered.

26

The cat shifted suddenly and sat, looking at him with green, unwavering eyes. It's waiting for me to make the next move, Lorimer thought, recognising a tactic he often employed himself. He was aware of Maggie keeping very still, holding her breath. The ginger cat continued to stare at him, its front paws neatly together. A sigh came from Lorimer's chest, breaking the spell, and he reached out and picked up the animal, cuddling it closely. Burying his face into the warm fur, he felt the thrum of purrs reverberate into his chest.

'Looks like we've got an overnight guest, then,' he murmured and looked up to catch Maggie's grin. *You're as big a softy as me*, her look seemed to say.

'I'll phone the local vet tomorrow, see if anyone's lost him. You never know, he might be microchipped.'

'And if nobody claims him?' Lorimer's question hung in the air.

'Well, I thought . . .' Maggie's eyes were on him, beseeching. 'We can't send him to a cat rescue place. Imagine being banged up in this weather.'

Lorimer had a vision of Janis Faulkner's face. She was incarcerated now on this hot July evening and Lorimer had a sudden urge to release her back into the wilds of Mull to wherever she had been going. As if aware of the change in his mood, the cat slipped out of his arms and strolled towards the kitchen and the open back door.

CHAPTER 4

Staying still had its advantages. If she did try to change position then the numbness in her limbs would wear off and she might remember what it felt like to be alive. That moment by the lochside, when the fresh morning breeze had wakened something inside her, seemed to be from a different age now, not a mere couple of days ago. She'd travelled up to Oban with a renewed sense of purpose; Lachie had said to come up any time. Why not? she'd asked herself. It would have given her a little respite, time to lick her wounds. Her mouth curled into a sardonic smile. Some wounds never healed. A little sigh escaped her and one leg moved as if of its own volition.

The springs of the other bed creaked, only inches from her face, and Janis froze. What if the woman were to wake up and try to engage her in conversation again? She might be a plant, for all Janis knew. Okay, her imagination was working overtime but she had reason enough to be paranoid. Running away from it all hadn't been the answer; it had only delayed the inevitable. Now silence seemed to be her only option. Silence here and now in this cell where the only sound was of another person's breathing; silence before all of their questions. She'd learned a long time ago to switch off her emotions. Nicko had been an unwitting teacher, not beating her into submission so much as driving her out of the place where everything hurt. It was a trick she could manage whenever things became too much, slipping into that other place where no voices could reach her, no eyes force her to face what she had chosen not to face ever again. They'd all tried already; a female solicitor they'd dug up from somewhere – a whey-faced woman with untidy hair escaping from a failed attempt at a French pleat – the police who had pressed her with questions for hours and now these prison officers with concern in their eyes and bunches of keys inside their pockets.

Janis sighed, remembering. They had looked at her with suspicion as if she was some sort of threat. Not to them, but to herself. She had seen the exchanged glances, heard the concern in the nurse's voice as she asked her, 'Are you feeling suicidal? Do you feel you might hurt yourself?' She wanted to say she was feeling just fine, thank you, never better, but as Janis lay there in the darkened cell, she knew that was a lie.

A rasping noise alerted her to the viewing hatch being lifted and she could imagine one eye pressed up against it, checking to see that she was all right. Holding her breath, Janis waited until the square flap was shut once more. They were watching her, waiting for her to make a mistake. But she wouldn't do that, she couldn't.

She'd endured the humiliation of being stripped and searched but the journey here had been the worst bit, Janis decided, remembering how she'd sat with knees bent in that dog box. At least they'd taken off the handcuffs once she was in the van, the bus, whatever it was. She couldn't remember these details. And then there was that other girl travelling with her, talking all the time. Desperate for Janis to answer her back, the girl had rambled on about how the *system* worked. Janis had pretended to ignore her fellow prisoner, aware of the officer listening to the girl's voice going on and on. But, as they'd been taken out from the prison transporter, she'd heard a whisper at her back, '*Dinna laugh or they'll think ye're on drugs. Dinna cry or they'll think ye're a psycho.*'

The young girl's words stayed with her now, like a mantra: *dinna laugh, dinna cry* . . .

'Janis Faulkner? Not a lot from background reports, I'm afraid.' The voice on the telephone sounded slightly apologetic. 'No criminal record. Very little to go on if her lawyer is looking to plead temporary insanity. But we have been keeping her under observation.'

Detective Chief Inspector Lorimer shook his head. There was something about the woman that troubled him. A plain old fashioned admission of guilt tempered with a good enough reason for her actions was what he was really after, but this strange refusal to speak did smack of something deeper. Was it more than simple shock at seeing a person fall dead at her feet? It was as if she'd reneged on any kind of human communication, the mental health nurse had told him. Maybe she was genuinely unbalanced, but she had driven away, she had taken money out of an ATM as if there had been some calculation in her thoughts and actions. Her psychological assessments were expected later this week. Now, having obtained the necessary permission from the Procurator Fiscal, he was going to drive out to the prison in Stirling to see her once again.

Cornton Vale women's prison had suffered badly at the hands of the press. A spate of suicides several years back had given the tabloids the opportunity to rubbish the institution and yet there had been several innovative and far-sighted changes over the years. But the institution itself continued to be a target for any adverse comments, with some liberal thinkers even suggesting that a women's prison was not a requirement of any civilised society. They hadn't seen the inmates, thought Lorimer. Many of them were in thrall to drugs, had been since late childhood, following a pattern that had become too well established within family circles. Half a century before they'd have been taught to knit at their mammy's knee, now it was a different sort of needle that took their attention and for some of them the prison was the only place where they could actually come off drugs. The staff included some pretty special people as he knew from his visits; it took a strong heart to cope with the variety of humankind that came and went.

Set in a housing estate on the outskirts of Stirling, one could be forgiven for thinking that this HMI establishment was in fact a continuation of the rows of white, pebble-dashed terraces. Lorimer parked the Lexus and walked back towards the main entrance, ready for the necessary measures that always accompanied such visits.

Janis Faulkner was waiting for him in a little room adjacent to the reception.

'Janis, this is Detective Chief Inspector Lorimer. He's the senior investigating officer in your husband's case.' The female prison officer made the introductions, her voice gentle, reminding Lorimer of that tone reserved for the bereaved, the grieving, but Janis Faulkner did not look as if it was grief that troubled her. That tense face was closed against something else, Lorimer thought. The female officer sat in a corner, her duty to ensure that the prisoner remained safe from this policeman and his questions. Admittedly, it was pretty unusual for the senior investigating officer in a case to actually visit the prison, but Lorimer felt they saw him as an interloper. That was not how he wanted Janis Faulkner

32

to see him, though why he was so bothered about her opinion he wasn't entirely certain.

'Janis?' he began, bending his head to see beneath the woman's fringe of fine, blonde hair. It reminded him of a child's hair and he wanted to touch it, to sweep it from her brow and take that heart-shaped face in his hands and tell her that everything was all right. But years of experience made him resist such impulses, knowing that they came from sheer pity.

She sat staring at the floor, her hands clasped together, unmoving. If there was an expression on that pale face it was impossible to read.

'Do you remember me?' Lorimer tried again. 'I was in Mull, waiting for the ferry as you arrived. Just coming home from my holidays . . . then we met in Glasgow . . .' He tailed off. For an instant her head was raised and a pair of grey eyes regarded him as if from far away. There was a flicker of recognition then the merest nod of her head before she relapsed into her study of the linoleum. Lorimer looked at the prison officer who gave an exaggerated shrug as if to tell him he was wasting his time.

'Hasn't your lawyer told you things will be much easier if you write a confession? Pleading guilty when the case comes up for trial can affect the sentence dramatically. Especially for a first offender,' he wheedled. But the woman made no response at all and Lorimer suppressed a sigh. He'd wondered about her state of mind on the day her husband was killed. She could have been pre-menstrual. There were plenty of cases where women had flipped under a rage of extreme hormones to attack their husbands. And some of them had been given fairly light sentences. Should he mention that yet? Probably not. But he might talk to the psychiatric doctor over in the medical wing. See what she thought.

Lorimer studied the woman in front of him. Her unexpressed misery seemed to fill the room. Could there be any possibility that she was in fact not guilty of this crime?

'Maybe you can tell us who you think killed Nicko?' he muttered, his voice barely reaching the officer. Janis Faulkner did not move but Lorimer felt her stiffen and for a few seconds he waited.

'Janis?' His voice was gentle, the tone reserved for calming a wild creature that had started from the undergrowth and stood caught between fear and flight. Only there was no flight for this young thing, he thought, unless she had already escaped to some distant place deep within her self. 'Janis? I'd really like to help you,' Lorimer said softly, but he sensed that she had left the room already, only her physical presence remained, and that he was speaking to himself.

—'If you change your mind,' he told her, slipping his card across the dark wooden table that divided them. 'I can always listen.'

CHAPTER 5

'We can't keep the media at bay for ever,' Ron Clark insisted. 'There's going to be a lot of speculation now they know that it's his wife. Why not simply hold a press conference now and get it over with?'

The man sitting hunched beside him on the empty terracing did not speak. His eyes wandered over Kelvin's grounds, visual-ising his team out there in the new season's strips: white shirts with a diagonal black band. It was an irony now. They'd have to issue black armbands for the opening match. He gritted his teeth. Faulkner would have raised their profile for a bit, put the wind up some of the clubs in their league, he thought. Even if the mid-fielder was a bit long in the tooth, they had bought him knowing he had still some mileage left, and some charisma too, he nodded silently to himself, remembering the man's roguish eyes and the engaging way he'd spoken with all of the backroom staff the day he'd signed for Kelvin. Letters and cards of sympathy had been received from his ex-club mates in Sunderland, all saying the same thing: how he'd been such a well-liked lad . . .

'Pat?' Clark's voice penetrated the chairman's thoughts, ban-ishing that vision of his new team. 'Look, I know Nicko's murder's been a helluva shock, but we need to say something. Even if it's just to tell them how devastated we all are.'

Patrick Kennedy sighed resolutely. 'Okay. But you talk to them, will you? Say we are being supportive of the family. Keep it vague. Don't mention anything about the wife if you can help it. And . . .' he paused for a moment, 'see if you can turn the spotlight on to Jason White.' Kennedy nodded to himself. That might be a good tactic. Concentrating on their other new signing so soon after Nicko's death might deflect attention from the bloodiness of it all, and White, with his nightclubbing lifestyle, was a potential headline grabber for quite different reasons.

'Ach, well, it's that time of year. Everyone's busy with new faces. Maybe this will all blow over once the season begins.'

'It had better,' Kennedy replied shortly. There was too much riding on this new team of his. What he really didn't need was a backlash from the fans or a slip in the team's morale. Support was required from every angle and it was Kennedy's job to see that it was forthcoming. Ron could handle the press. He'd been hired after the sacking of their previous manager when they'd suffered the ignominy of relegation. Ron Clark had come to Kelvin with an excellent track record and the respect of many in the world of sport. Kennedy trusted this man to put his message across.

The chairman of Kelvin FC stood up heavily, still gazing at the rows of empty seating. Alone at one end of the pitch was Kelvin's trusty groundsman, Albert Little. Kennedy watched him in the process of fixing new netting to one of the goalposts. Wee Bert, as everybody knew him, was ferociously dedicated to the club; not a pin would be out of place, not a striped line wavering when the turf was cut. Even today, under the hot July sun, the man was concentrating on his task with the kind of dedication that had won him the trophy for best groundsman in the Scottish Premier League in three consecutive seasons, a feat of which he was rightly proud. The chairman's eyes passed from one end of the park to the other, then, with his mouth closed in a determined line as if he had reached some unspoken decision, Patrick Kennedy made his way back down from the directors' box to the darkened passages that led into the club.

The cement steps echoed under his shoes and he glanced down at his feet, noticing the gleam of polish on black leather. Attention to detail, he'd told his players season after season, then repeated it to the string of managers who had come and gone from the club. As he walked out of the sunlight into the shadows, Kennedy passed a hand over his hair. It was thinning now but that didn't prevent him from having it groomed by the best stylist in Glasgow. Attention to detail, that's what made all the difference. If Janis Faulkner had killed Nicko then maybe the media would focus less on the club and more on the footballer, his wife and his background.

The last thing Kennedy wanted was a lot of journalists sitting on his doorstep, digging for dirt.

Maggie gave a deep sigh. Usually her husband's first week back at work after their summer holiday made her feel oddly bereft, what with his enormous backlog of emails and catching up in general, but today would be different. She peeked at the cat carrier on the passenger seat beside her, borrowed from a neighbour. The ginger cat was sitting sphinx-like, his paws tucked underneath his body. He'd slept outside somewhere but at the first sound of the back door opening he'd trotted into the kitchen, tail erect, greeting Maggie with a little meow of recognition. Now he stared ahead, quiet and alert. He must be used to cars, Maggie told herself; he must belong to somebody. She tightened her lips in resignation at the inevitable. They'd be bound to find the owner and give him back, wouldn't they?

The vet's surgery was situated in a small, pretty bungalow on a street full of similar residential homes. Maggie turned into the drive where a car park had long since replaced the original large front garden.

'Right, out you come,' she said and the cat gave a quizzical cry as it was lifted off the seat.

Inside, the reception area smelt of disinfectant and a draught of cold air came from a passage beyond the front desk, making Maggie shiver.

'Mrs Lorimer,' she told the girl behind the counter.

'Oh, yes, the stray cat. Just take a seat in the waiting room, Mrs Lorimer. The vet will see you shortly. Can you fill in this form while you're waiting, please?' The girl handed Maggie a black clipboard with a pen and paper attached.

The waiting room was empty of other pets and their owners, thanks to the appointment system and, Maggie told herself, the holiday season. But there was a large aviary in one corner of the room housing a pair of brightly coloured budgies; their squawking soon had the cat on its feet, head craning forward, a low growl issuing from its throat.

'Behave,' Maggie told him. 'You've to be good, now.' Then she sighed at such a proprietorial remark. What did it matter if he growled or not? She'd not have any say in his behaviour for much longer.

The radio was playing an old Abba number and Maggie found herself singing along as she drove home. The vet had promised to put up notices about the cat (who was not chipped and had not been a previous patient) and had given the animal a thorough examination. The sore back was the result of a dog bite, the vet had reckoned, showing Maggie a tiny hole puncturing the flesh.

He'd given her antibiotics for the cat, who had purred and wrapped his front paws lovingly around the vet's neck as he'd lifted him on to the scales.

'Lovely puss,' he'd laughed. 'Glad you've found a good home,' he'd added approvingly as Maggie had placed the animal carefully back into the plastic carrier.

'D'you think we could keep him if the owners don't turn up?' she'd asked.

'No reason why not,' he'd replied. 'But bring him back in for his injections if nobody claims him. He's been somebody's pet at one time. Been spayed, coat's not in a bad condition. Maybe you'll be lucky and find his owners. Or,' he'd grinned at Maggie's expression, 'maybe you'll be luckier and *not* find them at all.'

It was late when her husband finally reached home. No surprise, Maggie thought. A murder investigation took up so much time, and she should know. Lorimer had had his fair share of cases as Senior Investigating Officer over the years. Sometimes it irked Maggie that he had been overlooked for further promotion, though making the rank of Detective Chief Inspector in his thirties had been something to cheer about.

'Hi, we're through here,' she called.

Lorimer's head appeared round the doorway and he grinned as he saw them together; a woman and ginger cat curled up companionably on the sofa.

'Still here then, is he?'

'Yeah. The vet says there's no reason why we can't keep him. *If* nobody claims him, that is,' she added hastily.

'Better give him a name, then. We can't just keep calling him cat. How about Ginger?'

Maggie made a face and shook her head.

'What, then?'

'How about Second Chance?' Maggie suggested.

Lorimer snorted. 'Sounds like a racehorse.' Then he paused, 'Why not call him Chancer? That's what he is after all, a right wee chancer.'

Maggie looked up. Was there something of disapproval in her husband's tone? Or had it simply been a particularly hard day? Whatever, he needed something pleasant to ease the worry lines etched across his brow, she thought in a rush of affection.

'Okay, Chancer, off you go.' Maggie stood up and let the cat slip off her knees. 'Fancy some dinner or are you too tired?' She came up close to Lorimer, arms entwining his waist, and felt his breath warm on her face.

'Not that tired,' he murmured, pulling her tightly against his body.

'Sex-mad fool!' she murmured into his shoulder teasingly, but shivered as her husband's strong fingers traced the shape of her hips. Maggie closed her eyes as she felt his hardness against her, all thoughts of dinner vanishing as another sort of hunger commanded her senses.

CHAPTER 6

Jimmy Greer licked the salt from his lips. Crushing the crisp bag, he aimed it at an already overflowing waste bin but the bag unfolded itself mid-flight and landed well short of its target. No goal, he thought. Well, maybe he'd hit the mark with this latest story. Footballers' wives had that double allure of belonging to a man's world and still remaining glamour pusses, his editor had reminded him. They'd already sourced a picture of Janis Faulkner smiling into someone's lens from her poolside sun lounger. It was true what they said, a picture was worth a thousand words and this one told a lovely little story of self-gratification. It almost begged the reader to indulge in a bit of *Schadenfreude*. Greer smiled to himself. He'd see what other tasty bits he could rake up while he was at it. The *Gazette*'s senior reporter turned back to his laptop. A few more words to knock out then he was out of here.

Even with all the windows open, the newspaper office was stiflingly hot and underarm damp patches had spread like twin Rorschach ink blots across his blue shirt. Greer glanced at his watch. Time for a quick one in the press bar, he told himself, flicking the cursor to 'save'. Just a wee half before Kelvin FC held their press conference. Greer chuckled to himself, wondering what spin their new manager would have for them and what stories his rival journalists would have for tomorrow's editions. Well, his sources had brought him something better and he'd have an exclusive.

The boardroom at Kelvin FC was a testament to the club's long history. Founded in the late nineteenth century, its walls had echoed with the hopes and celebrations of Kelvin's directors over three different centuries. Old photographs hung on the wood panelling, their teams lingering on for posterity. Names could still be matched with the faces staring forwards to whatever lens had captured their images, some of them remaining forever young, their aspirations cut off by one of the wars that had ravaged the twentieth century. Ron Clark glanced around the empty room. It was his favourite place inside the club, somewhere he could come and feel at home among all these sporting heroes. His last job had been with another First Division team but it had lacked the history of a club like Kelvin. Clark liked it here. Besides, he and Pat Kennedy understood one another.

Chairs had been arranged in ranks facing the largest table behind which he'd placed the Kelvin Chair. This was a fine-carved affair, high backed with the club's crest emblazoned upon it, a chair normally reserved for Kennedy during more formal occasions. But today it seemed fitting that he should take it himself. Sitting there might give him the confidence he did not presently feel. Or was it because he was unconsciously taking Pat's place? And would he be trying to emulate the chairman's tactics?

The Kelvin manager shivered. He'd not felt as nervous as this before, even with a cup-winning match in prospect. But then, he told himself as he rubbed some warmth into his arms through his shirt sleeves, he'd never been involved in a murder investigation.

Sometimes players were difficult to handle; temperaments could flare up on and off the pitch and more than once in his career he'd had to step in to settle some belligerent character who'd threatened them with the press. A few pub fights and (once) the father of a teenage girl had caused him some sleepless nights. On the whole the boys here were great. They turned up on time for training sessions, worked hard at their fitness regimes and mainly stayed out of trouble.

But nothing like this had ever happened at Kelvin FC. There was absolutely no precedent for the murder of one of their star players. And, Clark thought sadly, a star who'd never even had the chance to put on a Kelvin strip. He recalled Pat Kennedy's bitter words. We've paid Sunderland top whack for him and now all that money's gone, the chairman had complained. Clark had remained silent, shocked that Pat could begin to think about hard cash in the face of the footballer's demise. What was money when a life had been so horribly cut off? But, he reflected, Pat seemed pretty obsessed by money these days. Ron's own nephew, Davie, who had come up through Kelvin's ranks and was now one of their regular defenders, had told him about the ill-feeling in the dressing room because of Kennedy's insistence that they wouldn't be paid extra for home wins next season.

Clark looked up, his train of thought interrupted as the first of the journalists was shown into the boardroom by Marie McPhail, Kelvin's administrative officer. Rising to his feet, the manager nodded to the reporter from the *Gazette*. 'Take a seat, will you. The others shouldn't be long.'

In truth the conference lasted a scant half-hour but for Ron Clark it seemed that it would never end. Questions about Nicko's background came up, the reasons they'd had for paying all that money for him, whether he had any ideas about the man's death to offer. The manager had shrugged his shoulders, bewildered that they'd think he could have any opinion whatsoever on the matter and wishing, not for the first time, that this particular press conference had not come within his remit as club manager. And as for getting in a mention of Jason White? That had been a non-starter.

Eventually he'd shaken all their hands and seen them out at the entrance to the club. It had felt as if he were accepting con-dolences after a funeral.

'Have the police been to see you?' Ron Clark turned to see a thin, cadaverous figure standing a little apart from the other jour-nalists. It was a man he had not recognised; familiar as he was with the sports writers, this one eluded him.

Clark's puzzled expression must have shown for the man thrust out a hand and gripped his own in a brief, damp clasp.

'Jimmy Greer. The *Gazette*,' he announced.

'The police? No they haven't,' Clark replied.

'They will.' The reporter flicked one long finger against the side of his nose. 'Trust me, they will,' he repeated, then with a grin that showed a set of unhealthy stained teeth the reporter turned on his heel and headed for the car park.

Ron Clark stood watching him for a few moments then he shiv-ered, despite the sun beating down out of a cloudless blue sky. There was something about the man Greer that made him more than a little uneasy.

He saw the floodlights looming over the motorway long before the actual stadium hove into view. Then some clever technology tilted the image and he was looking down at a manicured pitch, green beyond the dreams of any loving groundsman. Memories flooded back; the first time his dad had taken him to a league match. It had been Kelvin against Partick Thistle, he recalled, though what the score had been on that Saturday derby of long ago he simply couldn't remember. Flashes of the occasion were all that remained: Dad hoisting him over the black, metal turnstile, the Bovril he'd spilt down his new jeans and the roars of the crowd that crushed him on all sides as they'd climbed up the stone staircase to sit side by side on worn wooden bucket-seats. His dad had been a keen Kelvin supporter and some of that must have rubbed off.

Lorimer had played rugby at school, but he had always followed the progress of Scottish football. It was part of the male psyche, he thought, to know what fixtures were on and to remember the names of players, though these days that was becoming harder with all the foreign names mixed in with fewer and fewer Scots. Some of them, like Henrik Larsson, had stayed long enough to become feted almost as one of their own, but others were barely with a Scottish club for one season before they were off again.

Kelvin FC was one of those clubs that had retained a following among Glaswegians that was both loyal and parochial. Never rising to the greatness of the Old Firm, the club had nevertheless acquitted itself well in all its long history. And that, of course, was the main reason for such ardent loyalty. From its inception, Glaswegians had supported the club with a fierce devotion that was still reflected on today's websites. Lorimer was reading their latest offering right now.

It took only seconds to realise that this link to the website had not been updated over the weekend. Lorimer grimaced. Well, what had he expected? That the Kelvin Keelies would have posted up information about Nicko Faulkner's death? It was still holiday time, after all. Yet he'd expected something. After all, the transfer market had been hot for weeks and the new signings of Jason White and Nicko Faulkner had made headlines in more than just the sports section of the *Gazette*. White was one of the bad boys of the game, his name all too frequently in the tabloids for the wrong reasons. His flair on the park seemed to make up for his wayward bouts of antisocial behaviour though, at least as far as his past managers were concerned. Rumour had it that he'd been denied an English cap due to some of these incidents. How would he fare under the management of Ron Clark? The Kelvin manager was well respected in the game, one of those rare birds of passage, an articulate fellow who didn't talk in clichés all the time. Lorimer chuckled to himself; Clark had been the despair of Jonathan Watson, the TV comic who had taken off so many of the prominent figures in Scottish football.

Lorimer's mouse clicked on the last of the website's pages. At first sight it was simply a chat room for fans to have their say about the team's progress. The last batch of correspondence was dated 3 July.

Don't know why they have to put up the season ticket again. How many bums are they going to lose off seats if they keep this up? It's not as if we're even in the SPL this season – Chris

Well everyone says that Kennedy's going to have to put more money into the club or it'll be in trouble. Remember what happened to Airdrie? They had to crawl back up from Division Two after they'd gone broke – Danny

Aye, and Falkirk. They nearly went bust too, didn't they? Should've been in the Premier League as well, if it hadn't been for the condition of Brockville – Chris

Ancient history, pal. Though I suppose Kelvin's not exactly state of the art, is it? – Danny

'D'you want a cup of tea?' Maggie's voice broke into Lorimer's thoughts.

'Give me a minute. I'll be right out,' he called over his shoulder. He scrolled down to the last words on the page:

Well they must have plenty of money if they're throwing all that dosh at Nicko Faulkner. What d'you think? – Chris

But the chat came to an abrupt end, the invisible Danny failing to respond and leaving that question dangling in the ether. What *did* he think? What was the consensus of opinion among the fans? Had Nicko been unpopular with any of them? Lorimer gave himself a shake. That was a dangerous train of thought. Looking for some weirdo who'd had a grudge was just daft. Mitchison was almost certainly correct in his assessment of Janis Faulkner: it was so obvious that she must have killed her husband, but still Lorimer sat at the computer wondering that perennial question: why?

'It'll get cold,' Maggie murmured, her warm cheek against his. 'Come on outside while it's still light.' Lorimer put his hand on her waist, ready to encircle it, but she was off with a laugh and he could only follow her out into the garden where two sun loungers lay waiting. From the depths of one of them an orange face looked up.

'You again,' he grinned. 'Right wee chancer you are, pal.'

The sky was still light, the treetops dark against a pinkish haze that signalled yet another sunny day tomorrow. Maggie scooped up the cat and flipped it back on to her lap in one easy movement as she lay back on the lounger. A tray with two mugs sat on top of an upturned plastic litter bin, Maggie's improvised picnic table until such time as she could be bothered to buy a proper one.

Lorimer couldn't recall when the summers had been as hot as this one. Sitting out in their garden at the end of a working day had previously been more of a novelty; now it was a welcome routine. He closed his eyes against the brightness of the western sky and let his hand fall limply by his side. Somewhere in the shrubbery a blackbird's liquid notes came through the twilight. He opened his eyes, glancing at the cat, but it was curled contentedly on Maggie's knee, oblivious to any bird. That was good, he thought. Maybe it wouldn't be a nuisance after all. The idea of the animal stalking one of their garden birds and sinking its claws into a bundle of feathers made him wince, he could almost feel the sharpness of the points as they bit into the struggling bird.

Lorimer's imagination took another leap, this time into a kitchen where human flesh had been pierced by sharp metal and where a man had bled to death. Had he been stalked? Had that been a calculated act of cruelty?

The blackbird whistled again but this time Lorimer took no pleasure in hearing the bird and knew he would not recapture the peace he'd found on Mull until he'd come to find the truth behind Nicko Faulkner's killing.

CHAPTER 7

'We are the Keelies!' The rhythmic stamping of feet followed the refrain, echoing round the ground, then a huge cheer went up as their team ran out from the tunnel. Black and white scarves held high were waved in time to the chants, roars of approval met the loudspeaker's announcement of each team member. It was the first game of the season, the sun shone out of a clear blue sky, the score sheet was still pristine and anything could happen. Kelvin Park almost had about it a carnival atmosphere; music blared from the tannoy as a huge panda bear lumbered up and down in front of the stands, its immense paws held out to the front row of wee boys, clamouring to touch their mascot. Their spirits at least had not been dampened too deeply by the sombre aspect of a player's death.

'And you can hear the crowd as we look out over Kelvin Park. There's a sense of expectation in the air, don't you think?'

'I would agree with that. Kelvin FC playing at home to Queen of the South today surely have a real chance to go through this first round of the Bell's Cup.'

'You don't think the Dumfries side will progress past this game into the next round of the cup, then?'

'Well, Jim, I would say that Kelvin's reputation makes the home fans pretty confident of victory. Just listen to them!'

'Ah, but football's a strange game,' Jim Nicholson, the host of Radio Scotland's Sport Saturday, replied. 'Look at all the surprises from last season. And with Nicko Faulkner's death and Jason White not in the line-up, who knows what might happen?'

'Any idea why White's not playing today?' his co-presenter asked.

'No. A bit odd that he's not even on the bench, don't you think?'

Then the commentators broke off as a minute's silence began.

The ripple of talk died away leaving only the crackling static from the tannoy system and a whine like an air-raid siren as a motorbike started up. Its engine roared into life, then the noise faded into the distance until all that could be heard was a plaintive seagull crying above the stadium.

A minute is a long time to be silent, reflecting on one man's death. The mass of people stood, some with bowed heads, others staring at the two teams lined up on the pitch. In the quiet seconds ticking their way towards the start of the game, there was a sense of unease mingled with a desire to forget the recent tragedy and continue with the more important business of football. One man watched the clock, counting off the seconds. Then he put a whistle to his mouth and raised one arm skywards. Once again the noise erupted from the terracing, some handclapping endorsing the football club's respectful action.

From his vantage point in the director's box, Patrick Kennedy watched his team with something amounting to pride. They had all stood for the minute's silence, but now, like schoolboys released at the sound of a bell, his players were suddenly running into their positions, eager to begin this game. The pitch was in perfect condition. Wee Bert had spent days with the sprinkler, coaxing some energy back into the dried turf. The freshly painted goals gleamed white in the sunshine, no hint of a breeze disturbing the brand-new nets. Gordon Carmichael, their regular first-team goalkeeper, stood between the posts, eyes scanning the ball, but it was well up the park, no threat to Kelvin's six-foot-six goalie. He was a big, douce lad, was Gudgie Carmichael, thought Kennedy. Nobody meeting him off the park would dream that he was totally fearless when coming out to challenge an opponent.

Glancing around him, Kennedy could see the expressions on the punters' faces. Many of the men around him were recipients of the corporate hospitality that Kelvin offered at home games, and after a good lunch and a few drinks, they were happy to be Kelvin fans, if only for that afternoon. Last season's relegation was behind them now and all the talk was on getting back into the Scottish Premier League. Further along from the directors' box, people were getting down to the serious business of the new season, all eyes on the ball as it was booted across the park into the path of the oncoming Kelvin players.

A howl went up as Leo Giannitrapani missed an attempt at goal. Kennedy shook his head. Their Sicilian striker had disappointed them the previous season and if he didn't begin to fill the score sheet, the fans would expect him to be out this time next year. Still, it had been a chance for Kelvin to draw first blood and the crowd were applauding Giannitrapani's effort.

Kennedy's eyes followed the ball up and down the park, his teeth clenching in irritation as chance after chance went awry, Queen of the South's defenders nipping at his strikers' heels. Now if Jason White had actually been here . . . He sighed. All that money spent and what had the team to show for it? The new midfielder had been one of their great hopes. The player was still in custody after a night of riotous behaviour, despite all of Ron Clark's pleading. Relations between the local police headquarters and the football club were generally good but asking for favours like releasing the player for today's game had been a non-starter. White would suffer for this.

'Ohhhh!' The shout followed yet another missed shot on goal, this one from young John McKinnery. Kennedy joined in the hand-clapping. McKinnery's face expressed annoyance with himself. But his chairman nodded in approval. The lad was working his socks off today and deserved to score. Maybe the absence of Faulkner and White was giving him the chance to shine that he craved?

By half-time the score sheet was still blank and Kennedy trooped downstairs with the rest of the club officials and today's corporate guests.

'Well, Jim, still think Kelvin can win today? Queen of the South are giving them a run for their money, don't you think?'

Lorimer switched off the radio. Half-time commentaries annoyed him. He'd tune into the second half and then to *Super Scoreboard* to see what the rest of the day's results had brought to the opening day of the season. He'd had half a mind to go to Kelvin Park to see the game himself, but after the events of this week a quiet day with Maggie was infinitely preferable. Their holiday in Mull had brought them closer together again and he was loath to relinquish that feeling of deepening trust and affection. Still, he was curious to know how the staff at Kelvin FC were taking the sudden demise of one of their new strikers. Had Faulkner been playing today, he doubted that the score would be nil-nil right now. Monday would bring more reports on to his desk about Janis Faulkner. Then what? She'd been charged. The burden of responsibility was off them all for the time being. But there was something about this case that worried him.

What had happened that day? Had she really slammed a kitchen knife into her husband's chest? The forensic reports showed a missing blood spatter. Someone, somewhere must have been sprayed with arterial blood, spots so numerous and so minute that they might even have covered the assailant's hands and face. Had Janis washed off all that blood? And had she destroyed whatever clothing she had been wearing? There was absolutely no trace of her husband's blood on her person, no fingerprints nor any significant DNA to show that she had perpetrated that fatal act. But the woman's gym bag was missing. He imagined it stuffed with blood-stained clothing. Had she burned it somewhere? Or shoved it into a skip? Lorimer sighed. It was all far too speculative and he didn't like that at all. And another thing: why wasn't she protesting her innocence more vociferously? Why this dreadful clamming up that only seemed to confirm her as guilty?

'Now the teams are back out on the pitch and there are no changes to either side. And there goes Sweeney, passing the ball to McGrory who heads it across to McKinnery, and – oh, nicely intercepted by Logan. And Logan is running with the ball, passes – Rientjes, going fast down the line and, oh, gets himself into trouble there with the Dutch player who comes in again hard. Referee says play on and Rientjes hoofs it back up the park only to meet the head of O'Riley . . .'

Kennedy sat staring at the ground, his mind wandering. The industrial site at Maryhill was perfect. It would require a lot of upgrading but once the old football club was sold to the supermarket chain there would be enough money to give them a stadium they'd be proud of, and a decent backhander for himself. The only downside was the pitch itself. He'd had three separate

53

surveys done and they'd all told him the same thing: AstroTurf was by far the cheapest option. UEFA had deemed it a safe playing surface and the Scottish Football League had long ago endorsed it as an alternative to natural turf. Yet there were other voices that still rose in dissent. The chairman's gaze drifted over the terracing towards the high-rise flats that dominated the skyline. He could just make out faces at the windows, watching the game for free. His face creased into a smile of grim satisfaction. They'd have to pay up like the rest of the punters if all his plans came to fruition. There would be changes, lots of changes, but that was inevitable. Nothing stayed the same for ever, he told himself, his eyes flicking over the black armband of his captain, Andy Sweeney.

'And he's nutmegged him beautifully and Ross is going to go all the way! Can he put one past Gordon Carmichael? And he has! Beau-tiful goal by Ross, and Queen of the South take the lead!'

Lorimer banged a fist into his open palm. Carmichael! he agonised. The man they called 'the safest hands in soccer', just like his fictional counterpart in *Roy of the Rovers*, Gordon Stewart. He shook his head. Who would have believed it? But the commentator's voice continued and the policeman crouched over his radio, listening intently.

'Jim, can Kelvin come back from that? What d'you think?' the commentator asked as the teams regrouped.

'Well, they'll have to, won't they? Being knocked out of the cup at this stage isn't the best way to begin a season. Still, it's the league matches that really matter to them if they want to get back into the SPL. Now the game has restarted and Sweeney plays a clever cross to McKinnery.

McKinnery's off down the wing! Can anyone catch him? Oh! McKinnery's been brought down in a fearsome tackle by Logan but the referee says play on. Just listen to the crowd! McKinnery's still lying on the ground and now the physio has come on. That's a real let-off for Queen of the South's Logan. He's lucky not to have been sent off for that. You can't blame the fans for their outcry. That was a terrible decision. Well, they're bringing on a stretcher and McKinnery's being carried off. I saw Woods was limbering up a minute ago and, yes, it's Austin Woods coming on to replace young John McKinnery.'

Ron Clark sat down again, his fists clenched. What was the referee playing at? There would be some harsh questions asked at the close of this game. His face turned towards the action on the pitch, seeing his players' efforts to keep possession of the ball, trying to turn it in time to move ever forward in the direction of their opponent's goalmouth. For a time it seemed that every kick of the ball was deemed to find the blue shirt of a Queen's player and a see-saw of passing ensued. Then a lovely pass by Hugh McGrory was scooped up by Baz Thomson. Clark grinned as the number seven weaved in and out of the blue-shirted defenders, an impudent smile on his thin narrow face. He watched the player ducking this way and that, Thomson's dyed-red spiky hair making him an easy player to identify. A quick pass to Sweeney, then Thomson was screaming for the ball again. Seconds later he'd shimmied to one side and launched the ball into the net.

The crowd was on its feet, arms raised in elation, but it was short-lived. For a second time, Ron Clark sank into his seat, his expression thunderous. Thomson had never been offside! He watched as his players remonstrated with the referee, Baz among them, shouting something nobody could hear above the din from the crowd. And suddenly, there it was: a red card being held aloft and Baz Thomson was running towards the tunnel, hands held against his head as if to block out what was happening. Clark looked at the police and stewards as the air was filled with screams and obscenities. The noise took a while to die down; murmurs of anger were punctuated by yells of hatred for the referee. Clark checked his watch. Only a few minutes to go. Could his team possibly pull something out of the bag? Last-minute goals were not unknown. But as the minutes ticked by, the game deteriorated into a series of fouls that were rewarded by a rash of yellow cards and as the final whistle blew, the manager's mouth was a thin line of suppressed fury as he glared at the referee.

Nobody looking out at the team trooping back disconsolately to the dressing room could possibly have guessed that this would be their most memorable start to any season, and for all the wrong reasons.

CHAPTER 8

Norman Cartwright pulled into the driveway, hearing the crunch of gravel beneath his tyres. For a few moments he sat behind the wheel, too exhausted to move, glad of the silence now that the engine was switched off. It had been a hard game. The jeers and howls still rang in his ears. McKinnery's fall had been an accident. Scrambling boots had made contact with the ball, of that Norman was certain. It had been the hard ground that had concussed the Kelvin striker, not his opponent.

The referee sighed heavily, eyes closed, trying to relive the moments before he had blown his whistle, disallowing that Kelvin goal before all hell had broken loose. He'd made eye contact with the official running down the line. *He'd* known Thomson was offside, hadn't he? Well, they'd know soon enough when the match highlights were shown on tonight's television. And even if he had made a mistake, well, the referee's word was law and what was done was done, he thought, comforting himself in well-worn clichés.

There had been no post-mortem afterwards, the other officials wanting out of Kelvin's grounds and away as fast as they could. Norman had waited until most of the ground had been cleared before making his solitary way to the car park. If Rangers or Celtic had been Kelvin's opponents today it would have been quite another matter, and the referee would have had an escort from the grounds to his car, parked at a distance for his own safety. Norman sighed again. He would have welcomed that measure of security this afternoon. Had he made a mistake, though? *Had he?*

Perhaps if Norman Cartwright had not rolled the window down to feel the breeze from the passenger side of his Volkswagen he might have seen it coming. And, if he had not continued to sit so quietly and conveniently for the gunman who had him in his sights, perhaps he would have found the answer to his question.

But the projectile came whistling through the air, a malicious wrecking force crashing through the side of his skull. Norman slumped sideways from the sudden impact, any speculations he might have about the validity of Baz Thomson's goal cut off for ever.

'Not another one?' Rosie Fergusson protested. 'Can Glasgow folk not enjoy themselves on a Saturday without having to murder each other?' Her voice held a tone of jocularity that was at odds with the forensic pathologist's dedication to her work. A little levity helped in Glasgow City Mortuary, but never at the expense of a dead person's dignity. Once the body bag was opened and the corpse laid across her stainless-steel examination table, an atmosphere of intense concentration descended and any light-hearted comments disappeared like burst bubbles from a child's plastic wand.

Now she wouldn't even have time to shower and change before heading off to the scene of this most recent atrocity. A shooting: that was all the voice on the telephone had told her. Somewhere up in Lorimer's neck of the woods. Rosie had the satisfaction of knowing that someone else's Saturday evening was about to be ruined. At least if the DCI was there she could hope to salvage something of her plans with her fiancé, Dr Solomon Brightman. Solly had been a part of Lorimer's cases before, in his capacity as a behavioural psychologist. In fact, it had been a particularly grisly murder that had brought Solly and Rosie together. A little smile played around the pathologist's mouth as she conjured up Solly's image in her head. The dark eyes behind those horn-rimmed glasses could be solemn and pensive while he considered something in his work, but the moment he caught her glance they softened, making Rosie feel ridiculously girlish. She gave a delicious shiver then chuckled to herself. Behave yourself, woman, she scolded, concentrate on what's going on across the city.

Lorimer didn't muck about. He'd be thorough but he'd leave the messy bits to a whole team of dedicated officers who were at the crime scene already. And let me get on with my job, Rosie thought grimly as she gunned the BMW out of the mortuary car park. She had a good working relationship with the Detective Chief Inspector and even met up socially whenever the opportunity allowed. Maggie would be on holiday from school, lucky devil, Rosie thought. Maybe they could make a foursome some evening. Have a barbecue in the Lorimers' garden if this weather continued.

Thoughts of relaxed summer evenings disappeared the moment Rosie Fergusson stepped out of the car. The path leading to the semi-detached house was cordoned off with police tape, several vehicles were parked nearby and the pathologist identified the scene-of-crime officers' official van and Lorimer's ancient, dark blue Lexus. A uniformed officer stood on the pavement as if shielding the scene from prying eyes. But there was no need for that; the victim was still in his car but protected from view by a white scene-of-crime tent. Rosie turned around. Yes, there were several people staring from their open windows, she could see one at least trying to get a closer view, the sunshine glinting off a pair of binoculars. At least the police cordon had kept other passers-by at bay.

Rosie slipped on her white boiler suit and regulation overshoes, donned a mask and gloves, then, grabbing her medical bag, stepped carefully on to the metal treads that made a path towards the white tent. So many precautions were taken to avoid disturbing the scene and Rosie was as grimly vigilant as the rest of the team.

'Good evening, Dr Fergusson.' A familiar voice made Rosie look up. Lorimer nodded to her, his eyes shifting immediately to the man in the car.

'Here he is,' Lorimer murmured, pulling the flap aside, revealing the dust-covered Volkswagen and the body of Norman Cartwright. With gloved hands she opened the passenger door, careful not to touch anything on the upholstery, and looked at the victim. His head was turned slightly away from her but she could see the entry mark quite clearly, a large reddened hole a few centimetres from his left ear. Rosie would take exact measurements of the wound in time, but just looking at its size showed it had been made by a shotgun. Right now she wanted an overview of the whole scene. Carefully she stood up and edged around the vehicle, exclaiming as she bumped her upper thighs against the radiator grille. Reaching the driver's side, she saw that the door had been left open and the pathologist examined the body within the car, not yet touching it but taking note of every detail. The victim was still upright, held by the seat belt that now cut a groove into his neck.

'See that? I'll need to check for any post-mortem abrasion,' Rosie said, indicating the webbing that now supported the weight of the dead man's head. 'No exit wound so we will expect the pellets to have lodged within the cranial area. No excessive bleeding. Some powder residue scatters across the face. What are we looking at, I wonder?' she asked quietly. 'Something discharged from between two and three metres?'

Lorimer raised his eyebrows and gave a slight nod. 'The gunman must have been within shouting distance of his victim, don't you think?' he replied. Rosie nodded, concentrating on the size of the gaping hole in Cartwright's head. It was about two inches wide, surrounded by a periphery of scattered pellet holes. 'Unburnt propellant by the looks of this,' she murmured. 'Think we're looking at a sawn-off shotgun here,' she added, nodding almost to herself. They'd know more after the post-mortem and have a ballistics report on hand to aid the police investigation. But one thing was certain from this scene-of-crime examination: whoever had fired the shot that killed Norman Cartwright had done so in broad daylight, only yards from the man's own front door.

'Any idea of time of death?'

'Well, he's been dead less than six hours. Probably less than three, actually. No rigor and before you ask, I haven't taken his temperature yet.'

'Okay, let me know when you have. We know he left Kelvin Park around five-forty this afternoon.'

'At the game, was he?' Rosie asked. 'Wearing the wrong colours, maybe?'

'Worse than that,' Lorimer told her darkly. 'Norman Cartwright was the referee. He made some controversial decisions during the game. Okay, folk were crying for his blood, but that's just fans letting off steam. Didn't merit something like this.' Lorimer jerked a thumb at the scene inside the tent.

'Why? What happened?' Rosie asked suddenly and Lorimer gave her a quick precis of the match.

'So,' she said, straightening up and looking from the body to the DCI, 'your problem is several thousand disaffected Kelvin fans might have wanted to kill the ref. But how many of them would have had access to a sawn-off shotgun?'

Sunday mornings on call were not Rosie's favourite days. Yet she had parked her car beside her colleague Dan's in the mortuary car park aware of a quickening sense of interest in today's post-mortem. Two doctors were required by Scottish law so Dan would record all of the findings they made while Rosie conducted the more physical part of the business. It wasn't every day that they had to extract shotgun pellets from a murder victim, despite all that the press reports and the TV police dramas might lead the public to believe. Much of her work dealt with suspicious deaths, often due to the knife culture in the city, though she had had an interesting spell overseas in Rwanda. That was a time she remembered with sadness as well as satisfaction for a job well done. People who didn't know Rosie too well had been heard commenting on the pathologist's slim, slight figure, even wondering aloud what such a pretty young woman was doing in a job like hers. But looks, however fragile, were only skin deep and Rosie Fergusson was made from tougher stuff than most.

Norman Cartwright's body was waiting for them in the refrigerated wall adjoining the post-mortem room. Two of the mortuary technicians slid it out, placing it carefully on to a stainless-steel table. First they would examine the victim fully clothed, noting anything that might be required later. Giving evidence as an expert witness was never far from their minds as the pathologists performed their surgical work: everything would be noted and recorded with some degree of caution. *Most probably, most likely*, usually preceding any attempt to say exactly what had happened to a person whose death might be the subject of speculation.

Some time later, though, Rosie and Dan were pretty convinced by their findings. Their report would go straight to the Procurator Fiscal, of course, along with detailed ballistics analysis, but DCI Lorimer had a right to know just what sort of weapon had made an end of the football referee.

CHAPTER 9

WHO SHOT THE MAN IN BLACK?

Police man shot dead in his car has been confirmed as football referee Norman Cartwright. Witnesses heard a single shot being fired, though none of them admit to having seen the gunman. 'It was like a car backfiring, but really loud,' Joseph Tierney, a neighbour of the victim, stated. Mr Cartwright, who had been refereeing the match between Kelvin FC and Queen of the South on the afternoon of his death, was in his own driveway when the shooting took place. Police have already conducted a house-to-house inquiry following the incident and a report has been sent to the Procurator Fiscal. In a recent BBC documentary, the plight of football referees was highlighted when it was shown that death threats against referees and damage to property had frequently occurred at every level of the sport. There had been ugly scenes at Kelvin Park that afternoon following a controversial decision by Mr Cartwright during the game. Whether this has any bearing on his subsequent killing is something the police must surely take into account.

Lorimer read the byline with a sigh. Jimmy Greer! There was nothing malicious about the piece, nor anything to suggest that Greer was hinting at police incompetence. But it was early days and the DCI knew only too well that the journalist from the *Gazette* would muck-rake as soon as he had the opportunity. The friction that existed between Greer and the DCI had its origin in a previous case when the man from the press had stepped out of line during a murder inquiry. Lorimer hadn't missed him and hit the wall, as his mother-in-law was fond of saying. Now Greer sought to make life difficult for the DCI whenever he could. It was a hassle he could well do without.

It had been a long weekend and now, in the early light of Monday morning, there was more work to be done. Cartwright's house had been locked up after a preliminary examination to see what next of kin the man had. A divorcee with no children, his elderly mother in a nursing home, Cartwright had lived alone. He'd not even had a cat to keep him company, thought Lorimer, catching sight of Chancer's golden coat as the animal padded from the kitchen, an imploring expression on his face. Feed me, it said.

As he scraped the contents of a foil bag into the animal's saucer, he recalled the moment when they had entered Norman Cartwright's home. The dust motes had swirled thickly through a dark, narrow hallway that led to the sitting room and adjacent kitchen. Dirty pots and crockery were stacked up, half-submerged in a basin of scum-covered water. One fly had buzzed languidly against the window pane, others lay dead on the chipped wooden sill. The picture of neglect alone had rendered the dead man deserving of pity. Lorimer recalled the days he'd spent on his own after Maggie had gone to America to work; had he been as bad as that? He didn't think so. There was a sense of defeat about Cartwright's house, he thought.

It might be a good idea to go back with another officer in tow, just to see what else they could find out about the referee. The scene-of-crime officers had all the forensic material they seemed to require, but as the man had been shot outside his home, there had been little need to do a full-scale search of the premises. Normally Lorimer would leave a task like this to one of his more junior officers, but his visit today had a twofold purpose: he wanted to give Niall Cameron the benefit of his own experience – the lad had promise and could go far – and he felt an urge to satisfy his own curiosity. What might he find at number eight, Willow Grove? Some answers about the personality of the man who had been so mercilessly killed, he hoped. And, if he was really lucky, a reason to show why he had been gunned down in the first place.

It was only a short drive to the crime scene from the centre of the city. Great Western Road swept all the way out of Glasgow, through Anniesland Cross and Knightswood towards the Clyde and eventually Loch Lomond. In springtime the dual carriageway was intersected by a dazzling swathe of daffodils and row upon row of cherry trees, their pink and white blossoms scattered across the ground. Once, when they had been students, he'd taken Maggie down to Luss, a pretty little village right on the loch, after an all night party. It had been dark when they'd left the city and he could still see the daffodils in his mind's eye, pale and ghostly, sweeping along for mile after mile. Now he and Cameron were driving by the stately grey-stone terraces that marched all the way up towards One Devonshire Gardens, the city's most prestigious hotel. Lorimer gave it a cursory glance as they drove past. He'd taken Maggie there once, on their tenth wedding anniversary, and the memory of that special occasion lingered still. At night the trees outside sparkled with white lights but in daytime it might simply be mistaken for one more grand residence along this elegant row of Victorian buildings.

Norman Cartwright had lived in a pleasant, leafy suburb of the city, the sort of place where nothing much ever happens outside of school jumble sales and community coffee mornings. On this particular Monday the quiet of Willow Grove was disturbed by a small crowd of reporters and photographers anxious to catch up with the latest developments. As Lorimer pulled up to the kerb, he could see the next-door neighbours holding court at their front door. The DCI remembered them as Mr and Mrs Murphy who lived at number six, through the wall from the late Norman Cartwright. They had not been at home at the time of the incident, but that did not seem to be deterring them from putting in their tuppence worth. His mouth twisted in a grimace of distaste. Some people simply revelled in the chance to associate themselves with notoriety, especially when they could maintain a safe distance from its darker aspects.

'Okay,' he sighed, turning to his detective constable, Niall Cameron. 'Let's go in and hope we don't have them all knocking at the door.'

The two men walked briskly up the gravel path, ignoring the heads that suddenly turned their way.

Lorimer stood back to allow the DC space to unlock the front door, then they entered the stuffy hallway and closed the door behind them.

'What're we looking for, sir?' Niall Cameron asked, his eyes roaming around the dusty corridor.

'Nothing and everything,' Lorimer answered him. 'Just a feel for the place. See how he lived, what he was like. A person's home can tell you all sorts of things about them.'

'How d'you mean?'

'Well, what's your pad like? No, let me guess. Neat and tidy, everything in its place, right?'

The tall Lewisman flushed under his white collar, letting Lorimer know he'd hit the mark. 'Well, I do keep my bike in the hallway, near the front door, but only because there's nowhere else to put it . . .' he trailed off.

'An organised mind.' Lorimer chuckled. 'Dr Brightman would tell you that straight off,' he added, referring to Solly Brightman, the University of Glasgow psychologist. 'Seriously, you can learn quite a lot from how a person lived,' Lorimer told him, moving out of the hall.

Norman Cartwright's bedroom reminded Lorimer of an old student flat, filled as it was with heavy furniture that had gone out of fashion decades ago. The matching mahogany wardrobe and dressing table had definitely seen better days scratches and nicks around their bases told of years of abuse by some careless vacuum cleaner. Had he done his own housework? Or had there been a daily woman? No. It didn't look as if a woman's touch had been used here for a very long time. The carpet below his feet was stained and there were bits of dark fluff that could have come from the referee's socks. The beige cotton duvet had been pulled hastily into shape, one end hanging lower than the other as if Norman Cartwright had left for his match in a hurry. There was nobody to see his sorry attempts at making his bed, or so he'd have thought.

'No woman in his life,' Lorimer told the empty room. 'Nobody to care whether your bed's tidy or the place even smells nice.' Had *his* home been like that during Maggie's absence? he wondered, guiltily. Life without Maggie had certainly made him negligent about keeping house. But he'd been rescued by Jean, his gem of a cleaning lady. This place looked as if Cartwright had given up bothering about what his place looked like. Saturday's *Gazette* lay on one side of the bed. Lorimer picked it up. The referee had been reading the sports section then dropped it on the floor, meaning to pick it up later, he thought. An empty mug sat on his bedside cabinet, one more ring to add to the others staining the varnished wood, beside it a digital clock and a thin brass lamp, its shade an indeterminate brown. He switched it on but the colour was no better, an orangey wash illuminating that side of the bed. A paperback book lay behind the lamp and Lorimer turned it over to see what author the man had enjoyed. It was an American thriller by a writer he'd never heard of, its cover a lurid representation of a man being chased down some dark alley. He flicked the pages and saw that it was a library discard. So, there was no woman in his life but Norman Cartwright had had a penchant for fiction. Maybe he'd preferred the people of his imagination to those in reality. But, then, he was a sportsman who kept himself busy at weekends, not some recluse. So why did Lorimer have the feeling that this man had been a bit of a loner? Lorimer glanced around. No pictures on the walls, not here at any rate. Maybe the other rooms would yield more clues to the personality of a man who had been gunned down a few feet from his own front door.

Lorimer heard the doorbell ringing. 'Just ignore them and hope they'll go away,' he called to Cameron. 'What have you found?' he asked, entering a lounge that was depressingly similar to Cartwright's bedroom, all shades of browns and beiges.

'Wasn't a very tidy chap, was he?' Cameron observed, holding a sock between two fingers. 'Found this down the side of the settee.'

'Anything else of interest?' Lorimer asked, though from a quick look around this room there was nothing that stood out.

'I'd say it was quite the opposite; he wasn't interested in his home. Maybe he didn't spend much time here. Especially if he was a referee at weekends and worked full-time during the week,' Cameron said. 'Kitchen's not very clean either.'

Lorimer nodded, pleased to note how the DC's observations chimed with his own. Norman Cartwright seemed to have been a person who'd had no great desire to surround himself with the finer things in life. In fact, Lorimer doubted if this visit had yielded anything much at all except to enhance his pity for the victim.

'Think we're more likely to find out about him from the football people,' Cameron went on.

'Aye, his fellow referees, maybe,' Lorimer said. 'Nobody at Kelvin Park's going to give an unbiased view of the ref, now are they?'

They were waiting for the two policemen on Norman Cartwright's doorstep: a gaggle of journalists all talking at once. *Had he any idea who had killed the referee? Had they been looking for the murder weapon? What about the game at Kelvin Park?* The questions followed them all the way out into the street, Lorimer ignoring their shrill voices demanding answers. As he drove away, a silent Niall Cameron beside him, Lorimer suddenly felt a strange sort of kinship with Janis Faulkner. Had she ever been hounded by the press? Was that the reason behind her putting down the portcullis and retreating back into the safety of her inner sanctum? Something told him that he had to breach that particular fortress if he were ever to understand the truth behind Nicko Faulkner's murder. But, for now, this new case must take precedence in his thoughts and any sympathy he felt should be for this last victim and his family.

CHAPTER 10

'You're a fool!'

Pat Kennedy clenched his fists by his sides, to stop himself from lashing out at the man before him. Jason White tilted his chin upwards, a defiant and insolent expression on his handsome face. The footballer was silent but his demeanour said it all: that sneering, supercilious look that had Kennedy's fingertips itching.

'We've docked money from wages you've yet to earn! What the hell did you think you were playing at?' Kennedy raged. The man lounging by his desk raised one shoulder in an indolent shrug. 'Maybe it doesn't matter to you, but it matters to the club!' Kennedy continued to fume. 'Just don't you dare get into anything like that before a match again. What you do in your own time is *not* just your own affair. We expect you to be available for every match. Understood?'

The man looked away from Kennedy and sniffed. 'Can I go now?' he asked, no attempt to disguise the boredom in his tone.

'Yes,' Kennedy replied, then as Jason White strolled into the corridor he followed him out, a feeling of suppressed rage bubbling to the surface. 'And don't think you've got off lightly! Remember, White, nobody's indispensable in this game, and that includes you!' Kennedy's voice roared out after the footballer who walked away, pretending not to hear. He slammed the door of his office leaving a quiver of unease behind him.

'Big man's upset, isn't he?' Bert, the groundsman, remarked to Marie McPhail. The woman shook her head and laid a finger to her lips.

'Shh! Pat can hear every word you say, Bert. You know these partition walls are paper-thin. Anyway, who can blame him? After all that's happened . . .' She trailed off, the death of Norman Cartwright remaining unspoken between them. Marie shook her head as if unable to believe Kelvin FC had been associated with the death of two men. Many of the staff wore the same tight expression of shock whenever the subject arose: nothing prepared you for something as horrible as this. 'Anyway,' she continued briskly, 'Jason was totally out of order. Pat should have had his guts for garters.'

'Don't know why they had to buy him in the first place,' Bert grumbled. 'Or that wanker, Faulkner.'

'Bert! You mustn't say that. It's bad to speak ill of the dead!' Marie hissed.

'Och, who's gonnae hear me? S'not as if he was really a team player anyway. Not like our friend downstairs in the boot room.'

Marie McPhail raised a smile. It suddenly illuminated her thin, hard face. 'Has anyone ever actually seen Kelvin's resident ghost, then?'

'Well, one o' the young lads said he saw a shadow last winter. He'd jist aboot finished cleaning the boots when it loomed up at him. So he said.' Bert tilted his head enigmatically then lifted up his mug of tea and drained it. 'Thanks for the cuppa, lass. Back to work now, see you later.'

'Aye, not if I see you first,' Marie muttered under her breath. Wee Bert was a right doom and gloom merchant, never saying a positive word about anyone. Marie often suspected he was happiest when Kelvin got thrashed on a Saturday afternoon, it justified his morose predictions that the club would never again climb out of the First Division into the Premier League where they had once belonged. Still, he was right about one thing: Kelvin's glory days were truly epitomised by legends like Ronnie Rankin, the fleet-footed player who had won a place in Keelie hearts over four consecutive seasons before being blown up at Ypres. Rankin's picture hung in the boardroom, a sepia-coloured image that was pointed out to guests on match days. And legend had it that his spirit still hung around in the boot room downstairs.

She shrugged and turned back to the pile of correspondence on her desk. Wee Bert could moan all he liked, she was a Kelvin Keelie through and through and there was nothing that could sway her loyalty to this club, or to the man who sat feet away from her, divided from her by that partition wall.

For a long moment the woman looked at the blank space, imagining the chairman's massive body bent over his desk, his head drooping with fatigue and worry. What must be going through his mind? One player had been brutally murdered, another had landed in jail and now this poor referee shot on his own doorstep. Surely Jason White could have been a bit more sensitive towards Pat? Marie ran a hand over her spiky red hair and glanced at her reflection in the glass window that separated her from the club's main corridor. A thin-faced woman in a low-cut cream blouse looked back defiantly, gold hoops twinkling at her earlobes. She might be pushing fifty but she didn't look it. Plus she'd kept her figure, unlike Barbara bloody Kennedy, she thought, a curve of triumph softening her mouth. She'd give it ten minutes then take him in a good pot of coffee and some Tunnock's Teacakes, Pat's favourites. The thought cheered Marie up as she began to sift through the day's mail, putting aside the letters that were marked for the chairman's attention, with extra care.

Ron Clark put down the telephone, hand trembling. That hack Greer's predictions were right: the police were going to pay them a visit. But in the wake of Cartwright's shooting, that was hardly a surprise. Some inspector called Lorimer, or was it Chief Inspector? Ron felt the sweat break out on his forehead. He'd better get that right, hadn't he? It would never do to be on the wrong side of Strathclyde Police during something as serious as a murder investigation. This man, Lorimer, wanted to speak to all the players who'd been at Saturday's game. Ron shivered inside his tracksuit, despite the heat. Surely they couldn't imagine any of their boys had had a hand in that shooting? It was absurd. The police must think it was some mad bastard of a Keelie who had gone for the referee, surely? Or would they suppose it was nothing to do with the game at all? But, even as the Kelvin manager tried to reassure himself, a feeling of inevitable doom swept over him.

They were tainted with these deaths now and the club would never be the same again.

Lorimer looked up at the floodlights above the grounds, noticing a patch of cloud that was drifting across the vast expanse of blue. This summer was the hottest on record and already there were government directives about the use of hosepipes. How were Kelvin's groundsmen coping with it?

It was funny standing by the main door to the clubhouse when he'd looked towards it wistfully so many times as a boy, hoping to catch a glimpse of one of his sporting heroes.

That's where I saw Murray Crawford, he wanted to tell DC Cameron. But they were not standing here for him to blether on with ancient reminiscences. Today's purpose was infinitely more serious than that.

He'd pressed an intercom button just outside the massive doorway, a smoked glass affair etched with the crest of Kelvin FC and the motto *dum vivo spero*.

'While there's life there's hope,' Cameron translated, then blushed. 'We did Latin at the Nicholson,' he explained, almost apologetically.

Lorimer nodded, then a crackly voice came over the intercom.

'Detective Chief Inspector Lorimer, Detective Constable Cameron, Strathclyde Police,' he said firmly. The door opened with a click and, for the first time in his life, Lorimer entered the inner sanctum that was Kelvin FC.

'So, this is it?' Niall Cameron raised an eyebrow at the wood-panelled hall and the dark corridors that led off in several directions. Above them the ceiling sloped steeply, hairline cracks visible on the plaster.

Lorimer felt a sense of disappointment; it was altogether smaller and less imposing than the football club of his boyhood imaginings. Here was a tired and frankly run-down building. The door behind them had given a false first impression, what faced them was only a narrow lobby, its marble floor chipped and stained from decades of trampling feet, the plaster walls above the wood panelling a murky shade of nicotine yellow. The sole thing of interest was a row of photographic portraits hanging from a crumbling picture rail. Lorimer began to peer at the inscription on the one nearest to him and saw that it was of the present chairman, Patrick Kennedy.

Footsteps on the stairs above made him stand back even as he was thinking how different Kennedy had appeared in his younger days.

'Chief Inspector?' Lorimer recognised Ron Clark, Kelvin FC's current manager, his dark hair receding in a distinctive widow's peak from a weather-beaten forehead.

As Lorimer shook the man's outstretched hand he could see the expression of anxiety in his hazel eyes. The DCI had a fleeting thought that he was always destined to meet folk in situations that were fraught in one way or another; in his career as a policeman his outlook on humankind was inevitably distorted. Maybe this man was a good kind husband, a decent human being, certainly he had a good reputation among the football pundits.

'We're really sorry about what happened to poor Norman Cartwright. Coming after Nicko Faulkner's death . . . well, it's all a bit hard to take in,' Clark began, leading them up a flight of stairs from the darkened corridor. Lorimer glanced to one side, surprised to see another staircase running parallel with this one: that explained the architecture of the hall below at any rate.

'We have to ask questions of anyone who was here at the match or afterwards,' Lorimer explained, looking back at the Kelvin manager.

They stopped at the top of the stairs, a few feet short of a glass-fronted office where a red-haired woman sat typing. Her profile showed a sharp, determined face with lines around her mouth that suggested some displeasure with the world. She did not look up at the sound of their voices, Lorimer noticed, as they followed Ron Clark into a large room filled with glass display-cases and dark wooden furniture. A soft drinks machine sat somewhat incongruously in one corner and the walls were covered in large pictures of Kelvin teams throughout the club's long history, the more recent ones in colour dominating the room. At any other time Lorimer would have feasted his eyes on this exhibit but now he had to turn his attention to the matter in hand.

'Did you see Mr Cartwright leave the building after the game on Saturday, Mr Clark?'

'Yes, and I can tell you exactly when he did. It was at 5.38. I can be absolutely certain of that because we have a book for signing out at reception.'

Lorimer nodded, they had that sort of facts-and-figures information already, but now he was looking for first-hand impressions, something to gauge the antipathy that must have surrounded the referee before his final departure. 'Did you speak to him?'

Ron Clark averted his eyes and nodded. 'We didn't part on good terms, I'm afraid.'

'Not unreasonable, given the nature of the game,' Lorimer told him.

'You were there?' The manager's face registered surprise, as if a policeman could actually have a life outside the day job of catching criminals.

'Heard it on the radio,' Lorimer replied.

'You're a fan, then?' Clark's face creased into a smile, and for the first time since meeting the man Lorimer saw the enthusiasm that had been overshadowed by the deaths of two sportsmen associated with the club. But before Lorimer could reply he saw Clark's gaze shift to a spot behind the two policemen. Turning, Lorimer came face to face with a large lumbering figure who, for one idiotic moment, reminded him of Kelvin's panda bear mascot.

'Chief Inspector, Patrick Kennedy.' The bear proffered a massive paw and engulfed Lorimer's hand in its powerful grasp.

Kennedy's grey eyes bored into Lorimer's own, and for an instant the policeman had the sensation of being challenged. *Clear up this mess*, they seemed to be saying. *That's what you're here for.* As

79

he let go of Lorimer's hand, Kennedy attempted a sort of smile that was meant to show he was suffering the presence of Strathclyde's police officers with good grace, but the smile failed to reach his eyes, which remained cold and hard.

Lorimer felt as though he should apologise for even being there, then a sudden remembrance of Norman Cartwright's body, slumped inside his car, stiffened his resolve.

'We would like to question each of the players who were at Saturday's match, Mr Kennedy, plus anybody who had any contact with Mr Cartwright.'

'Oh? And why's that? D'you not think you'd be better off out there finding whatever madman was running about with a gun?'

Lorimer sensed DC Cameron flinch under the man's sarcasm, but the Chief Inspector was not to be put off by this sort of overbearing attitude. Lorimer had come across too many of his sort to be bothered by such tactics.

'The killing took place very shortly after the match on Saturday, a match that must have upset quite a lot of your players, given the nature of Mr Cartwright's refereeing decisions,' he said, smoothly. 'We need to investigate the time before his death in order to make sense of what happened.' Lorimer's tone was reasonable, no hint of apology to placate the man who continued to stare at them as though they were intruding on the chairman's time. He's a bully, Lorimer thought to himself, he's the sort who likes to dominate other people. He'd seen men like this before: husbands who kept their women subservient, bosses who controlled their workers through fear. Striving to restrain his instinctive dislike of the man, Lorimer continued. 'If I could speak to the team, to begin with, that would be a big help.'

A dry sound that could only be laughter issued from Kennedy's lips. '*The team*? Well, that's Mr Clark's responsibility, gentlemen.

I'll leave you in his good hands for the time being.' And with a nod to his manager, Patrick Kennedy turned on his heel and strode out of the boardroom.

Niall Cameron caught Lorimer with a questioning glance. The SIO was here as a courtesy to the club and its personnel. Were they supposed to let this man walk all over them? Lorimer's silent shrug seemed to say that they were, for now at any rate.

'The lads are downstairs, Chief Inspector. Usually they're at a training session, but when I knew you were coming . . .' Ron Clark tailed off, his unspoken words proof that at least one of Kelvin FC's staff realised the gravity of the investigation and had prepared accordingly.

'*He's* in a bit of a hurry,' Cameron commented, unable to keep the criticism from his tone.

Ron Clark shrugged. 'Mr Kennedy's upset. Such a lot's been happening.' The manager shook his head sadly, as if he could barely bring himself to speak of the two men whose bodies were lying in Glasgow City Mortuary. He stood up and moved towards his office door, the DCI and his DC falling in behind him. 'It's this way,' he said, leading the two policemen along a corridor, past the reception area. This time the red-haired woman looked up as they passed and Lorimer saw the thin, hard face turned their way and a fleeting expression that was not unfamiliar to the Chief Inspector, before she looked back at the papers on her desk. Whoever this woman was, Lorimer thought, his interest suddenly caught, she was scared. And that was intriguing, because in his experience people were only scared of the police when they had something to hide.

The players were sitting on benches around the wall of their changing room when Ron Clark ushered in the two policemen.

Whatever conversations had been going on before that moment stopped abruptly and Lorimer saw several pairs of eyes look their way. Yet his first impression was how young they all were, some still like schoolboys, and he laughed inwardly at himself; they say you know you're getting older when policemen look like laddies, he remembered his mother telling him. Well, he was becoming older now himself if this lot seemed like mere lads. Yet the longer he let his eyes roam over the group, the more he could see a few expressions that belonged to grown men: some calculating, others challenging.

'This is Detective Chief Inspector Lorimer and Detective Constable Cameron,' the manager began. 'They want to talk to you about Mr Cartwright's death on Saturday.'

Lorimer glanced at the man appraisingly; his tone of voice was that of a dad beginning to lecture his wee boys. Was there some sort of warning hidden in these words? And if so, to whom was it being directed? Another sweep of the changing room revealed nothing more than an attitude of respectfulness. They were all looking Ron Clark's way now, and Lorimer sensed that the manager controlled more than simply the players' tactics on the pitch.

Lorimer cleared his throat before speaking. 'The investigation into Norman Cartwright's death is still in its early stages and we are hoping that some of you might be able to throw a bit of light on to events that took place prior to him leaving the stadium. What we want to do is ask you all some questions. DC Cameron here will take notes of everything you can remember.' He nodded to the tall Lewisman who regarded the footballers with his usual grave expression, his PDA already to hand.

There was a shifting of feet and an exchange of glances that Lorimer took for acquiescence.

'We have already established the time Norman Cartwright left

Kelvin Park. What we need to know is who spoke to him after the match.' Lorimer waited, noting the heads that had suddenly bowed as if to hide from the reality of all that was happening. Once again he had that impression of recalcitrant schoolboys being dressed down by a headmaster. *It wisnae me*, he could almost hear them say. That was odd, surely. Why this atmosphere of collective guilt?

'Speaking harsh words to a referee you think cost you the match isn't exactly a hanging offence,' Lorimer joked, his smile wide and inviting. It worked. Some heads immediately came up and a few of the boys even managed a half-hearted smile.

'It isnae nice tae speak bad things when he'd deid, like,' one voice proclaimed.

'It's Simon Gaffney, right?' Lorimer asked, turning to a dark-haired lad who was sitting in the corner. 'You used to play for the Pars, didn't you?'

'Aye,' Gaffney said shortly, but his reddening cheeks showed more than a hint of pleasure that this Strathclyde cop had actually recognised him.

'You spoke to the ref, then?'

'Aye. An no jist me. We were blazin mad at him,' Gaffney continued, looking around at his teammates. 'Well, we were, weren't we? The man's right. He *did* ruin the game for us. Ah've seen wrang decisions but that was mental. Mean, we're really sorry he's deid an that, it's terrible, but it doesnae change whit happened on the park, ken.'

Mutterings of agreement drifted around the room and Lorimer saw that several more of the players were sitting up that bit straighter now, as if ready to say their piece.

'I called him a wanker,' one player offered and sniggers broke out among them, more in relief that the tension was broken than at the man's words.

83

'And you are . . . ?' Lorimer asked, though he recognised the striker's familiar narrow face and spiky dark hair tipped with red.

'Barry Thomson,' came back the reply.

'What else did you say to him?'

'Och, ah cannae mind. Ah wis that mad at being sent off.'

'Did you threaten him, perhaps?' Lorimer's words were spoken in a tone that belied their seriousness.

'Aye, mibbe. Cannae remember exactly.' Thomson turned a sly face towards the other players. 'Any o'youse mind whit ah said tae him?'

There was a general shaking of heads and Thomson turned back to shrug at Lorimer, a grin on his face.

'Anyone else?'

'Yes,' a voice spoke up from the shadows. Lorimer moved forwards to see better.

'Mr . . . ?'

'Douglas. Donnie Douglas,' came the reply and the policeman took in the shy expression and that unmistakable Highland accent.

'Could you tell me what you said to Mr Cartwright?'

The young man glanced around him as if regretting this sudden moment in the spotlight. 'I asked him why he'd done it,' Douglas said quietly. 'It didn't seem to make sense. I mean, one mistake you can brush off even if it seems unfair, but it was as if he was really out to get us . . .' The player's words fell away amid murmurs of assent from the others.

'And did you all feel that way?' Lorimer asked.

'No, of course they didn't, Chief Inspector. That was simply the knee-jerk reaction of disappointed players. And I can assure you that we're all completely horrified by the man's death.' Ron Clark spoke up firmly and once again the voices were silenced and Lorimer felt a short rush of anger. He'd just begun to gain their trust and now Clark had as good as told them to clam up again. Then the anger turned to curiosity. Was Clark really hiding something? And if so, was it more than a few well-chosen insults hurled at a man who was subsequently shot dead?

'Well, thanks for your cooperation. If you have any further information that might be relevant please don't hesitate to call us.' Lorimer's words were icily polite as he handed out cards with the HQ contact information.

'Well?' Niall Cameron ventured.

Lorimer shook his head. 'Didn't pick up much, did we? Except that Ron Clark's doing a good job as a nursemaid to that lot. We'll have to see what we can find from the club's external CCTV footage. At least that might show us exactly when everyone left the club and where they were headed.'

'There's the signing-out book,' Cameron reminded him.

'Aye, so there is, but that doesn't mean there wasn't someone waiting out in the car park for Norman Cartwright. Someone who might have followed him home,' he added darkly. 'We know that the weapon used was a sawn-off shotgun. That's easy enough for anyone to hide under a jacket. Sometimes they tie a bit of rope to the butt stock, loop it over their shoulder, then, bingo! No need to bring out the gun at all, just let it pivot around your hand, aim, fire, then simply let it fall and it disappears back under the jacket. If he's cool enough, he just strolls on by as if nothing has happened.'

Cameron raised his eyebrows. It sounded far too easy, the way Lorimer described it.

'The gunman could have fired the shot from a car parked by Cartwright's driveway, though, couldn't he?' he asked thoughtfully.

'True,' Lorimer replied with an approving nod in the DC's direction. Cameron was evidently using his imagination, trying to make a visual reconstruction of the scene in his head. That was good. The young man from Lewis had the makings of an excellent detective, Lorimer told himself. 'So far there's nothing to show if he was on foot or not. Hopefully that'll change. It also makes sense to see who else lived in the same neighbourhood as the victim,' Lorimer went on. 'We'll see if there's any link there. And if the house-to-house eventually turns up a witness . . .' He left the rest of the sentence hanging in the air.

Niall Cameron nodded his head. A whole lot of legwork had to be done before any tangible results might be found. They were heading back for a meeting with other members of the investigation team before Lorimer set out other lines of inquiry for them to follow. Cartwright's workplace, his family and friends – all of these would be subject to police scrutiny. The detective constable stifled a yawn. It was only Monday but it felt as though he'd done a week's work already.

CHAPTER 11

Lorimer looked carefully at the report to the Fiscal. It wasn't mandatory by law for him to have this document in his hand, but Rosie usually made sure he had sight of her reports in cases of murder, anyway. As he skimmed past the bits about issuing a death certificate he mentally blessed the blonde pathologist for her cooperation.

Norman Cartwright had died as a result of a shotgun wound to his skull: fragments of bone and shotgun pellet had penetrated the soft tissues resulting in trauma to the brain. In other words, Lorimer thought, instant death. Rosie's report included detailed descriptions of the entry wound and the pieces of shotgun pellet that had been removed from the victim's head. As she had already suggested at the scene of crime, the assailant had been only a few feet away, probably right on the pavement of Willow Grove. Lorimer read on. The angle of entry suggested that the gun had either been fired from a parked car or the gunman had crouched down, military style, to shoot his target. Pity none of Cartwright's neighbours remembered seeing a gunman flee the scene, he thought wryly, but one or two had mentioned cars passing along the street after the shot had been fired. That meant nothing, though, without a more definite link to the incident.

Meantime, the team was scouring the Glasgow streets for any

information that could be gleaned. Previous shootings of this type would be examined but it was never going to be easy to identify a specific gunman: shotguns were licensed to so many folk around the country and they would have to concentrate their search on those in the immediate area.

Something would turn up eventually, he told himself, in an attempt to bolster his confidence. It usually did.

Netta Cartwright sat clutching her handkerchief tightly, rocking back and forwards, a soft moan coming from somewhere deep inside her throat. Beside her the woman in black watched helplessly, her own face creased in pain. Having to identify Norm's body had been horrible but having to come here to tell Mum . . . Well, someone had to do it and of course it would be her, Joan Redmond thought. It was always her. On the few occasions that her brother had visited the nursing home, Mum had shown wee signs of recognising him, but on her own daily visits there was nothing. Until today. After she'd broken the news the old woman had turned to her and put up her hands in disbelief saying, 'Oh, Joan! Oh, no!' Then she'd lapsed into this quiet keening.

The police had been nice to Joan; that big tall man especially, the one who was in charge. There had been cups of tea and these trips back and from the mortuary in a big car. Yes, that had been nice of them, she thought. Pity they couldn't have been here to tell Mum . . . Her eyes filled with tears that she dashed away with the back of her hand. This was only self-pity, wasn't it? Or was she crying, like Mum, for the football-mad wee boy they could both remember?

Norman Cartwright had been an exemplary employee, according to the human resources manager. No record of poor timekeeping, few days lost through ill health and his work records always up to date. His nine-to-five existence in this government department belied the man who had scampered up and down the length and breadth of Scottish football pitches every weekend. 'A real stickler,' one of his fellow Scottish Football Association officials had told the officer who had called to ask about Norman Cartwright. 'Didn't stand any nonsense,' he'd added. That certainly tied in with the man's last match, one that would go down in the annals of football history for several reasons.

Lorimer looked at the sheets of paper before him. 'Good to his mum,' was how his sister, Mrs Redmond, had described him. So, if they were to look anywhere for a reason why Norman Cartwright had been murdered it would seem that they had to concentrate on that game in Kelvin Park after all.

Glancing at his watch, Lorimer saw that it was after nine o'clock. Maggie would have eaten long since, he supposed, feeling the hollow sensation in his empty stomach. And it wasn't fair to abandon her for hours like this. With a sigh that became a yawn, he decided to leave work for the night. Maybe tomorrow would throw something new into the mass of paperwork that lay on his desk, something that gave a clue into the killing of a football referee.

CHAPTER 12

It was still light when Jason staggered into the doorway of the club.

'Out!' The huge figure of Tam Baillie made to lunge at him but then stopped. 'Oh, it's you. Aw right then. Sorry.' And Tam, the bouncer, stepped aside to allow the footballer past.

The bouncer regarded Jason thoughtfully as he pushed his way into the brighter lights and music within. White hadn't learned his lesson, then? Tam's bushy eyebrows expressed a modicum of surprise. Some folk never learned, though, did they? With a shrug he turned back to regard the city street. Wasn't any of his business, but after Saturday's game and the referee's shooting you'd have thought even Jason White would have been keeping a low profile. Tam took out his mobile and tapped out the number he'd been given.

'Aye, he's here. Just like you said. I'll keep an eye on him. Okay?' The bouncer pocketed the phone and turned back to the street. Couldn't blame his gaffer for wanting to check up on him, could he?

The footballer blinked as he moved on to the dance floor. It was the second club he'd been in tonight. The first one had provided enough drink to get him going but none of the women had taken his fancy so he'd decided to move on. For once, Jason White was on his own. Normally he'd be accompanied by one or other of his mates, hangers-on who revelled in the glamour the footballer seemed to trail around him. But tonight Denis had cried off with the excuse that he had bad toothache and Jerry was down south on some business of his own. Were they deliberately avoiding him after last week's fracas? For a moment he thought about it. Maybe his mates hadn't liked seeing him being carted off in a police car. Or maybe they'd been spoken to by someone from the club. So what? Kennedy's tirade had fallen off him like water off a duck's back. Mentally he gave two fingers to the Kelvin chairman. It would piss him off if he knew he was here. What if he did frequent the clubs a bit more than the average player? He wasn't like them, anyway. *He* had star quality. That's what all the sports journalists were fond of writing, after all.

Jason sidled up to a blonde whose evenly clipped hair swung straight and smooth around her elfin face as if she'd ironed it specially in the hope of meeting some guy just like him. Jason jiggled up to her, moving his body suggestively and smiling his famous-footballer smile. She knows who I am, he told himself, the girl's sparkling eyes and tiny giggle giving it away. Her carefully made-up face shone with translucent blusher and she dropped her eyes coyly, revealing twin crescents of iridescent pink eyeliner. He pulled up the sleeves of his Armani jacket and danced towards her, making her shift back a little so that he took centre stage. He closed his eyes, knowing that when he opened them he'd see that adoring look they all had. Stupid cows! Still, he got what he wanted and they took home a story to tell their mates. I got pulled by Jason White! And if a few bruises took a while to settle down, so what? Girls liked a bit of rough with their tumble, didn't they?

Kelvin Park lay quiet under the darkening Glasgow skies. The car park was empty but one vehicle was parked beyond the main entrance, tucked out of sight from anyone who might be passing by. A man stopped by the metal gate and put his hand on to the padlock, giving it a slight shake, then, when there was no sound but the susurration of a little night breeze, he drew out a key and silently opened it. His footfall was silent as he crept towards the front door, nor was there any sound when he unlocked it. Only a tiny creak upon the ancient wooden stairs gave any hint to his presence as the man made his way up. But that didn't matter, he smiled to himself. They'd never hear a wee thing like that, not with the all-too familiar racket he could hear coming from beyond the chairman's office door.

He moved forward towards the passage near the top of the staircase and stopped, listening. Her moans sounded real enough, he chuckled to himself, stupid bitch wasn't even faking it. Then he stiffened as the woman's lover gave a shout that collapsed into a groan of relief.

They wouldn't be much longer, he told himself, slipping back into the shadows: a quick post-coital drink from Kennedy's private bar then they'd be leaving. She'd take a taxi, he knew that by now, all these evenings spying on them having paid off. The big man would slip into his Jag and be off back to his wife. *Working late again, dear?* she'd maybe ask him. He stifled a real desire to laugh as he made his way back into the night. Barbara Kennedy was in for a real shock one of these days, but it could wait till he was ready to deliver it: one more item on his insurance policy.

There was a sudden vibration from the mobile in his pocket.

'Yes?' he asked gruffly.

The voice on the other end told him what he wanted to know. Within minutes he was out of the darkness and into the brightly lit streets, heading towards his quarry.

*

93

It was dark by the time Jason was ready to go home. Candy (was that *really* her name or had she just made it up to impress him?) was in the ladies' toilet and Jason was lounging against the wall outside, his head ringing with the music, his body still swaying to the beat that throbbed from the nightclub. After a few minutes he pulled up a pink cuff to glance at his watch. Where the hell was she? Jason glanced back to the open doorway only to catch the bouncer regarding him with an expression of pity.

'What are you looking at?' he snarled at the bouncer, fists clenching in a reflex action. In the distance a siren whined, reminding him of that other night and, for once, sense prevailed. With the amount he'd drunk tonight he was no match for this guy. Directing a last glance towards the door, Jason shook his head. She wasn't coming out, after all. Another waste of time, all come-on and no delivery. Well, he wasn't in the mood now, anyway, so sod her and all the other bitches that made eyes at him but kept their distance.

Jason turned on his heel, attempting a deliberate swagger. He tripped instead, and cursed as the back of his hand grazed the stone wall, then, hearing laughter from the doorway, he spun round to see who was jeering at him. The bouncer had turned his head away, discretion being the better part of valour. Swearing again, Jason plunged into the shadows that loomed over the alleyway and headed towards the light of the street and the first available taxi.

Tam watched the footballer go. 'Eejit!' he muttered under his breath. The Kelvin player was going to hell on a handcart as far as he could see. 'Waste of good talent,' he told the night air, shaking his head. He'd been a Kelvin supporter all his days but on nights like this Tam Baillie's loyalty could be sorely tested.

*

94

The street was deserted when Jason rounded the corner of the alley. Looking up and down the street he could see the shop windows shuttered and still, only the lights of security cameras blinking from the darkened frontages. Squaring his shoulders, the footballer set off towards the city centre and the vague memory of a taxi rank. He hadn't been in this city long enough to know his way around much, and, besides, it was usually Jerry or Denis who organised things like taxi rides home.

The night air was cool against his face after the heat in the club and Jason gave a sigh that was partly relief and partly resignation at his failure to score with that girl, Candy. Stupid name, stupid cow, he muttered to himself, aiming a kick at an empty lager can that had been abandoned in the middle of the pavement. The sound of its metallic clanking as it skittered into the gutter seemed to resonate in the silence of the empty street. An echo – was it an echo? – made him turn around.

A figure stepped out of the shadows by the alley, walked towards him, then stopped.

Puzzled, Jason hesitated. Then he saw a hand raised, stretched out towards him.

The footballer's eyes widened in horror as a glint of light reflected off the gun.

There was no sound, no explosion bringing a crowd of people running, only a roar of light inside his head and a kick that carried the footballer off his feet. For a moment his limbs flailed in mid-air as if he were struggling to reach an elusive ball, then his body crumpled and hit the ground with a dead thud.

Nobody saw the figure that slipped back into the shadows, leaving the street as silently as it had arrived.

CHAPTER 13

The journey to HMI Cornton Vale prison had taken more than an hour this time. On a whim, Marion had chosen to drive along the country road through places she rarely saw these days, like Balloch and Buchlyvie. Now, stuck behind a tractor on a winding stretch of road, she regretted that moment of caprice. Squinting against the morning sun, she could visualise her sunglasses lying on the kitchen table. Fat lot of good there, she thought. Forgot them in all that hurry to ferry Caroline to the day nursery, Marion scolded herself. What was wrong with her these days? Was it true that part of a mother's brain shut down after giving birth or was it simply that she was trying to juggle too many balls in the air? What was she trying to prove? That she, Marion Peters, BA, LLB, could cope with the joint responsibility of motherhood and prospective partnership in one of Glasgow's leading law firms, a defiant little voice answered her. Other women managed it, didn't they? Women like the senior partner who managed somehow to have three kids and always appear immaculately turned out, Marion reminded herself with a twinge of envy.

Still, she shouldn't be late for this meeting. The prison had set aside a time for her to see Janis Faulkner and she had other duties waiting for her back in the office. That was probably why she'd taken this route, Marion realised. It was a form of escape. But, right now, all she wanted was to get away from this ruddy tractor.

Peeking round the edge of the tractor's massive wheels, Marion Peters gave a sigh. There were more cars coming in their direction. Mentally she apologised to the drivers in the line of traffic snaking behind her (they would all be men and they would all be cursing her) but in truth, there was nothing she could do about it.

Suddenly a pale blue BMW appeared out of nowhere, overtaking three cars plus the tractor, roaring into the lead and narrowly missing an oncoming silver saloon.

Marion's hands gripped the steering wheel in a moment of terror.

'Wanker!' she yelled and was gratified to see the same expression of disbelief etched on the face of the driver of the silver car as it passed.

For the next few minutes she resigned herself to the tractor's pace until, thankfully, it turned left at the end of the road.

Marion was already ten minutes late as she swung on to Stirling's ring road and headed through the town centre, past Tesco and into the Cornton area. Her heart was still thumping, but now it was with a sense of growing excitement. Could it be that she might manage to have the charge against her client dropped? And would this latest murder alter everything for the woman who was languishing so silently within these prison walls?

Janis read the newspaper with shaking hands. 'Three Murders at Kelvin' the headline proclaimed before going into details about Nicko, Mr Cartwright the referee, and now Jason White. For a moment Janis tried to remember if they had met this boy-about-town as the journalist had described him, but she could not recall the face that stared out at her from the front page of the *Gazette*.

What she saw was a good-looking man of about her own age with close-cropped hair, his friendly grin belying all the facts that were being spread down these column inches. He'd been a gambler, was used to mixing with dubious company ... She read on. Recently the footballer had been charged with assault and had missed Kelvin's opening match against Queen of the South as a result, a crime that seemed to gain disproportionately more lines than his other misdemeanours. And now he was dead, shot by an unknown Glasgow gunman. But it was the writer's thinly veiled hints that had caused Janis's hands to shake. Was he really suggesting that all three murders had been committed by the same person – that someone had a massive grudge against the club? She looked for the byline. Who was this Greer fellow, anyway? Was it the same reporter who'd made her look like a right little money-grubbing tart? If so, then he'd fairly changed his tune.

Janis raised her eyes and looked out of the square window towards the Wallace Monument and the hills beyond. Whoever he was, Jimmy Greer might well become her guardian angel. Her mouth curled into a tentative smile. Perhaps it was time to begin to speak again. And maybe it would be no bad thing to start with Mrs Marion Peters.

'Bit of a change in that one,' the prison officer remarked, walking past the closed door of the small room that led off from the prison's reception area. The interior of each room was visible due to the half-glazed door giving on to the corridor, but nothing of the conversation that was taking place could be heard. That was one advantage a prisoner's lawyer had over police officers: they were permitted to have private discussions alone with their client. The other woman glanced into the room. It was true. Janis Faulkner seemed almost animated for the first time since she had arrived at

99

Cornton Vale. It wasn't that unusual for prisoners to be withdrawn and scared in the early days of their remand, but this one seemed to have come back to life pretty suddenly. With a shrug of her shoulders, the prison officer moved on; her mind was already on other responsibilities, but a faint look of puzzlement remained on her face.

'Tell me everything you can,' Marion Peters urged. 'Anything that can make your case plausible will help to sway the judge.'

Janis Faulkner thought for a moment. 'Ask them about the bruises,' she said, slowly, aware of having been stared at by the two female officers outside. 'They wanted to know about them when I arrived. There was this form – all these questions – and I didn't let on. Too shocked, I suppose . . .' She ducked her head, hiding her expression under that swathe of corn-blonde hair.

Listening to the lilting accent, Marion wanted to believe her. There was something quite beguiling about her client's voice, she was not a Glaswegian by birth, maybe from Inverness, or even farther north. Wherever she had originated, her accent was pleasing to the ear.

'Tell me about the bruises, Janis.' Marion leaned forward across the desk, her tone confiding, woman-to-woman.

A huge sigh escaped the younger woman and she sat up again, tossing back that mane of hair with one slender hand. 'He hit me. All the time. For anything.' She shrugged. 'I just couldn't take it any more and that day I decided to go away.' A faraway look came into Janis Faulkner's eyes then as she added, 'How was I to know that Nicko would be . . .' She left the word *murdered* hanging in the air.

Their eyes met and for an instant Marion had the feeling that there was something being communicated between them that she could not put into words. Was it a plea for understanding? No, it was a lot more than that. There but for the grace of God, the woman seemed to be telling her: it could have been you, a woman, a victim of male brutality. And *had* she ended it all by sticking a kitchen knife into her husband?

Marion Peters, happily married wife and mother, put out a hand and touched her client's sleeve. 'How long?' she asked.

Janis looked away again, her lips twisted as if she were trying to stop the tears from spilling over. 'Ever since we were married. I never knew he could be like that, thought it was my own fault most of the time. Nicko made me feel bad, stupid, worthless . . .' The tears had started for real now and Marion fished in her pocket for a Kleenex tissue and passed it over.

'Especially when I . . . lost the babies.' Janis's voice had dropped to a husky whisper and she was shaking her head as if further words were simply not possible.

Marion Peters paused. Was it true? She could certainly check out the woman's physical condition from the prison's admission records and past medical history might well show a series of miscarriages brought on by so-called 'accidents'. Was this woman really more sinned against than sinning? If that was really the case, a jury might be prepared to show some sympathy.

CHAPTER 14

'He's on holiday, I'm afraid. Can I ask who's calling?'
'This is Strathclyde Police. We were hoping to speak to Dr Brightman.'

There was a short pause and a rustle of papers. 'I think DCI Lorimer has his home number,' the secretary's voice came back, crisply. 'We are not at liberty to give out details about our staff, you know.'

WPC Annie Irvine made a face at the handset as she hung up. Silly of her, she knew, but Lorimer had asked her to contact Solly Brightman asap and she had rung the university before thinking. Irvine dialled again. This time a man's voice answered.

'Hello?'

Annie Irvine felt a shiver up her spine. That dark velvety voice of his always had this effect on the policewoman. She instantly visualised his black beard and huge brown eyes, fringed with those thick lashes. That Rosie Fergusson was one lucky lady, she thought, wistfully. Maybe if Annie had the petite blonde pathologist's face and figure she might have attracted the man on the other end of this line, she told herself.

'Strathclyde Police here, WPC Irvine calling. Is that Doctor Brightman?' Annie added quite unnecessarily, but she was enjoying this call too much to let it end.

'Yes,' the voice returned, the vaguest hint of a question lingering in its assent.

Annie sighed inwardly. 'DCI Lorimer would like to speak to you, sir. May I put him through?'

'Certainly,' Dr Brightman replied, his tone simply courteous now, no overtone of curiosity provoking the policewoman's imagination.

'All right, I'll connect you,' Annie said, no longer trying to conceal her sigh.

'Lorimer.'

'Ah, it's you.'

'Solly, are you busy?' There was a silence at the other end of the line and Lorimer wondered just how long it might take the psychologist to decide whether he was or was not otherwise engaged. In normal conversation with him, the DCI was used to these lengthy pauses. Sometimes they aggravated him, but now, when he was anxious to have his friend's full attention, he was prepared to be patient.

'No, not really, that is—'

'Good,' Lorimer replied briskly before Solly could think up an excuse. 'Then you won't mind coming down to see if you can lend your weight on this one, will you?'

'Ah, it's the football murders.'

'That's right. I suppose Rosie filled you in on what's been going on?' Not waiting for an answer, Lorimer plunged on, 'We want you to come up with a profile for us. See what manner of nutter – sorry, I mean psychologically challenged person – we have out there.'

In the silence that followed, Lorimer could almost see the grin above that bushy beard. Solly would be shaking his head at Lorimer's political incorrectness. Never mind, it would be good to have him on board again. 'Can you make it down here this afternoon? Say about two o'clock?'

Lorimer put the phone down, staring thoughtfully at it for a bit. Dr Solomon Brightman had come into his life some years back when he'd been Senior Investigating Officer in a murky case involving the deaths of three young women. His expertise had been helpful then and the University of Glasgow's psychology senior lecturer had proved useful several times since. And now the Detective Superintendent had given his permission to use Solly once again. Lorimer drummed his fingers on the edge of his desk. This Faulkner case looked cut and dried in all but one respect. And it was that element that Solly would inevitably bring up. Were the three murders linked? Had the same hand that had pulled the trigger on two occasions also wielded a kitchen knife? Okay, the MO wasn't the same, Lorimer argued with himself, imagining Solly's objections and trying to counter them first. But even if a different weapon had been used first time around, the locus was similar: Nicko Faulkner and Norman Cartwright had both been killed at their own homes. Admittedly the referee's shooting had taken place outside his front door but, hey, that didn't mean all that much, did it?

The Detective Chief Inspector gave himself a mental shake. What was he trying to do? Prove to himself or to everyone else that Janis Faulkner was no killer? And for what? To show his superintendent that he'd been too hasty in his judgement? No. It was more than that, if he was to be totally honest with himself. He really and truly did not want to see that woman go down for a lengthy sentence.

And it was more to do with the way she had looked at him that day on Mull, a look that had gone straight to his heart.

*

105

Dr Solomon Brightman sat quietly, hands folded, his dark brown eyes taking in the face before him. Lorimer was in persuasive mode today, and the psychologist wasn't surprised.

'Take a look at the whole picture, Solly. Here's a Scottish First Division club with a glowing history, no sectarian issues, just a good old-fashioned family club. Now all of a sudden there are three men dead: two of their newest signings and a well-known referee. Now, call me a simple soul, but that can't just be coincidence, can it?'

Solly smiled and looked away. There was so much earnestness in the DCI's tone. It would be a pity to burst his hopeful bubble. Still, Lorimer was used to having his pet theories questioned, Solly thought. And maybe that was really what he wanted, after all – a fresh perspective in a case where he might have lost a sense of objectivity.

'The modus operandi—' he began.

'Right. I knew you'd ask about that. Frankly I can't see why a gunman can't also be a knife-man. There are plenty of both in this city,' Lorimer grumbled.

'The MO,' Solly continued, unabashed by Lorimer's interruption, 'is quite different. On the one hand you have a crime committed within the victim's own home—'

'A rented place that Kelvin had sorted out for them until they'd bought somewhere permanent,' Lorimer interjected once more.

'And on the other there are two killings that look as if the victims have been stalked. One happened at night in the street after the victim had been in a nightclub; the other at the victim's own doorstep. Each of these strikes me as calculated. Wouldn't you agree?'

'Maybe someone calculated when Nicko Faulkner would be at home, too,' Lorimer argued.

'But it has all the hallmarks of a crime of passion,' Solly reasoned. 'The kitchen knife came from their own set of knives, the injuries suggest a suddenness that is concomitant with this scenario and we now know that the widow was an abused woman. So you have it all, really: means, method and opportunity, not to say motive.' Solly sat back and folded his arms.

'Well, let's say for the sake of argument that you're wrong. Jason White and Nicko Faulkner had a lot in common. They'd both been new signings, they'd come up from clubs south of the border and they were expected to make a difference to Kelvin's prospects.'

'And the referee? Where does he fit into this picture? Anyone who had a grudge against the club would have welcomed Mr Cartwright's decisions, surely?'

Lorimer bit his lip. Solly was right. And he'd asked himself that very question over and over again. 'What if . . .' he tailed off, reluctant to voice a theory that had been gnawing away at him ever since the discovery of Jason White's body. 'What if we have someone who has no axe to grind with the club itself? What if this is a class-A lunatic? Someone who has killed these people in a fit of genuine madness.'

'You mean a multiple killer who has experienced some sort of trigger that sets him off?'

'Well, perhaps . . .'

'There doesn't appear to be anything to link these deaths at all, does there?' Solly began, his gaze wandering out to the parts of the city he could see from Lorimer's window. 'Still, it might be interesting to look at the geography of it all,' he murmured to himself.

'I can give you a map of the murders right now.' Lorimer handed over a sheet of paper with a photocopied area of the city

107

of Glasgow on which circles had been drawn in red ink. The DCI came round the desk and leaned over the map as Solly took it from him.

'There's where the Faulkners were living, there's Norman Cartwright's house and that's the street where White was gunned down. All within ten minutes' drive of Kelvin Park.' He pointed at a green dot on the map.

'How would somebody know where to find this referee?' Solly asked.

'Telephone book. Or by asking one of the club officials.'

'And did anybody do that? Ask them, I mean.' Solly turned up his face to see Lorimer frowning.

'No, we thought of that and no one can recall anybody asking where Norman Cartwright lived. Anyway, they're careful about giving out that sort of information.'

'So, we might want to begin looking at the personnel within the football club itself,' Solly mused. 'At those people who did have access to the victim's home address, perhaps.'

'Look for someone who wanted rid of two footballers and a referee?'

The psychologist gave a sigh. 'No, Lorimer, for someone who wanted rid of a referee and one football player, who had been making headlines for something other than his skills with a ball.'

'But you will accept that there is a possibility that all three are linked?'

Solly smiled wryly. 'When did you ever know me to have anything other than an open mind, my friend?'

'There's no direct correlation between them,' Rosie said, waving the ballistics report for Solly to see. 'Cartwright was killed with a shotgun, White was killed with a pistol,' she continued. 'Can't determine the exact type of weapon from the injury itself but I reckon it'll have been something like the MSP.'

'What's that?'

'It's one of these silent pistols. Its Russian nickname is *groza*, it means thunderstorm.'

'And can you say that's what caused this death?' Solly shook his head in astonishment.

'We can't,' Rosie replied. 'This is just me ravelling a thread about what *might* have been used. Won't bore you with the science, but actually it's the injury itself that shows it wasn't a rifle.' Rosie turned her head away to conceal a smile. Her fiancé was squeamish about the finer points of her work. Rosie reckoned that was a true and certain mark of his love for her; to hitch yourself to a forensic pathologist for life was no mean feat when you had a stomach as weak as Solly's. Suddenly a memory of the evening they'd met came back to her. She'd been in her white coveralls, examining a woman's blood-soaked corpse and Solly had almost fainted at the sight. He hadn't been the manly knight-on-a-white-charger sort, Rosie thought to herself, but there had been something about him that had warranted a second look. She smiled for a moment, grateful that her day job hadn't driven him away.

'Anyway, whatever type of pistol was used could well be an assassination weapon and Ballistics will love to have a look if Lorimer ever gets his hands on it.'

She watched as Solly merely nodded in reply. The report was fairly comprehensive and if ever they were to catch the perpetrator, the investigating team would want to see just where he'd obtained a firearm like that. Trouble was, her ballistics man had told her, the market was full of stuff the average career criminal could pick up in Pakistan or Eastern Europe. But the MSP was a bit specialised. *If* that had been his weapon of choice. Rosie looked again at the facts surrounding each of the shootings. Did a different weapon necessarily mean that a different finger had pulled the trigger? Or was Solly's involvement justified? For a moment she looked at him, head bent over a paper of his own, and she longed to run her hands through his dark curls. Later, she thought, later. And with a little smile of satisfaction, Rosie Fergusson sat back and continued her own evening's homework, wondering about these victims and her meticulous examinations of their remains.

'So, you might have three different killers on the loose?' Maggie said slowly, her fingers caressing Chancer's golden fur as he lay curled on her lap, half-asleep.

'No, I don't think so,' Lorimer replied. 'Either it's one man with a strange sort of vendetta against the club or, if Solly is correct, the same man plus Janis Faulkner.'

'You don't think she killed her husband, though, do you?' Maggie asked, her eyes troubled.

Lorimer heaved a sigh and shook his head. 'Don't quite know what to believe right now. If there was some sort of logical pattern to it then I'd say no. But she's well in the frame for it now it appears she has a motive as well. Battered wife,' he added, glancing up to see what Maggie would make of it.

'But why would she have to kill him? Why not simply walk out?' Maggie bit her lip, suddenly wishing she hadn't spoken those words. *She'd* walked out, hadn't she? Well, sort of – those months away on that exchange programme in America had been a time of separation, a time to sort themselves out.

'Hah! You should see the number of women who ask themselves

that very question. Cornton Vale's full of them. Think they're somehow in the wrong, stay because of the kids, oh, all sorts of reasons but usually it's because they're in thrall to some bloke with a power complex.'

'The Faulkners didn't have kids, did they?'

'No, but that's not because she didn't want any. Her lawyer tells us that Janis had several miscarriages following his brutality.'

'I still can't understand it. Why on earth would you stay with a horror like that?'

'Hm.' Lorimer sifted through a pile of papers until he came to a photocopy of a newspaper cutting. 'Here. Take a look.'

Maggie studied the picture of the man and woman. They were laughing and having fun on some exotic beach somewhere. Janis Faulkner looked like something out of a fashion magazine, her tiny tanga showing off a gorgeous body, and as for that mane of glossy hair, well, there was nothing to show that the woman was unhappy with the man in the photograph or ill-treated by him.

'You think she's making it all up?'

Lorimer shook his head. 'No. There were bruises all over her body when they brought her in. Marion Peters, her lawyer, has asked for them to be photographed as evidence.'

'But that might just as easily go against her, surely?'

'That's a risk her defence counsel is going to have to take. If they decide that all three murders were committed by someone else then she may well get off scot-free.'

Maggie Lorimer put her hand on her husband's shoulder. 'And do you think she should?' she asked softly.

Lorimer glanced at his wife. What was she really asking? Did she want his professional opinion or was she probing more deeply into a sensitive area that he didn't want to acknowledge right now?

111

'Not for me to decide,' he mumbled vaguely then planted a swift kiss on her forehead as if to conclude the conversation.

Lock-up was the worst time of the day, especially during a summer that seemed to be lasting for ever. The thin green cotton curtains failed to conceal the brightness outside and Janis had stopped bothering to pull them shut. Now she sat cross-legged upon her narrow bed, gazing out at the sky. The last wisps of pink had vanished from the space between the heavens and a horizon that was framed by the prison window. A darker blue had swept in from the east and it would be a matter of minutes before the clouds gave way to deepening shades of sapphire.

Weren't there fourteen different words in Gaelic for the colour blue? She couldn't remember. Lachie would know. It was the sort of thing she could have asked him. For a long moment Janis visualised the man she had been trying to reach on that fateful day when the police had stopped her. There was something timeless about Lachie's face, she thought: those twinkling blue eyes that could laugh or be so suddenly penetrating and that look he used give her that said so much more than words could ever say – that he understood her as no one else ever could. Janis breathed deeply, seeing again the hills behind the croft; they would be purple with heather now. She imagined herself there, turning to see the loch below, its fringes of grass and reeds alive with summer insects, the occasional ripple of a trout glistening in the day's last light.

Suddenly she shivered and realised that her arms were cold from sitting so still. It was time now to close the window on these memories and to hope that the dreams that came would be as kind.

CHAPTER 15

The reporters were all clustered around the main gate when Albert Little came to open up for the day.

'Wasters,' he muttered under his breath, scowling at them and standing aside as they pushed in. 'Like a lot of jackals,' he spat out after them, but nobody seemed interested in the opinions of a mere groundsman. Still, that suited him; he'd work to finish and it wouldn't do to fall behind his schedule.

One by one the newspaper men and women came to a halt at the front entrance and turned to see if Albert would open up for them.

'You'll need to wait for the polis,' he told them, a smile of satisfaction spreading across his weather-beaten features as the protests began. 'This is a secure area now,' he added and, as if to prove Albert's point, at that moment a police van rolled into the car park. 'Youse cannae get in without a special permit.' He grinned, then, opening the main door, he stood arms folded, as if daring anyone to pass. 'Ah've got ma orders, so ah have, an ah cannae let onybody in.'

There was a muttering, then one man stepped out from the crowd and stood directly in front of the groundsman. He was a tall, spare individual, a nicotine-stained moustache giving him the look of a dissolute cowboy villain, but the eyes that stared into

Albert's were sharp as flints. Albert felt the folded notes being pressed into his palm and heard the whispered words: 'Jimmy Greer. The *Gazette*. Just you give me an exclusive. More where that came from, pal. Round at the Wee Barrel, six o'clock, right?'

Albert grunted and looked away as if he was completely disinterested but his gnarled fingers pocketed the money.

Greer stepped away and made a face to the crowd, pretending that Albert had given him a flea in his ear. 'Wee Hitler!' he exclaimed then pushed through the lines of journalists to where the uniformed officers were alighting from their van. The others turned and followed the *Gazette*'s senior reporter, the groundsman temporarily forgotten.

'Bunch o' sheep!' Albert snorted in disgust, but he fingered the notes in his pocket, calculating their worth and wondering if he would meet up with this chancer, Greer, later on or not.

Kelvin Park was virtually in a state of siege, thought Patrick Kennedy, as he gazed from his vantage point upstairs. If it had been match day then all of this rabble could have been sent packing by officers from the local division who came as a matter of routine to keep order among rival groups of fans. But no opposing teams would meet out on the pitch today. For the players it was the business of training as usual. He was glad that Ron Clark believed in hard work as a panacea for all ills, even for the shock of knowing your colleagues might have been picked off by some nutter on the loose on the streets of Glasgow. There had been some frightened faces among the players as they'd arrived for training.

Kennedy had been wakened in the wee small hours by DCI Lorimer telling him about White's death. Since then he'd hardly had a good night's sleep. When he'd opened his eyes this morning it still seemed like some wicked dream he'd been having and it was only his wife Barbara's hushed tones that had brought him fully awake and facing reality. Now the chairman stood, hands behind his back, gazing out at the empty expanse of green and Wee Bert walking around the perimeter of the pitch with his white paint-marker. There was something infinitely reassuring about the groundsman's activities, he realised, watching the man mark out the lines with military precision. Thank God someone was behaving normally at least.

Pat Kennedy pursed his lips. Things weren't going right at all. By now the newspapers should have been full of the success of his two new signings, White and Faulkner, plus the news that he'd so far kept to himself of Kelvin's putative new stadium. Kennedy clenched his fists so hard that his fingernails dug into the flesh. He'd worked and planned meticulously to achieve it all and Barbara's control of the shares would be meaningless once he'd finished . . . He'd imagined the headlines in all the local papers, especially after the hype they'd written about his promising new players being sure to take Kelvin into the Premier League this season, but nothing could have prepared the chairman for what had actually appeared instead. 'Kelvin Killer at Large' one of them had written; 'Football Club Seeks Protection' another one had proclaimed. And it was true: Kennedy had insisted that Lorimer provide them with some form of security. The DCI had listened to his harangue on the telephone and answered politely that while Strathclyde Police could not offer continuous police protection, they would make every effort to give advice to the players and staff and in fact a senior liaison officer had been promised at the club within the hour. Kennedy had ended the call with a sense of dissatisfaction. It was one more instance of things slipping out of his control, he thought, as he watched the groundsman mark out the pitch.

He should really speak to the players, give them some reassurance, let them know that 'Big Pat' Kennedy wasn't standing for any nonsense. An official from the Scottish Football Association had already been on the phone to ask if the fixtures were to continue as planned. Kennedy had said Yes, of course, and had merely grunted when the fellow on the other end of the line had gone on at length about offering commiserations and did he want the association to send anything to White's family? With a sigh that seemed to come from his boots, Kennedy contemplated that other, necessary, call. What on earth was he to say to White's mother? Had the player disclosed the bollocking he'd been given? Kennedy chewed his lip for a moment. No, probably not. The wee toerag wouldn't have wanted his mammy to know he'd been in trouble with his new boss.

Kennedy shuddered. This wouldn't do at all. Thinking ill of the dead was just as bad as speaking it, and it would make things a lot worse if he should blurt out exactly what he had thought about the late Jason White.

Despite the manager's best intentions, business was anything but normal for the players that morning. Usually they'd be training outside with Ally Stevenson, their coach, but today they had been making do with the facilities in the gym. Stevenson looked as glum as they all felt. By this time of the morning he'd usually be bawling them out, running back and forwards with them, his thickset figure belying the man's strength. Stevenson had been a professional footballer years ago but now he resembled more a wrestler or a prop forward. Some players hinted that years of steroids had altered the coach's physique, but none of them would ever have dared ask him.

'Where's Donnie Douglas?' Stevenson growled.

'Dunno. Not everyone came in this morning,' Baz Thomson mumbled.

'Well, he's supposed to be here,' the coach objected. 'Anyone else missing?' Stevenson looked round at them. What he saw were boys whose heads were bowed, not only avoiding the coach's stare but deliberately failing to look at one another. There was a collective sense of grief about them that Stevenson suddenly admired. They were good lads, all of them. Even if White had been a bit of a Jack the Lad, he'd been their teammate and his murder was a huge shock.

'Ally, d'you know what we're meant to be doing?' Gudgie Carmichael spoke up at last.

Stevenson shook his head. 'Waiting for Mr Clark and Mr Kennedy to come down and see us all,' he replied. A few heads shot up at his words. They weren't used to hearing Ron Clark being referred to as *Mister*, Ally thought. But it had seemed right to speak in that way even if such formality had a strange, funereal foreboding about it. Why had he said that? The manager, whilst not being their bosom buddy, was an approachable sort and they had begun to have a good rapport with him. But everything was different now; all their relationships with one another were under scrutiny and would be until they found who had killed these three men. And the sooner these boys realised that, the better.

Pat Kennedy strode into the gym, followed by the manager and a uniformed police officer.

Kennedy introduced the stranger. 'This is Sergeant Cornwell. He's from Strathclyde Police and will be helping you to . . .' He broke off, turning to the policeman who had moved into the centre of the room to give a full explanation.

'Good morning.' The officer turned slowly, making eye contact with each and every one of them. 'There are various matters that

I want to discuss with you, but mostly to let you all know that there has been a special police protection unit set up, should you wish to avail yourselves of that.' Seeing a few blank looks, the policeman stifled a sigh and added, 'We can arrange for CCTV cameras to be set up in your own homes if you so wish. Not that we think any of you are in any immediate danger.' He finished off with a tentative smile.

'What're you gonnae do?' Baz Thomson demanded of the man sitting next to him in the club coach.

Andy Sweeney, the Kelvin captain, gave a shrug. 'Do what they've suggested. Make sure I'm travelling with someone else to and from the club,' he said. 'Mandy'll kill me if I don't,' he added, referring to the dark-haired beauty to whom he was engaged.

'Is it yer bird ye're scared of or some nutter?' Baz jeered.

Sweeney gave a sheepish laugh then asked, 'What about you?'

'Och, I don't know. Kind of ruins your street cred tae have a mate follow ye around, know whit ah mean?'

'That's daft,' Gudgie piped up from across the aisle. 'They said it would only be till they caught the guy. Why take a chance?'

'And what if they don't catch him, eh?' Leo Giannitrapani, the Sicilian striker, cut in. 'What if this is some sort of vendetta?'

'Ach, away ye go, Leo. Glasgow's no like Sicily. We've nane o' yer Mafioso gangsters here,' Baz protested.

'Want to bet?' came a soft voice from behind them. The other players turned to look at John McKinnery. No one spoke. McKinnery's family were all drug dealers and it had been his passion for the sport that had hauled the young footballer away from that ghetto.

There was a silence after that while the coach sped down the strip of motorway that led to their training ground. But John

McKinnery's gaze travelled from one player to another as though he were sizing them all up. He'd come from a world where life was cheap and sometimes short, but murder seemed to be no respecter of persons or places. Being on the right side of the tracks no longer seemed the safe option and McKinnery was experiencing the first bitter taste of life's ironies.

CHAPTER 16

Willie shoved the last pair of boots into the dookit and sat back on to the floor with a groan. It wasn't so bad polishing them all after every training session and the boy really didn't mind doing them post-match either, but the heat down in the boot room was oppressive. The smell of polish mingled with an older, mustier odour: decades of sweat and toil overlaid by the dust that gathered in each dark corner of the room. There was no window in this place and the only light came from the partially opened door that led to the stone-flagged corridor.

He closed his eyes and tilted his head back, then rolled it from side to side, just like the physio had shown them. The dizziness was probably just from bending forward for so long, that and this stuffy atmosphere. If only the place had decent air conditioning, he thought, but Kelvin FC still lacked some of these useful devices. Those other more modern clubs had it all. His mate Derek had told him about the new stadium at Falkirk with all its mod cons. The boy sighed. He was happy enough where he was for now and if he stuck at it maybe he could have a real chance of making it into Kelvin's first team in years to come.

His body slumped against the wooden bench that ran around the tiny room and for a moment he let his mind slip into a fantasy where he was running out on to that green pitch wearing Kelvin's black and white strip. He saw a ball cross over his way and suddenly it was at his feet and he was running, running down the park, his marker trying to keep up with him. But his feet were speeding over the turf and the goal was in sight. With one eye on the goal mouth he aimed, kicked and shot. The roar of the crowd sang in his ears and he was being raised up high on several pairs of shoulders.

A cold current of air woke the boy from his reverie and he opened his eyes. From the corner furthest from the door he sensed a movement that made him turn and stare.

'No!' he cried, backing away from the figure that loomed towards him, shielding his face with both arms. With a whimper he scrambled for the half-open door and staggered into the corridor.

Just once he risked looking behind him. And what he saw made him run headlong towards the back stairs, and safety.

'It was real. I tell you I saw it!'

'Okay, calm down, Willie. Hey, you're shaking, son.' Jim Christie, the kitman, put a hand on the boy's shoulders, feeling the tremble through his thin T-shirt. 'Tell me again, what happened?'

Willie closed his eyes as he began to speak. 'I wis jist sitting there, right? I'd just finished polishin a' the boots and I wis jist havin a wee rest. Then it all got cold and . . .' The boy opened his eyes wide and Jim saw him try to blink back tears.

'I saw it.' His voice dropped to a whisper. 'I saw the ghost of Ronnie Rankin!' he said, one hand clutching the kitman's sleeve, as if he needed the reassurance of holding on to something safe and solid.

*

Ron Clark groaned. Three murders and now another sighting of the legendary Kelvin ghost: it was simply too much to bear. The manager bit his lip. It wouldn't be so bad if they could keep it to themselves, but he doubted that would be possible. The evening papers would be full of it. He could just imagine the headlines suggesting that Ronnie Rankin's shade had been disturbed by what was going on at Kelvin Park. It was a load of bollocks. All of it. There was no ghost down in the boot room, just a wee daft laddy with an overactive imagination.

He knocked on the chairman's door and pushed it open.

'Well? What are we to do about all this nonsense?' Big Pat began, leaning back in his captain's chair and glowering at his manager.

'Nothing.'

'Eh? I'm not standing for this sort of tosh, Ron! Sack the wee blighter.'

Ron Clark sat down in the chair opposite and shook his head. 'I don't think so, Pat. Jim Christie said the boy was genuinely terrified. The press would make a meal of it if we kicked him out. Why not just ignore it? Treat it as another nine-day wonder.'

Pat Kennedy pursed his lips and for a moment he seemed ready to argue. The manager kept his gaze steady, waiting for the chairman's response.

'Ach, I suppose you're right, Ron. It'll all blow over eventually. But tell the boy he's relieved from boot duties, meantime. And find a lad who'll do the work and not end up having bad dreams down there!'

'Fine.' Ron attempted a smile. 'What about Saturday's fixture?'

Kennedy returned the smile with a nod. 'Aye. A league match

123

against Dundee will suit us fine. And they've promised us maximum security.'

'Who's the ref?'

Kennedy managed a smile this time. 'Graham Dodgson.'

Clark breathed a sigh of relief. 'Well, that's one problem solved. Dodgson's never been known for a truly controversial decision.'

'No, but he doesn't suffer fools gladly either,' the chairman growled. 'It'll be fine, Ron. Just stop worrying. Okay?'

'A ghost, eh?' Jimmy Greer grinned at the man sitting opposite him in the Wee Barrel. He slurped his pint, letting the foamy head settle on to his moustaches, then licked them slowly, never taking his eyes off the Kelvin groundsman.

'Aye, that's what ah said. A ghost.'

'And who's it meant to be – Norrie Cartwright?'

Bert looked sourly at the journalist. 'That's not very funny,' he replied with a sniff of contempt.

Greer laughed, then, looking over his shoulder to check that they were out of earshot, he leaned forward. 'What about my other story, though? I thought we had a deal.'

Bert looked intently at his glass, his mouth a straight line of disapproval. He'd hardly touched the whisky, somehow it seemed better to down it once this business was done. After all, the man was paying for it.

'Ah'll tell you what ah know but only on condition that ye never let on who told you, right?' As his eyes met Greer's, he saw the grin fade from the journalist's face. Then a nod of agreement told him that they had a deal, but one that was on Bert's terms.

'Listen.'

'I'm all ears.'

'Look, Greer, less of the cheek, right? This is serious stuff we're talking aboot.'

'Okay, okay, keep yer hair on.' Greer raised his hands in a conciliatory gesture. 'I'm listening. Sure I am.'

Bert leaned closer. 'There's a lot goin on at this club. Mair than you or onybody else knows aboot.' He paused then sat back, as if unsure of what to say next.

'If it's the money . . . ?'

'Well, it's got tae be worth my while. This could cost me ma joab, know whit ah mean?' Bert's voice took on an aggrieved tone.

'I'll see you all right, pal,' Greer replied. 'Double what I gave you today and the same at the end of the month. For three months. Okay?'

Bert seemed to consider this. 'Aye, ah suppose so,' he said at last.

Greer took another long draught of his pint and set down the glass with a thud. 'Right, let's be having you, then.'

'Big Pat Kennedy had a real humdinger of a row wi Jason White jist afore he died,' Bert said.

Greer's eyebrows rose. 'Go on.'

'Well, ah wis in the next room but you couldnae help but hear him. He wis yelling at the lad as if he wis gonnae knock his block aff. Then,' Bert paused for effect, 'then he says if White ever pulled a stunt like that again he'd have him. Says nobody wis expendable,' he added, nodding solemnly.

Greer made a face. 'You really expect me to think that Big Pat Kennedy had something to do with White's murder?'

'Well,' Bert said, still nodding, 'he's got one hell of a temper.'

Greer frowned. 'What're you trying to say? Do you actually know something about all this? I can't write something that's mere speculation, you know.'

Bert looked hard at the journalist then picked up his whisky and downed it in a shot. Wiping his mouth with the back of his hand, he gave another sniff. 'Mibbe ah do, and mibbe ah don't.' He stood up, ready to leave the pub.

Pushing aside his chair he fixed Greer with a different look, his head to one side, a thoughtful expression on his weather-beaten face. 'Oh, and there really is a ghost. More than one person's seen it over the years. Ask Jim Christie if you don't believe me.' And with that Albert Little walked away, leaving the *Gazette* reporter staring after him.

Jimmy Greer gave a slow smile as he watched the groundsman leave. He was an arrogant little shit, right enough, but he could be useful. Greer knocked back the last of his pint then put down his empty glass. Aye, he could be useful but, though he might think it, Albert Little sure as hell wasn't his only source of information at the club.

CHAPTER 17

Maggie stretched slowly, her toes pointing towards the end of the bed. If she didn't disturb him maybe he'd stay a little longer, warming her body. It felt so good to have him in bed beside her, his breathing deep and regular, his head tucked against her breast. It was after eight o'clock and she really should have been up and about. Her husband would be at work by now, this case was making extra demands on his time. She smiled ruefully. Their holiday in Mull had done them both the world of good but how long would he feel its benefit? Already his eyes had taken on that all-too-familiar look of intensity, heightened by darker circles that spoke of sleepless nights spent puzzling things out.

It was funny how life turned out. They'd met as students at the University of Glasgow, she was studying English Lit, Bill immersed in History of Art. Maggie had kept to her vision of teaching English but her husband had dropped out and become a policeman, though his passion for art had never diminished. Maggie remembered the nights they'd spent in bed when they'd first been married, whispering plans about their futures: they'd have two kids, a rambling house in the country with dogs and cats, maybe hens at the foot of a long back garden. She'd had an image of herself as the earth-mother type, tending her young, her husband coming home after a hard day's work to a pot of something wholesome bubbling on the stove. Well, she'd certainly become a damned good cook, even if she said it herself, but other elements of that faraway dream had melted to nothing over the years.

She turned slightly but it was enough to disturb the slumbering cat and he slithered away from her side and landed on the carpet with a gentle thump, leaving a warm spot where he had been curled beside her. Maggie sighed. The soft fur against her bare skin had been such a sensuous pleasure. Now she may as well get up and be about her day, there was plenty to be done. Still she lay there, relishing the sense of freedom and considering the day ahead. Summer holidays were for catching up with things that were neglected during term-time and she had made good inroads into the garden, but there was also the forthcoming term to prepare for. A load of paperwork was waiting for her downstairs. Maggie had ignored it during this fine weather, telling herself it couldn't last: the rains would come eventually and she'd tackle it then. Yet this spell of heat had gone on and on for weeks now and there was no sign of it breaking. Maybe she'd potter in the garden and then have a look at the Edinburgh Festival guide. There was plenty she wanted to see at the book festival, for instance, and she'd miss her favourite authors if she didn't book up soon.

Chancer jumped back on to the bed with a meow that Maggie had come to recognise as *feed me*. She was out of bed and on her feet before she had time to think about it.

'You've fairly got me trained, haven't you, wee fellow?' Maggie laughed, wrapping her cotton dressing gown around her.

Downstairs in the kitchen, Maggie watched the ginger cat scoffing his breakfast. 'Wonder if anyone'll phone today,' she thought aloud. It was a while now since she had put up all those posters of Chancer with the message that he was a stray and asking if anyone wanted to claim him. She'd left her number but she'd also left a postscript saying she was happy to give him a home if he remained unclaimed. Her eyes rested on their back door. A good joiner could cut a cat flap out of the bottom panel. She'd seen different ones in the pet shop where she had left one of the flyers. Chancer would have to have a collar, she thought, and she would need to have him chipped. Stop it, woman, Maggie scolded herself. This was daft. She was simply setting herself up for a disappointment if Chancer's owner suddenly materialised.

Life had brought her too many disappointments already, she thought sadly. She could just imagine somebody like Solly Brightman telling her that this wee cat was simply a substitute for the baby she couldn't have. Or would he? The psychologist was a gentle man and somewhat other-worldly. Maggie smiled. He and Rosie Fergusson made a good pair: the pathologist's brisk common sense a foil to her fiancé's dreamy manner.

'Wonder what sort of kids they'll have?' she addressed the cat. Chancer ignored her, head down in his bowl.

Dr Solomon Brightman gazed out across the Glasgow rooftops. The skyline was hazy today, the view on the other side of the river Clyde blurred by the heat that shimmered over the city. He stared at the familiar dark spire with its distinctive spikes that so reminded him of a knight's mace. Glasgow University's tower was a landmark that could be seen from many points in the city and Solly was fiercely proud to be part of it. The new university term was still weeks away and he had plenty of time to think about next year's intake of students but he continued to look at the buildings on Gilmorehill as if seeking inspiration.

These murders were far from simple. Despite what DCI Lorimer wanted to think, there was more than one hand at work. It had happened to them before: jumping to the conclusion that a serial killer was on the loose when in fact that had not been the case at all. Solly had considered the locations of each crime and thought long and hard about the modus operandi: two different sorts of guns had killed the referee and Jason White, a kitchen knife had fatally wounded Faulkner. There were so many possible permutations for motive. But it was all conjecture. What if someone had a grudge against players from south of the border? That ruled out the referee, of course. Or what if someone from inside the club was trying to prevent any new signings taking over from existing ones? Again, that precluded Norman Cartwright. Or, to look at it another way, what if Janis Faulkner had killed her husband in a fit of passion? Was it a mere coincidence that another team player had been subsequently gunned down and that this other player had also been a new signing from England? Solly absent-mindedly ran a finger through his beard. He'd never felt any hostility from a single soul in this city, only kindness and helpfulness. Even late-night drunks had been generous in their garrulity, plying him with their life stories as if he were one of their mates, not a man whose accent still betrayed his London origins. No, he would confidently rule out any racial motive.

What he had to do was to put himself inside the skin of these killers. Why had someone mercilessly shot the referee? Spectators shot their mouths off about what they saw as a bad decision, they didn't stalk the man in black to his own home and then shoot him dead in cold blood. It was more than that, Solly decided. There was a calculation about this killing, and of Jason White's, that spoke to him of an agenda. This man (and he was certain that it was a male killer) had a reason for killing these two sportsmen.

130

Perhaps a person of normal mentality might not see whatever had driven him as a valid reason for killing, but Solly knew that the mind behind these killings saw things in quite different terms. The deaths had been necessary to him, a logical conclusion to whatever mental pathways he had taken.

And Solly was beginning to feel that the man who had pulled those two triggers had also watched Kelvin football team from somewhere other than the comfort of his own armchair.

'We need an update,' Lorimer said. 'The press are snapping at our heels and Mitchison's on my back demanding public reassurance before Kelvin's next game.'

The DCI was walking towards the nightclub where Jason White had last been seen before his death, DC Niall Cameron loping along by his side. Lorimer's brow was furrowed in a permanent crease these days, the Lewisman observed, glancing at his boss. He'd hit the ground running after his holiday and, as usual, was breaking all the rules about working-time procedures. Cameron had been happy to do overtime, his daily cycle through the city becoming earlier with each passing day, a fact that had so far gone unnoticed by Superintendent Mark Mitchison.

They reached the black door of Jojo's, one of the city's classier nightclubs, with its familiar bright pink logo. Lorimer rang the buzzer and waited. Niall Cameron noticed his boss shifting from one foot to the other, his impatience barely concealed. The Detective Constable knew how he felt; they all wanted something, anything that could provide a clue to untangling this triple killing.

A muffled voice sounded from the intercom.

'Strathclyde Police,' Lorimer announced to the grey metal box, then an unseen lock shifted and the door clicked open.

Pushing the black door open, they entered an unlit reception area with a door marked 'cloakroom' to their left. Footsteps coming from a basement room below made them step further into the darkness.

Lorimer looked around him, trying to see each shape in this claustrophobic place, aware of the breath tightening within his chest. It was a weakness he had struggled to overcome in his job, but sometimes it still caught him unawares. It was a relief when a figure loomed towards them and snapped on a light switch on the corridor wall.

'Sorry about that,' the man said. 'Forgot you were coming in. Tam Baillie,' he announced, offering his hand to each of the officers in turn. 'Assistant manager,' he grinned. 'Jist – *just* promoted,' he corrected himself, as if the job description had included the need for brushing up his spoken English. Or was it the presence of two of Strathclyde's finest?

'Detective Chief Inspector Lorimer. Detective Constable Cameron.'

Lorimer felt the strong grip that matched the assistant manager's physique; those broad shoulders and athletic frame told him that Baillie was a force to be reckoned with. But the man's grey eyes were smiling at him.

'Hell of a business, isn't it?' Baillie began, motioning them to follow him to where the light now showed a spiral stair descending downwards. All three men had to bend to avoid the low ceiling slanting across the turn of the stair.

'In here, if you don't mind. It's a bit cramped but at least we can sit down,' Baillie grumbled, adding, 'If we can find some chairs.' In one easy movement he heaved three plastic chairs from a stack in the corner resting against a towering pile of empty drinks crates. 'There we are, sit yourselves down.'

Lorimer resisted the temptation to dust down the seat. Baillie's attempts at friendliness might just as easily turn to pique if he showed any sort of criticism of the place. Truthfully, it was a shambles. The walls were dingy with age and grime, dotted here and there with bits of Blu tack where posters had been. Behind Baillie a flyer had been pinned, showing forthcoming events. Lorimer recognised one of them, a local indie band called Micronesia. Tam Baillie sat down in front of the poster, obscuring the date of the band's next gig.

'Right: Jason White. Your lads came down already to ask us what happened that night,' the recently promoted bouncer began, his eyebrows raised. 'Something come up, then?'

Lorimer bent his head in a neutral gesture. 'We're still looking into the events of that night,' he began. 'What I'd like is for you to cast your mind back to the other incident,' he said, 'the one where White ended up in custody.'

Tam Baillie slouched back in his chair, the friendly expression vanishing in a sudden scowl.

'Know what, Chief Inspector?' he said. 'That wee guy was an accident waiting to happen, if you want my opinion.'

'Oh? Why's that?'

'Och, he had attitude, know whit I mean? He was full of himself. Had money to burn, paraded it all the time. Pulled the birds like it was a game to him. Him and these two mates of his. Right wankers, they all were.'

'And on the night White was arrested . . . ?' Lorimer pulled Baillie back to the matter in hand.

The man rolled his shoulders as if sitting still for any length of time would make him seize up. He didn't look as if he'd had much experience of a desk job. Lorimer wondered briefly about his change in status. Was the promotion a way of rewarding faithful service or shutting him up?

'He was wasted,' Baillie began. 'Don't know what he'd had before he came into the club. This is a clean place, we don't tolerate substance abuse,' he continued, sounding as though the phrase was a practised one that rolled off his tongue whenever authority loomed. 'But he had a real skinful in here and then just started the aggro.'

'Can you describe what took place?'

'He had this bird.' Baillie made a grimace of distaste. 'Wee lassie she was, all gooey-eyed to be fancied by a footballer. They're all the same,' he complained, 'daft wee lassies running after the Armani suits, sniffing a bit of glamour. And money,' he added cynically. 'Anyway,' the bouncer caught Lorimer's warning glance at this further digression. 'He has this girl up against the wall and she's screaming blue murder. Then a lad appears from the dance floor and tells White to leave her alone. Next thing we know he's laying into the boy and then, before I could step in, there's a real free-for-all going on. Lassies screaming and bottles being flung across the room; White in the middle of it all. He'd head-butted the lad and there was blood runnin' down the boy's face. I grabbed White and told him to cool it, but he just went mental, so we called the police and had him carted off.' Baillie looked from one to the other. 'That's it, really.'

'So,' Lorimer began, 'how did you react when he returned to the club the night he was killed?'

Tam Baillie dropped his gaze and the DCI sensed his discomfort.

'Ach, the boss said to let him in if he came back again.'

'Is that company policy? Don't you normally ban trouble-makers from your club?'

Baillie met Lorimer's intent stare. 'The boss is a Kelvin supporter. Obviously. Likes to encourage the lads,' he muttered.

'You didn't approve of that?' Cameron asked quietly.

'Naw, ah didnae,' Baillie retorted, his attempt to match the DCI's fluent tones suddenly deserting him. 'Ah follow Kelvin an all, but if it had been up tae me ah'd have banned the wee nyaff!'

'But your boss thought differently?' Lorimer asked.

'Aye.'

'Who exactly is your boss, Mr Baillie?'

Tam Baillie's eyebrows shot up. 'Mean, youse didnae know?' The man looked from one officer to the other. 'It's Pat Kennedy.'

Lorimer tried not to look surprised. 'And he didn't ban White from his club?'

The former bouncer shook his head. 'Naw. I even phoned Kennedy up that night, like he'd asked me to.'

Lorimer swallowed hard. This was one bit of information the Kelvin chairman had not thought to share with the investigating team. Still, it wouldn't progress things to take out his displeasure on Tam Baillie.

'So White was no trouble that night?' he asked, keeping his tone as diffident as he could.

'Naw,' Baillie smirked suddenly. 'Tried tae pull a bird but she wasnae havin any of it. Gave him a right dizzy. So he jist left.'

'And that was the last you saw of him?'

Baillie sat up suddenly as if he had heard something in Lorimer's tone that he didn't like. 'What're you saying?'

Lorimer stared at the bouncer, his blue gaze unwavering. 'Just that. Did you see him after he left? Which direction did you see him take?'

Baillie's relief was palpable as he answered, 'I was in the doorway. On duty. Saw him go down the lane. But I didnae see which way he went. Told your other lot that,' he added, sticking out his lower lip petulantly.

'Thank you, Mr Baillie. It's really helpful to have an idea of the background,' Lorimer said, rising to his feet and extending a hand.

'Tam,' the bouncer told him, 'jist call me Tam.'

Tam Baillie waited until the two men were out of sight then pushed the black door hard-shut. He clenched his fists and found that they were damp with sweat. Rubbing them on the seat of his new Slater suit, Tam shook his head. That hadn't been so bad, the busies were just doing their job, checking up. And he'd told them the truth, hadn't he? The boss couldn't fault him for that, surely.

CHAPTER 18

'There's something I think you should see, sir.'

Lorimer looked up from the mess of papers that littered his desk to see WPC Irvine hovering at his doorway. He frowned at her, from sheer habit, though the interruption was not unwelcome.

'Yes?'

'One of Kelvin's first team, sir. His background report . . .' Irvine hesitated, tucking a wayward strand of dark hair behind one ear. She approached his desk. 'Thought you should know.'

Lorimer glanced at the A4 page then leaned back into his chair with a whistle.

'Interesting,' he remarked, then gave her a smile that made her own face light up with a mixture of pleasure and relief. 'Let me know if you find any more like that, will you? And thanks,' he added, catching her eye and nodding his approval as the policewoman slipped out, leaving the door ajar.

Lorimer's smile faded as he read the report. So, it seemed that Donnie Douglas had a bit of a past. The footballer had been signed during the previous season from Inverness Caledonian Thistle, a team that had rocketed up the league tables in recent years. Lorimer remembered his performances on the pitch; he was a solid mid-fielder but a sharp eye could see that he hadn't really settled into the team. According to the report, Douglas lived in digs in Glasgow's West End. But what really interested the DCI was the note about his father. Douglas senior was currently being detained at Her Majesty's pleasure in Peterhead prison for manslaughter. Lorimer read on. The victim's death had been the result of a bar-room brawl. But it had not been his first conviction for violence, which included the illegal possession of firearms, and Douglas had been sent down for fifteen years.

Lorimer felt a stirring in his blood. Donnie Douglas had not turned up for training since Jason White's body had been discovered. He'd not been the only one, but there was a yellow Post-It note stuck to a page quarter-way down the heap on his desk that was meant to remind the SIO to find out why. Lorimer nodded to himself. The boy might've gone to ground deliberately, feeling threatened by his father's criminal record. Whoever said that mud sticks was right; few people ever managed to escape their past, though the footballer must have been making a real effort to do just that. Still, it might be a lead, and should be followed up.

'Donnie Douglas? No, he hasn't. Yes, we've tried to contact him at home. No, there wasn't a reply. No, we couldn't reach him on his mobile either. Sorry. What? Why d'you have to do that? Oh, I see. Oh. Well . . .'

Ron Clark put the phone down, his hand trembling. It was a stupid oversight on his part, he supposed. The out-of-towners had been allowed a bit of time off from training this last week and the Kelvin manager had simply lumped Douglas with them. His Highland accent was to blame, perhaps, making Clark forget that he was a Glasgow resident now. So, where was Donnie? He bit his lip. The police were going to obtain a search warrant for the

138

player's flat. With a sick feeling in the pit of his stomach, Ron Clark tried to wrench his thoughts away from what they might find there.

'Strathclyde Police.' DC Niall Cameron held up his warrant card for the man to read. A pair of treacle-brown eyes glanced at the card then came back to look him up and down. Mr Singh, a turbaned man in his late fifties with a luxuriant pair of well-oiled moustaches, stood in the doorway. Then with a show of reluctance he stepped aside, letting Cameron and his colleague enter the flat in Barrington Drive. They'd taken the underground to Kelvinbridge then walked along the tree-lined avenue, noting several tiny well-tended gardens. The small patch that hugged the entrance to Donnie Douglas's flat had a resplendence of crimson-coloured roses, their stems bent under the masses of blooms. As they'd waited on the front steps for Mr Singh to answer the bell push, Cameron had drawn in their scent and for a fraction of a second he'd been reminded of home; a fleeting image of the garden with its waterfalls of climbing roses came to mind before the landlord's voice had obliterated that fragile memory.

'We don't have any trouble here,' Mr Singh began. 'No trouble. Ever,' he said firmly.

Niall Cameron kept his expression neutral. The man's protestations might well be an indicator of some incident in the past, or maybe he really did run a strict regime in his flats. It didn't matter either way; the warrant in the DC's pocket gave him immediate entry into Donnie Douglas's rented rooms.

'Would you be good enough to show us Mr Douglas's flat, sir?'

The man glared at Cameron then turned wordlessly, leaving the DC and his colleague to follow him into the darkened hallway.

Cameron gave a nod to the young man who trailed just behind him. John Weir was fresh out of uniform and this was his first day in CID. His dark suit and pristine white shirt were as brand new as the slicked-back haircut. DC Weir smiled nervously and nodded back. It gave Cameron a peculiar feeling to be in charge of this outing.

As the landlord unlocked the door to the footballer's rooms, Cameron remembered all that Lorimer had told him about reading a person's surroundings. It wasn't enough to look for evidence of a crime, you had to see what a place could tell you about the people who lived there. The main door was a solid enough affair with a bell push on the polished frame. Underneath was a metal plate where names of tenants could be inserted. A scrap of paper bearing the footballer's name in childishly formed capitals had been pushed into the space, a temporary measure until something better came along.

Afterwards he would tell Lorimer that it was the smell that hit them first as they moved into the flat. Not the pungent rotting smell of a decaying corpse, an expectation that had been hovering unspoken at the back of their minds. No, it was a sweet and sickly smell that wafted across the living room. Cameron glanced towards the top of the sash windows; there was not even a chink of space allowing fresh air to ventilate the room, a fact he must remember to report to the DCI.

'Looks like he left in a bit of a hurry,' Weir murmured, pushing open the bedroom door. It was true. The room bore every trace of a panic-stricken exit, particularly that bottle of DKNY aftershave lying where it had spilled on to the bedroom carpet, its fumes leaching into every corner of the place.

Cameron rifled through each drawer and cupboard, turning over papers and bills.

'No,' he said at last. 'No passport or credit cards.'

'Were we expecting to find them?' Weir asked and Cameron shook his head, sighing. The comment was justified, given that the sliding wardrobe door was open, exposing a gap in the rail with only empty coat hangers. It was obvious that Donnie Douglas had cleared out, and in something of a rush.

'Got to be thorough,' Cameron growled in rejoinder. 'Let's see what else we can find.'

Weir might have been impatient to get out of the flat but Niall Cameron wanted to linger, taking in what he could of the rented rooms, following his SIO's advice to read a place for clues as to the personality of its inhabitant. It was a real boy's flat, he decided eventually. The porn magazines were there, right enough, but they were at the bottom of a pile of comics, lurid things with strip cartoons, the sort of stuff they'd giggled over in primary school, Niall thought.

'Look at this,' Weir remarked, pointing into the kitchen cupboard. 'D'you think he suffered from the munchies?' Weir joked, pointing to packets and packets of breakfast cereals.

'Na. Probably some kind of special high-carb footballer's diet,' Cameron replied.

'I don't think so. Take a butcher's at that.'

Cameron followed his gaze. There, at the back of the kitchen table was a row of wee plastic spacemen all lined up in formation.

The two men exchanged a glance. It was just the sort of thing a young kid would have done. Cameron could just imagine Douglas playing with his Kellogg's freebies before he set off for training each morning: a lonely boy struggling with the responsibilities of a grown man.

'Where d'you think he is now?' he heard Weir asking as he wandered out of the room, but it was a question that Niall Cameron could not answer.

He felt an unexpected rush of sympathy for this young man who had run away. Standing in that kitchen, he thought he could understand what had happened. Donnie Douglas's safe world had been ripped apart. First his childhood had been thrown into chaos by a violent parent, now some other menace had infiltrated the footballer's life.

But who was it that had made the boy feel so threatened? Or was it something he knew that had made him flee?

Lorimer sank back into the sun lounger with a groan of pleasure. This was definitely the best time of the day. The fierce heat had left the sun and there was a tiny breeze stirring the plants. He watched absently as a peacock butterfly alighted on the purple tip of a buddleia. The cluster of cone-shaped flowers swayed slightly in the evening air, the butterfly clinging on, sucking from one tiny floret before hovering and landing on another. Down beside him in a patch of shadow, Chancer was watching it too. Lorimer put out his hand to stroke the animal, a ploy to keep it from pouncing on the butterfly, and was rewarded with a thrumming purr. He closed his eyes, enjoying the feel of warm fur under his fingers and the draught of cool air kissing his face. For a moment he slipped into a doze, all thoughts of the day forgotten, his body utterly relaxed. Then he opened his eyes and realised the cat was no longer there by his side.

He was too late. The cat was already heading towards the shrubbery, one peacock butterfly in its mouth. Lorimer watched the animal slip under the trailing leaves and disappear into the shadows.

Gazing up into the pink-stained sky, Lorimer's mouth tightened. He'd dropped his guard for just those few seconds. Was that some sort of an omen, perhaps? If he took his eyes off the case is this what might happen? He remembered what Niall Cameron had told him about Donnie Douglas. Butterflies, footballers: hedonistic creatures both, he mused, but so vulnerable to whatever might be stalking them.

Lying there in the gathering twilight, Lorimer felt a chill creeping over his flesh.

CHAPTER 19

Rosie stood in the shower, towelling herself dry. She bent her neck one way then the other. It had been a long day. Sometimes the physical effort of post-mortem surgery left her feeling drained, like she was now. But maybe, too, it was this relentless heat. The mortuary was air-conditioned and the refrigerated room kept things reasonably cool. But it was the nights at home that were worst. Hot, windless nights that failed to breathe a whisper of fresh air through their open windows high above the city. For a moment she leaned against the glass of the shower cabinet, luxuriating in its chilly surface. Closing her eyes, Rosie thought about their honeymoon. She and Solly had opted for a winter wedding with a trip to New Zealand afterwards. It was supposed to be much like Scotland at that time of year, but hotter. Normally she'd have welcomed anticipating a break from the long winter months, but now, with this extraordinary weather, she found herself longing for cold, clear days and the sharp frosts of a February morning.

Rosie pushed her body away from the glass with a soft groan and wrapped the towel around her, then stepped out on to the cork mat. She could hear voices from the corridor as some of the technicians made their way to the staffroom. The place was never silent; day or night, there was always some activity as bodies were

145

brought in from all parts of the city. The latest, a stabbing, had been brought in from a bar in the East End, the result of a drunken brawl. The police had the perpetrator in custody: the dead man's cousin, someone had told her. He'd bawled his eyes out once he'd realised what he'd done, so the story went. It didn't matter how contrite they were, Rosie and her fellow pathologists still had to perform the surgery just as meticulously.

Rosie shook the drops of water from her hair. She was dressed now and ready to go home. The hot air would dry her blonde locks by the time she was back in the flat. Giving a sigh of pleasure at the prospect of being home, being with Solly, she gathered up her belongings and headed for the car park beyond the back door of the mortuary.

The High Court stood right across the road from where she had left her car, its pillars of justice intended to command respect. Often during the daytime Rosie would glance up at the knots of people standing on the steps: some would be smoking, flicking their ash on to the pale stones that had been trodden by those who were guilty of heinous crimes and those who sought justice for their victims, as well as the plethora of advocates whose business it was to determine how far the system served its clients. She'd been in countless times, seen some murderers sent down for custodial sentences and a few others who had slipped out on some legal technicality, thanks to the unstinting efforts of their sharp defence lawyers. Mostly it worked, but there were times Rosie had to bite her lip when she felt justice had not been done and remind herself that it was her job to present evidence that showed possibilities, rarely definitive truths.

As she pulled away from the mortuary, Rosie turned on the radio just in time to hear the end of the weather report and the latest warning about misuse of water. Shaking her head, she

146

turned the air conditioning up full-blast and concentrated on negotiating her way out of the evening traffic.

She didn't see the green lorry until it loomed up so close that she took her hands off the wheel, throwing them up in an involuntary gesture of protection. A sound like an explosion hit her as the side of her car was ripped open. Rosie was flung backwards, her neck jarring against something hard.

Then all noise, light and feeling disappeared into oblivion.

Solomon heard the buzzer and smiled. She'd forgotten her key. Again. What a woman, he thought. But the voice from the intercom was not Rosie's.

'Strathclyde Police. May we come up, Doctor Brightman?'

Solly murmured words of acquiescence and pressed the button to open the door. It would be something being delivered from CID, no doubt. He waited by the front door warily, watching through the spy hole. Once before he'd been conned by a bogus policeman, but the two uniformed officers, though unknown to him, seemed real enough and he opened the door to let them in.

'Doctor Brightman?'

Solly nodded, feeling his stomach muscles tensing, suddenly aware of the gravity of their demeanours.

'I'm afraid we have some bad news for you.'

'How bad is it?' Maggie clutched Lorimer's sleeve. His arms were holding her tightly as if he couldn't bear to let her go.

'We don't know yet. She's still in intensive care. Solly's down there now.'

'Will she . . . ?' Maggie left the words unspoken, the tears spilling over and coursing down her cheeks. 'I can't believe it,' she whispered. 'Not Rosie. They had so much to look forward to. Not fair,' she added, burying her face into her husband's shirt.

Lorimer stroked her hair, his expression sombre. The news from the Royal Infirmary was not good. The BMW was a write-off and preliminary reports suggested that the air bag had done some damage to the diminutive pathologist's upper body. That was as much as the officers on the scene had let him know. And the hospital staff had issued the usual 'serious but stable' bulletin. It would take the next twenty-four hours before they could properly assess the damage, and Rosie Fergusson's chances of recovery.

Lorimer heard a noise by his side and looked down. The ginger cat had jumped up on the settee beside them and was regarding them, head to one side as if he could sense their anxiety. Lorimer put out his free hand and caressed the animal's soft fur. The responding purr brought a lump to his throat. He remembered telling Rosie about the stray, recalling her amused delight. She loved cats. She'd even wanted to come over and meet him. Would that ever happen now?

CHAPTER 20

There were times, thought Solly, when all the years of study-ing psychology counted for nothing. Nothing prepared you for this awful numbness.

He had been sitting by her bedside for what seemed like hours. The sky had grown dark for a while but now the light was return-ing over the city's outline of tower blocks and the misty-covered hills beyond. They'd whisked her off to theatre for emergency surgery – exactly what he couldn't tell, he'd been too shocked to take in all the salient details. Pressure on her chest cavity had been the main issue, though her poor face was bruised in several places.

Solly bent forward and ran a finger across her hair, glancing at the monitors beyond that recorded the performance of her vital organs. When it came down to it, was that all a person consisted of? A heartbeat that pumped fluids around the circulatory system; lungs that breathed gases in and out; a brain with synapses flick-ing here and there, signalling what a person thought, wanted, desired? Rosie wasn't a believer in anything beyond this life. She'd made no bones about it. But Solly, gazing at her now, wanted to think that this woman he loved with a passion was wrong. Just for once. He couldn't bear the thought that her spirit – that laughing, zany spirit – would suddenly be extinguished like a candle being snuffed. She had to come back to him, he thought. Then, closing his eyes, Solomon Brightman bowed his dark head and began a silent, imploring prayer to the God of his fathers.

Across the city another head was bent, another mouth was silently intoning words. Words that were directed not at an unseen deity but to those anonymous readers of Kelvin FC's website. The letters were tapped out slowly by unaccustomed fingers, their image filling that stark white space on the computer screen. It had been easy. There was no need to provide a genuine identity, no way of the message finding its way back to the user of this particular server. Bit by bit the fingers continued their tapping, stopping now and then to see if that was the right word, the salient phrase. At last the hands drew back, then, with the cursor hovering over 'send' one finger reached out and the words disappeared into the ether.

The police presence at Dundee's football ground was much greater than usual, augmenting Tayside's usual numbers with some of Strathclyde's own. Uniformed men and women strained their eyes gazing into a crowd that was hyped up by the recent events at Kelvin FC and the fact that Dundee and Kelvin were rivals for the top spot in this season's league. Lorimer had driven up with Maggie. It was a good way to distract themselves from Rosie's condition. He was keen to see the match, observe the players and it would be a day out together, he'd promised her. Now they were here, sitting amidst the sea of black-and-white scarves held aloft as the Keelies sang their alternative version of 'Lord of the Dance'.

The detective's eyes scanned the ground. There were TV cameramen on the opposite stand, their cameras covered in grey tarpaulin, and others situated behind each of the goals next to the sports photographers. Once this fixture was underway, their cameras would be swivelling this way and that, according to the pace of the game.

'Now let's hear it for Blake Moodie, today's mascot,' a voice called from the loudspeaker and a scatter of handclapping broke out as a wee tow-haired lad trotted out, clutching the hand of one of the club officials.

'Now make some noise for your home team, Dun-deeee!' Yells and stamping followed as the home team emerged, followed by a mixture of catcalls and whistles as Kelvin's players ran on to the pitch.

Maggie gave her husband a quizzical glance but he just grinned back, his spirits lifted by the familiar sounds. This was par for the course, after all, at an away game. He looked down, noting a white metal gate set near the mouth of the tunnel, bearing the club's familiar insignia of laurel leaves and the date of its inception, 1893. Further along, the advertising hoardings displayed the name of a local blacksmith specialising in wrought ironwork and Lorimer nodded to himself, making the connection. Now the players and match officials were on the pitch, the latter wearing bright turquoise strips to differentiate them from the players' more sombre colours.

'And you can hear the sound that reverberates down the tunnel and that familiar anthem of theirs sung with passion and expectation,' the commentator insisted. 'Now we're just moments away from kick-off. Looking at today's team it seems very much that Ron Clark has decided to play a three-three-four formation. Referee is looking at his watch and yes! The ball is way up into Kelvin's half and Farraday is chasing after it . . .'

151

Lorimer glanced at Maggie. Her cheeks were flushed with the sun and she seemed to be enjoying the atmosphere. It wasn't often he had the chance to combine work and home, he thought ruefully. They'd go for a decent meal afterwards, maybe even drive over to St Andrews. He watched as the ball sailed off the boot of Farraday, the Dundee striker, and passed within inches of the goal. A huge 'Ohhh!' went up, then chants of 'Easy, easy, easy!' came from the Dundee fans. Lorimer nodded. Farraday's shot hadn't been too far off. Kelvin's defence would have their work cut out if the striker was on form today.

'And now Gemmell has passed to Devitt who beats Baz Thomson – Thomson, you remember, who made that terrible error last season, saw Kelvin relegated – now it's picked up by Sweeney who passes back to Friedl, ball's played down the middle . . . oh, too long for McKinnery. And Dundee keeper O'Hagan kicks it back up the field. Now Morgan is sprinting for the ball but the whistle goes and Kelvin take possession once more.'

Maggie followed Thomson's progress as he passed under their view, heard the thwack of boot on leather then joined in the groans around her as he lost the ball in a hard tackle. Dundee's dark blue jerseys seemed to outnumber the opposing team's black-and-white and she found herself counting the players in each team just to make sure. Bill had told her on the drive up that Kelvin had not beaten Dundee at home in any of their Scottish cup ties. Ever. It seemed an astonishing statistic, especially when Kelvin had reached the ranks of the Scottish Premier League when Dundee had still been languishing in the first division. Football was a funny game and she doubted that she could ever have the same passion for a team that all these fans seemed to feel. Round about her, the expressions of the Kelvin fans showed a determination bordering on fanaticism as they watched the players move back and forwards. Had the killings been the work of some obsessed fan? Maggie gave a shudder, wondering what sort of personalities lay behind these faces. Her eyes strayed back to the perimeter of the pitch where a linesman was directing his lime-and-orange chequered flag towards Kelvin's half.

'Now the whistle goes and Sweeney takes the free kick, sending the ball across to Rientjes who runs with the ball, passes it to Thomson, back to Sweeney, away to McKinnery who can't quite make it and it's a throw-in to Dundee. Kelvin need to keep possession of the ball, make more of their chances, if they are to have any hopes of regaining their Premier League status this season. Dundee is their Achilles heel, of course. They've never beaten a team at Dens Park. Can they defeat these odds today? Now Dundee's Farraday is screaming for the ball. He's onside and Gemmell is moving forward, opens up the middle of the field, quick shimmy to Devitt and – oh! A lovely little one-two, outwitting Rientjes, and Farraday has the ball at his feet and he drives it . . . Oh! What a shot! Just hit the post! The Dundee striker has shown an early determination and I'll be surprised if he doesn't open Dundee's account soon.'

'What's the referee stopping them for?' Maggie asked.

'Offside,' Lorimer told her briefly, eyes on the pitch.

'Rubbish!' snorted the Kelvin fan at his side, overhearing them.

Lorimer didn't respond. There was no way he was going to let himself be drawn into an argument with a belligerent Keelie. Nor did he feel like stopping to explain the offside rule to Maggie. The Dundee striker had the ball at his feet once more and, illuminated by the silver light of camera flashes, he took his second shot, but Carmichael threw his body sideways, his punch sending the ball out of play. Lorimer joined in the clapping, nodding approval of the Kelvin keeper's save, but anxious too for the corner kick that it gave to the home team. There was a scramble for the ball and it see-sawed between opposing players until Carmichael scooped it up once more with a massive kick that sent it way into Dundee's half.

'Fancy a pie and Bovril?' he asked Maggie.

She wrinkled up her nose, but then laughed. 'Och, go on, why not. Show a girl a good time, why don't you?'

Lorimer squeezed past the spectators in his row, then headed for the stairs that would take him to the catering stalls behind the stand. It wasn't quite half-time but, going now, he'd avoid the rush. Besides, he had a notion to check out the directors' area, see who had come across from Glasgow to watch their team today.

Maggie Lorimer listened to the chat behind her. The teams had disappeared back into the bowels of the stadium following the referee's half-time whistle and she was being entertained not only by the Seventies music blaring from the loudspeaker system but also by snatches of dialogue from Kelvin supporters.

'Rubbish game. Whit's Clark no playin Thomson up front fur? Can he no see the wee man's gaggin fur the ba?'

'Aye, like he was against Queen of the South?' came the dry response. 'D'ye no think he's bein a bit cannier today? Mean, he disnae lose out on a league match efter bein red-carded, but he'll need tae watch hisself, know whit ah mean?'

But Barry Thomson's fate at the hands of his two erstwhile critics was silenced as the fans moved out of earshot just as Lorimer arrived bearing a grey cardboard carton full of half-time treats.

Maggie had no sooner finished the scalding cup of Bovril than the players were back on to the pitch and she glanced from left to right, familiarising herself with the change of ends.

'Yes, it looks as if Celtic are making a play for Hammond. Taking him on a loan basis if they can. After he scored that vital goal against Kelvin last season,' the radio commentator continued. 'But, back to today's game against Dundee. And it's a magnificent day here at Dens Park, sun splitting the stones. Great turnout too, and despite the nil-nil scoreline the fans seem to be enjoying this game. Kelvin haven't really shown any great pace today – one wonders if recent events have any bearing on the players' morale – and question marks remain about their defensive capabilities, though I must say that was a cracking save from Gordon Carmichael to deny Farraday the opening goal. Now we're into the second half and let's see if the home side can capitalise on their excellent start. No goals so far, if you've just joined us, but this Dundee side have entertained us for the first forty-five minutes with some great football. And Sweeney kicks the ball high into the air, it comes down on to the head of Clark who passes it to Friedl. Now the mid-fielder takes it steady, tip-toeing it forward, but there's a terrific challenge by Morgan, typical of him, then he passes it down the line, taken by Knight – not seen too much of the ball this afternoon – but Knight sends it down to Morgan . . . a terrific pass, but Morgan couldn't quite control the top spin and the ball's gone out of play . . .'

Maggie yawned, gazing over the rows of spectators. The sky seemed to beat down on them, a relentless blue devoid of any trace of cloud. In Mull she'd welcomed the occasional nightly showers that had left a sweet scent in the air before the day's heat had turned the grasses harsh and brittle. They'd passed a low-lying place between their cottage and the village of Craignure, a flat area jutting out towards the water, two sets of goalposts staring blankly across the green. Maybe there would be a couple of teams there right now, knocking a football back and forth between them. Could the locals muster enough talent for a proper match, or would it just be five-a-side? Somehow Maggie found it difficult to imagine that pristine patch of ground being kicked up into sods by a crowd of tackety-booted islanders, but she'd overheard someone talking about local teams: the Tobermory Tigers and the Dervaig Bears.

'. . . and Woods is onside, dodges his marker and strikes, but the effort was just a bit too obvious and O'Hagan takes it with no difficulty. Now Devitt picks it up and turns to pass it and – oh! Gemmell goes down, clutching his leg. Looks like a sore one. You can hear the crowd shouting abuse at Clark and the referee seems to agree. Yes, there's the yellow card . . . now Gemmell's back on his feet . . . no harm done and Dundee have the free kick. Sweeney comes tearing in, forcing Devitt to play it long. Kelvin's forwards are staying up the field and I can't help but think this is allowing their markers to mark them a little bit more easily – Kelvin will have to be sharper on the ball. And here comes Thomson, intercepts Morgan's pass and runs past one, then two defenders, takes a shot at goal but puts it straight into O'Hagan's arms. Nice try though, and you can hear the fans clapping their approval. Best chance Kelvin have had all afternoon . . .'

Lorimer gave a sigh. Some games were like this. Try as they might, the strikers simply couldn't put the ball past the post. Dundee had had more chances and their striker Farraday would probably earn himself the accolade of Man of the Match. He watched, dispassionately now, as the Kelvin players struggled to take and keep possession of the ball. It was as if they were trying to pick their way through a minefield; Dundee were piling on the pressure, forcing the Glasgow team into making just too many mistakes. Twice he'd watched, hope soaring, as Kelvin rattled the woodwork. But this simply epitomised the afternoon's play. It was a nervy and edgy Kelvin side and he wondered, not for the first time, just what was going on inside the heads of these eleven men.

CHAPTER 21

Ron Clark tried to remind himself that gaining one point was a damn sight better than none, but he experienced a sense of failure nonetheless. If only he could concentrate on the players, the forthcoming matches. They were due to play the Pars at home next week, maybe things would be better by then, back to some semblance of normality. An atmosphere of disquiet still hung about the dressing room and sometimes he sensed the unspoken fears that clung to his players. A sense of horror had gripped the entire community; the tributes of flowers that had been left by the club's main entrance included messages expressing a collective grief. But instead of being a comfort, their daily presence had made the manager feel increasingly depressed.

Clark climbed the stairs to his den, glad for once that his wife was still out shopping. A bit of a browse on the computer would settle this disquieting feeling he'd had all day, take his mind off things. He logged on to the sports pages, though he'd listened to the round-up programme on the way back from the match. It was still interesting to see who'd scored what and when, who'd been sent off. A shiver went down his spine as he read of a controversial decision from a well-known referee. He flicked from page to page then, as if his fingers had a life of their own, he logged on to Kelvin's own website, curious to see if anyone had remarked on today's non-event of a game. There was no comment as yet so he went on to the club's unofficial page where anyone could log on, without having to register.

Ron Clark's mouth opened as he read then reread the words. Hands shaking, he reached for his mobile phone.

'I can't believe it either,' Lorimer told the Kelvin manager. 'It must be some sort of a hoax.' He bit his lip before adding that there must be any amount of nutters who could have sent the message. A copy of it was up on his own screen now.

Patrick Kennedy will be next. For disservices to Kelvin Football Club.

The sender had signed himself **The Kelvin Killer** in bold lettering as if to flaunt his self-conferred title.

Ron Clark's voice was becoming agitated; Lorimer could hear a rising note of panic as he requested police protection for his chairman.

'Has *he* asked for it?' Lorimer wanted to know.

There was a pause before Clark answered, 'Not exactly.'

'Does he know about this message, Mr Clark?' Lorimer enquired.

'Well . . .'

'Look,' Lorimer began with a sigh, 'we can't authorise any further police presence at the club or at his home unless Mr Kennedy asks for it himself. Even then it's doubtful that an officer would be detailed to stand guard. I suggest you make him familiar with this and let him decide what he wants to do about it.'

Lorimer scrolled down the unofficial website's chatroom page to see if there had been any response to the threatening message.

So far the rest of the page was blank. But for how long that would last was anyone's guess and as it was out in the public domain, there might be any number of replies. It was probably just some daft wee boys logging on in their bedroom, bored out of their minds during the long school holidays, especially as today's game had been guaranteed to disappoint anyone looking for another sensation. Not something Strathclyde Police should take too seriously. Patrick Kennedy would throw a fit if he heard that his manager had tried to gain special police protection for him.

He sat back, his mind drifting away from the case. His initial enthusiasm for it had waned in the aftermath of Rosie's accident. Suddenly what became of the pathologist figured far more prominently in his thoughts than this latest development, if he could dignify it in such terms, ever could.

Glasgow's Royal Infirmary sat close to the M8 motorway on one side and near to the mediaeval cathedral and the Glasgow Necropolis on the other, a symbol of hope sandwiched between life, death and all its mysteries. Solly watched the traffic streaming along on the main artery that connected Scotland's two major cities. Thousands of commuters flashed past, oblivious to the quiet drama being played out in this hospital room. Life went on regardless, people speeding towards the city, to nights out at the concert halls, dinner dates or simply to the safe sanctuary of their own homes. His flat on the hill above Kelvingrove had become home to them both these past months, ever since Solly had asked her to stay for Christmas. And they'd made plans, talked about a wedding, a trip Down Under, how many children they'd have: Solly smiled at the memories even as he felt the tears run down his cheeks. What dreams they had! What glorious beautiful dreams! And was that all he would have left: dreams of what might have been?

Looking down at Rosie's still, pale face, Solly shook his head. No, he wouldn't give up hope, not now, not until they came to tell him that there was nothing left to hope for. The sounds of the machines by her bed whirred and clicked in subdued monotone, discreet and necessary. He examined the monitors, afraid to see any sudden change that might break that slender thread of existence, but there was no change at all, simply patterns repeating themselves over and over.

Outside, things were happening; Lorimer's triple murder case was no doubt spawning reams of paper down at the divisional HQ but they would have to continue the investigation without his input. At least for now.

'You did *what*?' Patrick Kennedy's voice rose in a crescendo that made the man before him take one step backwards. 'When did you suddenly become my keeper, Ron?' The chairman's tone contained a sneer that made Ron Clark's cheeks flush.

'I just thought—'

'You're not paid to think, Ron, you're paid to manage a football team. When I need you to cover my back I'll ask you. Okay?'

The Kelvin manager nodded, tight-lipped, and turned on his heel. The door behind him closed with a shudder as if he wanted to slam it hard but lacked the guts to do so.

Pat Kennedy glared at the door for a moment then gave an enormous sigh. That had been a bit stupid. He needed Ron on his side. To alienate him was not just daft, it was potentially lethal. Still, DCI Lorimer was right: this crazy website message was probably a schoolboy prank. He'd not give it any more thought than it deserved.

Kennedy drummed his fingers on the desk. The incident had ruffled him, though. Maybe it would be best to keep a low profile for a bit. Tell Marie to cool things off until all this had blown over. It was too dodgy to have her here after hours or even in a country house hotel where he might be recognised by the media. They'd pick up again at some future date, he thought. Better to spend time with Barbara doing family stuff. Safer, too, added a little voice. Kennedy's mouth twisted in a grimace. He just needed to keep his head straight then he could gain total control of the club, and be shot of his wife into the bargain. To show his hand too soon was risking everything. He hated all this enforced caution with the press at every gate. The club had suddenly become smaller and more confined, as if there was no place to hide. But from what, Pat Kennedy asked himself, was he hoping to hide?

The telephone's shrill note disturbed his train of thought.

'Kennedy.'

'Ah, Mr Kennedy. Just wanted to check something with you. You didn't tell us that you were the owner of Jojo's nightclub.'

'Common knowledge, Chief Inspector. Didn't think to mention it.'

'Nor did you tell us that Baillie had told you Jason White was at the club on the night he was killed.'

There was a silence between the two men until Lorimer said, 'Hello, are you still there, Mr Kennedy?'

Pat Kennedy's mouth was suddenly dry as he remembered exactly where he had been on the night of the footballer's murder. 'I didn't take any call from Tam Baillie that night, Chief Inspector,' he said slowly. 'And if he says he called me, then he's lying.'

Lorimer clicked his mobile shut. The voice on the other end had sounded husky, disbelieving. It was amazing how voices could reveal things. And that little conversation assured Lorimer that the Kelvin chairman was telling him the truth. He'd dispatch DC Cameron and DI Grant to Jojo's to check up on Baillie's story. Someone had been telephoned by the bouncer, that was clear. And if it hadn't been Pat Kennedy, then who was it? Lorimer closed his eyes tightly. Progress in this case was maddeningly slow. Already there were veiled hints about the case being reviewed. That would mean another officer coming in to check up on all the work his team had already done. Performance management, Mitchison had reminded him yet again, as if he hadn't been measuring each and every action with infinitesimal care. But maybe this would give them the lead they desperately needed. He fervently hoped so.

CHAPTER 22

Maggie closed her eyes. It seemed wrong to make a pact with God, but under the circumstances ... Please, she implored, please let her recover, let her be whole and strong and ... just Rosie again. She swallowed hard to fight the lump forming in her throat. I'll give up Chancer, you can make his owners turn up, just make her better, will you?

As if on cue, the ginger cat sprang on to her lap, making her open her eyes. Was this an omen? Don't be so silly, woman, Maggie scolded herself. The cat jumps on your knee every time you sit down.

The house seemed too quiet. There was no sound from outside, no children shouting, no strimmers buzzing their way around neighbouring lawns, nothing to disturb the silence of her home, just the muffled purring of her cat. But today Maggie would have welcomed some reminder of human existence. Her immediate pals were all away, Mum was off on a senior citizens' bus run and she couldn't think of anyone to phone for a chat. Maggie tried to imagine what her friends might be doing on holiday. With their families. Playing by the fringes of continental beaches, perhaps, or exploring the delights of art galleries and museums? If she'd had that first child, it would be twelve years old by now, she mused. But there had been no first baby or second, or third. In the early days they'd always said three kids would be great. But none had survived the early stages of pregnancy and now there would never be any wee faces to look at and see whose features they'd inherited.

The art galleries aren't just for families, she thought suddenly. And it will be cool in there, away from this blistering heat. Chancer made a meow of protest as she stood up and let him slip from her knees. That's what she'd do, Maggie decided. She'd go and see some other old friends, ones she'd neglected for far too long: the Monets and Rembrandts, for instance. It would also take her mind off Rosie Fergusson. And that was what she really wanted, wasn't it? The idea of Rosie lying there between life and death was simply too horrible to bear.

Kelvingrove Art Gallery and Museum had undergone a transformation in recent years with a new educational facility and basement restaurant, not to mention the revamped exhibition areas. Maggie had been one of the first to visit it after its reopening, a day full of families with excited children pointing at Sir Roger the huge stuffed elephant and the cheetah and the penguins, as well as the Spitfire suspended from the gallery's ceiling.

Today it was quieter. Several mothers with wee ones in buggies were in evidence but for the most part it seemed as if Kelvingrove was playing host to visitors from overseas. A gaggle of Asian tourists with their cameras slung around their necks passed Maggie as she made her way along the corridor towards the Dali. It was good to have it back home, she thought. St Mungo's Museum of Religious Life and Art had given it a glorious place of honour for a few years but *Christ of St John of the Cross* belonged here, within the sanctuary of the city's famous old galleries.

Maggie Lorimer gave a sigh. It was easy to lose oneself inside that painting; the shores of the Sea of Galilee looked so cool, and inviting, the Christ's eyes on the land below, arms stretched out to encompass his little world. You didn't feel the pain, Maggie thought. It wasn't like those paintings designed to horrify with an emaciated figure hanging like a bloodless corpse, with ashen-faced women mooning around. No, this was different. It spoke of a triumph over death, the cross almost floating away to heaven as you gazed and gazed.

'You wouldn't think that such a death could have been so beautiful,' a voice remarked.

Maggie turned, startled at the words. She'd been so lost in her contemplation of the painting that she'd failed to notice another person step up beside her. A man of around her own age was looking at the Dali, not at her. And what was that accent? Canadian, she decided. Maggie nodded, unsure of how she was expected to reply, for it *was* beautiful, the landscape a masterpiece, the Christ figure utterly compelling.

'First time you've seen it too, huh?'

Maggie shook her head. 'No. I've known this painting all of my life,' she said.

'That so? You're one lucky lady, then. It's taken me a pretty long time to make my way to this place.'

Maggie smiled. 'Worth waiting for?'

'You bet!' the Canadian replied, turning his gaze away from the painting to appraise the woman who stood by his side.

What were those green eyes seeing, Maggie wondered: a Scottish woman, well past her youth but still with a girlish figure, her dark unruly tresses falling below her shoulders? Or did he see the faint lines around her eyes and mouth, that yearning look that she sometimes glimpsed when she caught sight of herself in a mirror? Whatever it was, his expression seemed to tell her that he liked what he saw and Maggie experienced an unexpected thrill of pleasure.

'This might be a little forward,' the Canadian began, 'but would you let me buy you a coffee? I'd love to hear what you think of our friend here.' He nodded back towards the picture. Maggie thought about it for a moment. Did he mean to begin a discourse on Christ? Was he a religious nut of some kind? But no, surely he meant the painting, Dali's fabulous masterpiece, rather than its subject? Besides, it was only a coffee and the man's voice suggested a cultured background that might be fun to explore.

'Yes, thank you. Coffee would be fine,' she replied at last, her eyes meeting his, noting how they crinkled in delighted satisfaction.

Maggie grinned back, suddenly, half-shocked at herself. Was she being picked up? Never go away with strange men, she thought to herself, laughingly. And surely a policeman's wife should know better!

'There's a place on the ground floor,' the Canadian began.

'The basement will be quieter,' Maggie told him firmly. 'And cooler,' she added. He stopped and half-turned towards her, hand outstretched. 'Forgetting my manners,' he began. 'Alan Osborne.'

Maggie returned the handshake, feeling his fingers strong and warm. 'Mrs Lorimer,' she said, immediately adding 'Maggie', aware of how formal she sounded – like being back in the classroom.

'Well, Maggie Lorimer. What can you tell me about Salvador Dali's painting?'

Alan Osborne was sitting opposite her, stirring his coffee (black, no sugar, Maggie noticed), his eyes twinkling again, leaving her unsure about where his interest really lay. They'd indulged in a bout of small talk while waiting for their coffees and Maggie had found out that he was a professor of logic and semantics at McGill University. Her teaching career seemed to interest him, though, especially her sojourn in Florida schools. But now the Canadian was back to where they had started, with the Dali.

'Well, it's been about a bit over the years. It was slashed by a fanatic a long time ago, then repaired.' She frowned. 'I remember being told about it but I think the damage was done before I was born.' And I'm not telling you how old I am, she thought swiftly. 'Then it was here for years and years before being moved to another museum in town. Have you been on a Glasgow tour bus?'

'Sure have. Found out a heap of things from a very interesting tour guide.'

'Do you remember Glasgow Cathedral and St Mungo's Museum? That was where the *Christ of St John of the Cross* went for a while. Now it's back here,' she said fondly.

'Okay.' Alan Osborne sipped his coffee. 'But what does it mean to you, apart from being a bit of your city's history?'

Maggie cocked her head to one side as if unsure of his drift.

'I saw that look on your face. That's what stopped me in my tracks. I said to myself, Here's someone who can see into this painting.'

'What sort of look?' Maggie asked.

'Like . . . supplication, I suppose you'd call it. Like you were asking that figure for a big favour.'

Maggie shivered suddenly, remembering the pact she'd made with God that morning.

'Cold?' Alan Osborne put out his hand and brushed her fingers gently.

She shook her head, drawing her hands back under the table. 'No, just a bit surprised. I wasn't aware of letting my feelings show

169

back there,' she began. 'A friend of mine had an accident – a bad car smash – she's not in a good shape.' Maggie bit her lip, astonished at the powerful emotion welling up inside her.

'That's too bad,' the Canadian murmured. 'Hard on you, too. Not being able to do anything for her, I guess.'

Maggie nodded, unable to speak.

'Know what it says to me?' the man continued, his voice low and gentle. 'That painting tells me that death isn't as bad as it's made out to be. And maybe there's more good stuff still to come . . .' He paused.

'Do you have any experience of beautiful deaths, then?' Maggie asked, trying to keep her tone light.

'As a matter of fact I have, Mrs Lorimer. My wife died in my arms three years ago. A beautiful experience I'll never forget. Brain tumour,' he added.

'I'm sorry,' Maggie mumbled.

'Don't be. We had some great times together and memories that'll never die. Not unless I succumb to old-timer's disease,' he joked.

'My husband has a lot of experience of death too,' Maggie said suddenly.

'What does he do?'

'He's a policeman, Mr Osborne. He solves murder cases,' Maggie replied, looking her companion straight in the eye. 'And none of them ever seem to be beautiful at all.'

CHAPTER 23

'Would you look at this.' Lorimer moved to one side, enabling his colleague to see the computer screen. 'We've got a reply.'

Alistair Wilson pulled at the knot on his tie. The DCI's room was a bit cooler than his own; a desk fan ruffled a pile of papers that were kept from flying away by a bit of quartz-crazed pink rock that Lorimer had brought back from his holiday.

'So it was a nutter, then?' Wilson murmured, looking at the response to the purported killer.

Have you absolutely no respect? Idiots like you should be barred from Kelvin.

'There's more,' added Lorimer.

Do you not think that Mr Kennedy has enough to think about without fools like you making stupid threats? Get a life, will you! From: A real Kelvin fan.

'He's saying exactly what we think, isn't he? Some daft kid's idea of a joke.'

'Well, there's nothing anyone can do about it. There's no way we can trace a sender. Looks like our irate fan will nip that nonsense in the bud, though, doesn't it?' Lorimer replied.

'Why d'you think their manager was so upset by it, though?'

Lorimer shrugged his shoulders. 'Who knows? I got the impression Ron Clark was a bit tense when I met him. Not surprising, under the circumstances. Losing two key players like that . . .' He looked thoughtful. 'I will say this, though, he seemed to have a bit of a guilty conscience about the referee.'

'Oh?'

'Nothing sinister, at least I doubt it. Just a case of wishing he'd left certain things unsaid after the match. My guess is he had a real go at Cartwright then felt bad about it after the man's death.'

'Aye, who wouldn't,' agreed Wilson. 'Well, where do we go from here?'

'Any luck yet in tracing the person Tam Baillie called?'

'Nope. He'd received an email from someone who was definitely not Pat Kennedy, instructing him to call when Jason White turned up at the club. Why he hadn't spotted that it wasn't Kennedy's usual email address, God alone knows. Technical support reckons it was probably sent from an internet cafe. And the number he was asked to phone has drawn a blank.'

Lorimer leaned back, still gazing towards the computer screen as if somehow he could draw inspiration from it. Where do we go from here? Wilson's words seemed to ring in Lorimer's ears. That was the million-dollar question, wasn't it? He felt uneasy about using a psychological profiler that he didn't know and trust, especially after working so closely with Solly Brightman. They were just going to have to tackle this case with all the other means at their disposal. Had it been a case of multiple killings with the same MO there might have been some sense in having the case screened on *Crimewatch*. They got results from time to time, after all. But this case was so full of twists, he just couldn't see his way forward.

'How's Dr Fergusson?' Wilson ventured.

'Don't ask,' Lorimer answered shortly. He had to keep thoughts of Rosie from his mind. Concentrating on three murders was all he could cope with right now.

Wilson nodded. The closed face staring ahead of him could have suggested a hard, unfeeling officer to anyone who didn't know him. There was real suffering under that grim exterior. For a moment the Detective Sergeant was tempted to place a hand on his boss's shoulder, but he resisted. They had to pretend a strength they might not feel – it was par for the course in this job, sometimes.

Fingers tapped on the relevant keys to enter Kelvin FC's unofficial website then rested limply against the edge of the table while words formed upon the screen. *Idiot*, the fan had written. *Fool*. Well, perhaps it was best that way. The fingers came together in a handclasp, thumbs tapping together, considering. If everyone else, including the police, thought this was the work of a crank then Patrick Kennedy would have lost any chance of protection, wouldn't he? The hands unclasped slowly then one formed the shape of a gun, two fingers pointing towards the screen.

'Bang!' said a voice, then the mock barrel was raised, and fingertips blown gently from lips that curled into a smile.

Chapter 24

He was coming after her again. This time the knife was in his hand and he turned it this way and that, to make her see the overhead light glancing off the blade. He was smiling, eyes bright with malice, sandy hair flopping over his forehead, that white sports top accentuating his golden tan. Janis thought she'd never seen him look so good, but it was a dispassionate appraisal: there was no flicker of desire, no bits tingling. That was something she'd stopped feeling long ago.

The sound of a key turning in the lock made her eyes open. For one panic-stricken moment Janis imagined he was back, coming in to get her, then she lay back on her narrow bed, relieved to remember where she was. It was all right. She was safe in Cornton Vale, though for how much longer?

A patch of brightness shone opposite the window, heralding yet another sunny day. It wasn't so bad, Janis thought. She'd imagined being incarcerated within a tiny cell all day, every day, but the reality was quite different. In some ways it was like being back at school with a timetable to follow, educational classes to attend and a decent gymnasium. The women were even split into different houses and placed on work teams like laundry or kitchen duties. It wasn't all hard graft. Already she'd been to beauty therapy and hairdressing sessions run by the inmates themselves.

'No whit ye're used tae, hen,' the woman who combed out Janis's wet hair had remarked. But there had been nothing bitchy in her tone and Janis had just smiled and shrugged.

'See when ah git oot o' here, ah'm gonnae open ma ain salon,' the hairdresser had told her. Janis had made some innocuous reply but later she'd been surprised to learn that it was true. The woman was being given a prison grant to start up her own hairdressing business.

There had been lots to wonder at in this place. Many of the girls were self-confessed junkies, repeat offenders who were glad of the chance to get clean in the sanctuary of Cornton Vale prison. Their life outside was what really trapped them, not this institution. A lot of them looked like wee lassies and Janis was appalled to find that some had been mothers three times over. She'd blanked out her feelings whenever they went on about *the weans*; her miscarriages were out in the public domain now that the papers had a hold of her story. But the women seemed sensitive enough not to pry. They might find out what you were in for, but it was an unspoken rule not to ask questions. Some of them were just poor souls who were caught in a spiral of theft or prostitution to feed their drug habit and pay their dealer. Funnily enough, they were the easiest ones to talk to, once they'd come out of their self-enforced lock-up.

Janis was allowed out into the grounds every day now. The gardens were extensive and well maintained by the women themselves. At first she had been wary of these hard-faced women with their hoes and spades but none of them ever brandished their tools as weapons as she'd imagined they might. She walked past them each day, keeping her eyes close to the gravel pathway before finding sanctuary in what was called the family centre. In reality this was a chapel where services were conducted by a friendly priest, Father Joe, but behind the main hall that doubled as a spare classroom was a series of smaller rooms that were kept especially for family visits. Mums would have time to see their children in these bright, toy-filled rooms and for a time it would seem almost like a church crèche. They put on a brave face, these mothers, but once the visits were over Janis had seen them suffer inconsolable storms of weeping. More than once Janis had felt a strong compulsion to reach out and give them a hug, but she'd controlled these urges, fearing the consequences of what a physical touch might bring.

There were other surprises, too. The idea of prison brought with it an image of stern guards who could mete out punishments at random. She'd been frightened of them at first, these officers in black, chained to bunches of jangling keys, but gradually Janis had come to recognise their humanity. Most had a sense of humour and could josh with the girls just as easily as they might restrain them. The members of the medical staff were far and away the best, perhaps because of their different uniforms and the fact that they were there to make the women feel better. Janis had been amused by one nurse who had a predilection for brightly coloured tunics with cartoon animals. It seemed to work, though, and the younger women were more relaxed with her than any other health official.

She lay looking at the light shift around the room. In some ways this was the best part of the day, a quiet respite before the clatter of washing and breakfast. It gave her a bit of peace, a chance to reflect. But that dream had disturbed her and she could still see Nicko's laughing face coming at her.

All she could think of now was what had happened and, more to the point, what was to come. She recalled Marion Peters' words: 'It would be an admission of guilt if I didn't try to have you granted bail, Janis.' It was the available evidence that was crucial, the lawyer had explained. Once there was deemed sufficient evidence to link all three murders, the words hammered a rhythm in her brain, she'd be let out, granted *bail*. That word was spoken in here like something religious. Since Marion Peters' last visit they'd been watching her, the prison officers, watching and wondering. Why? Were they in cahoots with the police? Did they report back to them for any reason?

Janis Faulkner squeezed her eyes shut and shook her head as if all these thoughts were flies buzzing around her. She'd go mad if she didn't watch out. She needed to play it cool now, act as if she had all her emotions under control. That wouldn't be so hard, now, would it? After all, she'd had years of practice.

'Anything yet?'

'Depends on what you're looking for, Mrs Peters,' Lorimer replied. He paused, considering. There was no need to go into details about Donnie Douglas's disappearing act.

'But my client needs to know,' the woman persisted. 'She's locked up in there for a crime that she didn't commit, and you and I know fine well there is not a scrap of forensic material to link her with her husband's death.'

'She ran away from the crime scene,' Lorimer began slowly.

'Because she was afraid of her husband,' Marion Peters objected. 'And how do you know she didn't leave before he was killed?'

'Mrs Peters,' Lorimer tried to contain the impatience in his voice, 'we've been over this before. The door was locked and there was absolutely no sign of a forced entry.'

'And who else might have had a key? Weren't there key holders at the club?'

Lorimer didn't answer. The house had been rented out through an agency. Sure, the agents had keys, but only for emergencies. That had been checked thoroughly right at the beginning of this investigation. Peters knew that well enough. She was clutching at straws, but the DCI couldn't blame her.

'Look, this is a very complicated case,' he said. 'I have every sympathy with your client's position but until we have enough new evidence to show that the deaths were committed by one and the same hand, I doubt if your client will be granted bail.'

'Oh, I'm sure you're very sympathetic, Chief Inspector.' The lawyer's voice was heavy with sarcasm. 'Very sympathetic indeed.'

Lorimer listened as the line was cut, and put down his phone with a sigh. What he would give for something to show that Faulkner had been stabbed by the same person that had gunned down White and Cartwright. The forensics team had been over Nicko and Janis's place with a fine toothcomb and all that had emerged was that someone had made a damn good job of clearing every trace of blood from that kitchen. There was nothing in the wife's car, either – even the mess of soggy paper tissues had been scrutinised to see if any traces of blood were on them. Marion Peters was right. There was no way the footballer's wife should be locked up in Cornton Vale prison *if* she was innocent. But that hadn't been for him to decide; that was a decision taken by a member of the justiciary.

For the first time in a long time DCI Lorimer felt that things were spiralling out of control. Solly, who would have been giving him some sort of guidance, was out of the picture and what evidence there was could easily point to three separate killers. And as for Rosie? No, it was better not to think about Rosie.

How had it all begun? With the death of a footballer, he thought. Had Nicko Faulkner been such a good buy for Kelvin

FC? And what about Jason White? Lorimer leaned back in his chair, hand on chin, wondering. When it came down to it, each of these new signings was a bit of a puzzle. Why would Clark want to saddle himself with a load of trouble like Jason White? His current mid-fielders were a fairly talented bunch.

Then he remembered. Donnie Douglas had been a new mid-field signing last season. The lad had shown promise, even scoring a few goals. So why go to the expense of buying a player past his prime and one that was never out of the headlines for his off-the-park antics? Had anyone at the club tried to dissuade the manager and chairman from these purchases? And was there any possible link between the two English footballers and Norman Cartwright? It was time to ask more questions, he thought. And this time he wanted the right answers.

CHAPTER 25

Kelvin Park was situated in one of the quieter parts of Glasgow's West End though it was in easy walking distance of the underground station or any of the buses that trundled along Great Western Road. Lorimer had opted for the latter, leaving his Lexus in the car park, and now he was making his way across the bridge spanning the river Kelvin. He ran a curious fingertip over the wrought ironwork, and was rewarded by the metal's warmth. It was something he and his pals used to do on sunny summer days, long before their curiosity had been tempered by basic chemistry lessons in high school. They'd warmed their hands up then placed them on their faces shouting 'Iron Man!' and running down the road, giggling. Lorimer stopped for a minute, looking down at the river's sluggish progress. Rocks, usually concealed, were sticking up like hump-backed seals basking in the heat of the day. There was a smell, too, of something rotten and sickly. Maybe it was the river itself, the weeks of drought failing to carry off whatever detritus had been chucked in by the local neds. He couldn't recall when it had been so shallow.

Lorimer loosened his tie and slipped his jacket over one arm, glancing back towards the west, noting the faded grandeur of grey granite terraces looking down their middle-class noses at the colourful huddle of shops on the opposite side of the road. The West End was a melting pot of classes and creeds, he thought, and as if to sum up its diverseness, a bicycle whizzed by, smart leather briefcase strapped to its rear pillion, causing a small draught of air to disturb the saris of two Indian women coming towards him. Lorimer stepped aside to allow them passage, noting their heads bent together intimately, their low voices speaking in their native tongue. They were mother and daughter, he decided, out for a spot of shopping if the carrier bags clutched in bejewelled fingers were anything to go by.

Lorimer rounded a corner and headed towards the football grounds. The leafy drives swung away from Great Western Road and marched purposefully towards Woodlands Road and the foothills of Kelvingrove Park. With a glance up to his left, Lorimer took in the curve of flats that dominated the skyline – that was where Solly and Rosie lived, he thought, then looked away, suddenly refusing to pick out the windows of their home. It was too much to bear, this not knowing whether the pathologist was going to make it or not. How the hell Solly was coping was anybody's guess. Best not to dwell on it, he decided. Instead he swept his gaze across the park and beyond to where he could see the floodlights reaching into a cloudless sky.

As usual, the sight of Kelvin Park filled Lorimer with mixed emotions. His boyhood had been dominated by football, going to the matches with Dad had been the highlight of most weekends during the season. Hot pies and Bovril just didn't seem to have the same taste nowadays. But the club held more for him now than mere childhood memories; it was a place full of secrets and ghosts that had more to do with the current custodians of Kelvin FC. And if he was right, there were people in that club who were hiding things that could give him a clue about why these three men had been killed.

*

Ron Clark was standing outside the main door, cigarette in hand. Had he been waiting for him? Lorimer couldn't decide.

The Kelvin manager stubbed out his fag in the sand-filled metal ash-box, wiped a hand down his tracksuit trousers and took a step towards the DCI.

'Good to see you, Chief Inspector,' Clark began, a tentative smile working on his mouth. Lorimer took the hand that had been extended, wondering at the man's words. Good to see him? He didn't think so. But folk tended to hide behind platitudes in his game.

'Any sign of Douglas?' Lorimer asked.

The Kelvin manager shook his head, not meeting Lorimer's eyes. 'Nothing. We contacted his mother in Aberdeen, like you suggested. Don't think I gave anything away, just blethered on about things in general. Gave her a chance to ask about Donnie, and she did. Wanted to know how he'd been since the *tragedies*, as she put it. So it's clear that he's not been in touch with home.'

Lorimer nodded towards the door. 'Can we go inside? It's a bit hot out here.'

'How about taking a walk up to the East stand?' Clark suggested, pointing up at the ranks of seats blurred among the shadows. 'It'll be cooler there.'

Lorimer spread his hands in a gesture of acquiescence and followed Ron Clark around the building and through a metal gate. It was odd to be here, inside Kelvin Park, the stadium yawning like an empty mouth around the pitch. The sprinklers were on and as they climbed up a flight of steep stone stairs he could hear a swish as the water scattered droplets on to the metal safety barrier. At the far end of the park he could see the figure of the groundsman who appeared to be sorting through a pile of white netting, oblivious to any visitors who might be watching him.

'I wanted to talk to you about the team,' Lorimer began.

Clark looked at him, his features composed and alert, but said nothing.

'Why did you want to buy Nicko Faulkner and Jason White?'

The manager sat back further into the shadows, a frown gathering across his face.

'What a strange question, Chief Inspector. Why does a manager usually buy new players?' he countered.

'To improve the team,' Lorimer answered sharply. 'But did you really think they would do that?'

'Of course.' Clark's eyebrows rose and the ghost of a patronising smile twitched at the corners of his mouth. 'But you evidently don't agree with our choices,' he said.

'No,' Lorimer replied, 'I don't. Why spend a lot of money on a player who's seen better days and one who's more trouble than he's worth? I mean, White cost you an arm and a leg, didn't he?'

'We considered him a good investment,' Clark replied, then laughed bitterly. 'I suppose it's easy to be critical with hindsight, Chief Inspector.'

'But it was such a big investment,' Lorimer persisted. 'Faulkner's transfer fee was pretty spectacular too, and you've got a really good young squad as it is.'

'Yes, we have, but that's not going to get us back into the Premier League next season, is it? We needed some quality players with experience: a couple of mid-fielders who weren't afraid to go in and make something of the game.'

'Not like Donnie Douglas,' Lorimer replied quietly.

Clark looked at him and for a moment their eyes met. The Kelvin manager looked away first, shaking his head. 'Donnie was a fine mid-fielder, Chief Inspector. But we needed a bit more creativity, if you know what I mean.'

Lorimer thought he knew what Clark meant: for creativity read not being afraid to go in hard, to risk red card situations, suspensions, whatever it took to win a game. White had had that sort of creativity on and off the park. And Nicko Faulkner had never been far from controversy on the pitch.

'You say Douglas *was* a fine mid-fielder, Mr Clark. Have you any reason to think he's unlikely to return to your club?'

Ron Clark looked out into the green void before them, considering. 'Why should he want to disappear like that, Chief Inspector? Unless he's got something to hide?'

Answer a question with a question, Lorimer thought. The Kelvin manager would make a good politician. Still, it didn't make him feel any better about Clark's slip of the tongue.

'How did Patrick Kennedy feel about your choice of new players?' Lorimer asked, turning the conversation back again.

'Oh,' Clark smiled properly for the first time, his eyes brightening. 'That's an easy one to answer; you see it was Pat's idea in the first place to go after Jason White and Nicko Faulkner.'

'And you? What did you think?'

Ron Clark laughed mirthlessly. 'Me? Oh, Chief Inspector, I'm not paid to think. I'm paid to do what I'm told. Haven't you picked that up yet?'

Lorimer did not reply for a moment, considering the politics that were involved within a football club. Usually things happened behind closed doors with juicy titbits leaked here and there to the press. He'd not taken Ron Clark for Kennedy's poodle. Far from it, the manager had a good reputation in the game. Still, a murder case could suddenly strip bare a lot of the facade; it wasn't uncommon for a man to reveal his innermost fears and desires when confronted by issues of life and death.

'So,' Lorimer countered at last, 'what was your own opinion of Faulkner and White?'

Ron Clark's smile had already faded as he took in the policeman's words. 'If I said I didn't want them in the first place does that give me a motive for their murders, Chief Inspector?' The question was spoken lightly but Clark's expression was deadly serious.

Lorimer shrugged, letting Clark's own words hang in the air.

'Okay, I wasn't happy with Pat's idea to buy Jason White. I knew he'd be a load of trouble, but I was overruled. For the record, Chief Inspector, I wasn't totally against the purchase of Faulkner. The man had plenty of style. He was a charismatic player and still had plenty to offer a team like ours. Pat felt he could've inspired a lot of the younger boys.'

'So you don't think anybody at the club would have wanted Faulkner out of the way?'

Ron Clark turned to look Lorimer straight in the eye one again. 'No. And if you want my opinion you've already got the only person who could have killed Nicko.'

This time it was Lorimer's turn to avert his gaze. Simply wishing Janis Faulkner innocent wasn't going to make it true. Like he'd told the lawyer, he needed more evidence to link the three killings. And now it looked as if Ron Clark would be the last person to offer him that.

'Mr Kennedy will see you shortly, Chief Inspector. Can I offer you a cup of coffee?' Marie McPhail regarded Lorimer gravely, making him recall the woman's expression on that first visit to the football club. She hadn't been too happy to see Strathclyde's finest on that occasion.

'Thanks. Coffee would be lovely. Just black, no sugar,' he

added, sliding open the glass door to the receptionist's office and stepping inside.

The woman had begun to turn away but looked up, confused as she saw the policeman standing right by her desk, a silent 'Oh' of alarm forming on her lips.

He folded his arms and smiled at her. 'Must be terrible for you having us coming back and forward,' he began, chattily. 'Eating you out of house and home,' he joked, indicating the packet of biscuits that Marie McPhail had pulled from a cupboard behind her desk. He was rewarded by seeing her shoulders relax.

'Och, it's no bother to me. Besides, we're used to the police coming in to do pre-match inspections, and the ones who are on duty on match days are no trouble. Very polite.'

'Bit of an upset for the club having CID on your doorstep, all the same,' he persisted.

'Your lot aren't nearly as bad as all those newspaper folk hanging around every day,' the receptionist declared. 'It's been terrible here. S'not the same place any more.' She looked up at Lorimer, an appeal in her eyes. 'All we really want is to get back to normal, Chief Inspector. We'll be glad once you get the man who's done these terrible things.'

'Think it's a man, do you?' Lorimer teased her.

'Oh, yes,' she assured him. 'No woman could have done a thing like that, shooting those poor chaps.' She handed him a mug of coffee emblazoned with the club crest.

'Including Nicko Faulkner?' Lorimer asked lightly.

For a moment she looked uncertain, then she made a face. 'Maybe I shouldn't say it but see, if he *was* knocking his wife around the way they say in the papers, well, he deserved everything he got!' Then, as if suddenly realising to whom she was speaking, Marie McPhail covered her mouth with her hand.

187

'It's all right,' Lorimer assured her with a shrug. 'Everyone's entitled to their opinion.' He took a sip of the coffee, regarding her over the rim of the mug. 'By the way, did you ever meet Janis Faulkner?'

'Aye. A nice lassie. Quiet. Well mannered. But then they say it's the quiet ones you have tae watch, eh?'

'Chief Inspector,' Patrick Kennedy's booming voice echoed along the corridor. Lorimer and the woman looked up to see the chairman standing just outside his door. 'Marie's been looking after you? Just bring your coffee through here,' he added, disappearing into his office.

'Better go. Thanks for the coffee,' Lorimer grinned conspiratorially at the receptionist. 'Mustn't keep your great man waiting.'

Marie McPhail looked as if she were about to reply but thought better of it, her cheeks reddening.

It was a simple thing, but it immediately gave away the woman's secret. Lorimer nodded to himself. So, Pat Kennedy was playing away from home, was he?

'Chief Inspector, you wanted to see me.' Kennedy grasped Lorimer's hand in one great fist, then let it go, seating himself behind his desk and motioning the policeman to take a seat opposite. It was a gesture typical of a powerful man, putting something physical between them and establishing his authority from the outset. Lorimer responded by crossing his legs and sitting back as though in the presence of an old chum. It might irritate Kennedy, but that was what he wanted; a chance to rattle the man's gilded cage.

'Yes, Mr Kennedy. Can you tell me a bit about the club's financial state at present?'

Pat Kennedy looked mildly surprised as if he had been prepared for a completely different sort of question.

'Well, now, you'd have to ask our accountants.'

'I'm asking you,' Lorimer persisted.

For a moment Kennedy glared at him, but there was something in the policeman's expression that brooked no nonsense and he sniffed instead.

'We're doing fine, Chief Inspector. The club has a well-documented investment portfolio that our shareholders can have access to any time they like. Our gates have been pretty much as expected, season tickets are at an all-time high.' He attempted a smile but failed to bring it off. 'What more can I tell you?'

'How about your financial position regarding the transfer fees of Nicko Faulkner and Jason White?'

'They were paid!' Kennedy protested.

'And recouped from the players' life insurance policies, I suppose?'

Lorimer's blue stare was met by a single 'Ah' from the Kelvin chairman.

Kennedy cleared his throat and licked his lips nervously before continuing, 'Why do you ask?'

'It's our business to find things out, Mr Kennedy. If your insurance policies cover more than players' injuries then the club might stand to make quite a killing on these two victims, if you'll forgive my pun,' Lorimer said.

'I don't know who you've been speaking to, Chief Inspector,' Kennedy replied, bunching his fists on top of the desk, 'but you've been totally misinformed. Kelvin FC does *not* stand to gain by these players' deaths.' He thumped hard, making some sheets of paper tremble on the smooth wooden surface. 'In fact,' he leaned forward and Lorimer saw the rage in his eyes, 'we have made a huge financial loss with the deaths of White and Faulkner.'

189

Lorimer nodded slowly. He'd suspected as much, but his questions had been designed to get under the chairman's guard and it looked as though he had succeeded. 'Can I ask how you intend to recoup these financial losses, Mr Kennedy?'

'We don't have to pay two rather large wages, Chief Inspector, and we won't be making any more offers for players this season. Simple.'

'So nobody in Kelvin FC would have a financial motive for their deaths, then?'

Patrick Kennedy sank back into his chair, a frown upon his face as he realised just what sort of a trick Lorimer had played.

'I think that's a pretty cheap shot, Lorimer,' he began. 'Money isn't everything you know,' he continued, in such a sanctimonious tone that Lorimer wanted to laugh. Were Solly here, the psychologist would have spotted the lie straight off. He'd bet his police pension that money mattered a hell of a lot to that big man sitting behind the desk.

'You'd be surprised what money – or the lack of it – can do to some people, Mr Kennedy,' Lorimer countered. 'It's not unusual for us to see that as a motive for murder,' he murmured.

'Well, I doubt if anybody murdered these poor lads for money, Chief Inspector,' Kennedy went on, his voice still heavy with the kind of false pity that made Lorimer's stomach churn.

'And Norman Cartwright?'

'What about him? He was shot by some lunatic fan, surely? Isn't that what your people think?'

Lorimer didn't reply. He wasn't about to reveal what his team were thinking to the Kelvin chairman, but it was interesting to note that there was no sorrow in Kennedy's voice for the referee.

'And you're quite happy that this website message is also a bit of madness?'

'Look, the serious fans all register on our official website. This rogue one was just a bit of sick fun on somebody's part. I really don't think anybody is out to get me or anyone else in the club.'

'Someone tried to pass themselves off as you in that email to Tam Baillie, though, didn't they, Mr Kennedy?'

'Looks like it,' Kennedy muttered, avoiding Lorimer's stare.

'Baillie was quite certain that it was your voice on the telephone when he made his call.'

'Well, he was wrong, wasn't he?' Kennedy snapped.

'Somebody has gone to a lot of trouble to make it seem as if you were keeping tabs on Jason White,' Lorimer mused. 'Wanted you in the frame for it, perhaps?'

'Look, Chief Inspector, I've told you repeatedly I was not in contact with Baillie that night. Nor did I ask him to inform me about White's whereabouts.'

'And you still say you were here all of that evening?'

'Until I went home, yes.'

'And can anyone here at the club confirm that?' Lorimer asked.

Kennedy merely shook his head. Then the chairman's gaze looked beyond Lorimer, making the policeman turn around. There, through the obscure glass panel of his office door, was the shadow of a figure. Neither man spoke, fully expecting the person to knock and come in. But instead, the shadow shifted and Lorimer glanced at the chairman who simply shrugged.

'Whoever it was will come back if they want to see me,' he said. 'Now, if you have no further questions, I really have rather a lot to do.' Kennedy looked down at his desk and rustled the papers as if to make his point.

'Thank you, sir. We'll be in touch if there are any more developments.' And with that, Lorimer stood up. Kennedy remained where he was, not deigning to show the chief inspector out.

191

Once out in the corridor, Lorimer looked around to see who had been waiting to speak to the Kelvin chairman but the place was deserted and even Marie McPhail's tiny office was empty. With a twist to his mouth, Lorimer started for the stairs. He didn't trust Kennedy but did that mean he was a cold-blooded killer? And what on earth would he have to gain from losing yet another player?

Maybe it was time to speak to Donnie Douglas's teammates. And maybe they'd have some notion of where the mid-fielder had gone.

CHAPTER 26

He'd taken a taxi back to the Division, picked up the Lexus and now Lorimer was heading out of the city towards the leafy suburbs of Milngavie and Bearsden. Behind him the city shimmered in the heat, the grey silhouettes of high-rise flats and church spires hazy and indistinct, the river a winding ribbon separating north from south. Now he was driving down an avenue shaded by mature trees, catching the occasional glimpse of fine houses beyond their front gardens. Purple wisteria tumbled about the arched doorway of one red sandstone mansion, the unmistakable shape of a sleek Jaguar glinted from another driveway. This was one of Glasgow's most favoured locations, expensive and understated like a sophisticated woman, rubbing shoulders with the country set nearby.

All the players had been picked up and taken to the training ground, and Lorimer could hear shouts from the field as he parked his car outside a modest-looking building with a wooden sign, 'Kelvin FC', painted in black on a white background. He walked towards the field, seeing the lads spread out along the width of the playing area, moving in diagonal steps to warm up their muscles. Beyond them he could see a groundsman who was pulling a roller behind him. It wasn't Albert Little, his territory began and ended at Kelvin Park. These grounds were rented from the local authority and were maintained by a variety of parks department staff.

Lorimer strolled in the direction of the football coach, hearing him bark out instructions to his players. Despite the aching heat, every one of them sported a plastic bib over his black T-shirt: this coach didn't pander to his boys. The game was a serious affair and pre-match training meant taking sides and going through tactical motions as if they were really playing an opposing team. It would be interesting to see just how careful the players were of each other, Lorimer thought. A bad tackle in training could put some-body out of the game for weeks. And footballers were notoriously selfish, chasing these few eager years while they lasted. Members of the Kelvin first team might be paid a small fortune but their glory days wouldn't last much more than a decade unless they were particularly lucky, or played in goal. The sensible ones invested their big money though a few, like Jason White, squandered it with as much alacrity as the prodigal son.

He wondered about Nicko Faulkner. The English player had had some good years and would probably have lent a bit of glamour to Kelvin's team, but would he have delivered the sort of skilful football that had marked him out ten years ago? And had he put away enough for a long retirement? Lorimer recalled the press photos of Janis Faulkner and her husband and wondered if they had enjoyed the champagne lifestyle. It might be interesting to see just what the footballer's wife had stood to inherit. Though, somehow, he could not bring himself to believe that she was cold-hearted enough to have killed him for his money.

He was inside the training park now, leaning against a wooden fence, watching as the coach organised the players into two teams. The sound of a lark made him look up and he strained to see the exact point in the blue blue sky where the soaring bird poured out its liquid notes. There it was, a moving speck of darkness fluttering almost out of sight.

Lorimer wrenched his gaze away from the heavens and looked back at the game beginning on the field. Ally Stevenson was yelling something at one of his defenders who turned to acknowledge the coach. For a while the play moved up and down the field, the ball criss-crossing in arcs between the players until Lorimer realised the nature of this particular game: Stevenson was making them play aerial balls as much as possible, yelling instructions about weight and balance as the players sought to follow his demands. Eventually he called a halt and the players went through a series of stretching exercises before jogging gently round the perimeter of the pitch.

'Keepie-uppie for big boys, eh?' Lorimer smiled as Stevenson came to join him.

'Aye, well, they think they know it all when they come up to senior level, but there's always a lot to learn about fitness, stamina . . .' The coach broke off, following the players as they ran past. 'Some of them are naturals, some like to think they are. It's my job to sort them all out and make them do the job properly. See him?' Stevenson pointed to the final runner who had jogged past, elbows pumping rhythmically at his sides. Lorimer looked at the footballer, a tall lanky lad. 'We had to hire a specialist to teach him how to run. He spent all day for weeks doing slaloms in and out of traffic cones. Cost a bloody fortune.'

'And was it worth it?' Lorimer couldn't help asking.

Stevenson shrugged. 'Don't know yet. He's certainly changed his gait and he hasn't lost too many balls in tackles so far, but we'll wait and see.' He paused. 'My money would be on him to come back big-time this season. Reminds me of Peter Crouch: same gangly frame but effective, know what I mean?'

Lorimer nodded. The English internationalist had shot to fame for outstanding performances in the last world cup, his familiar beanpole figure making headlines all over the world. He could see the physical resemblance, but he wondered if the Kelvin lad had the same star quality.

'Donnie Douglas,' Lorimer began, moving on to the reason he was standing on the edge of the field.

'Have you found him?' Stevenson's eyebrows shot up and the detective saw the hope in the man's eyes. As he shook his head he felt guilty, seeing the coach's head turn away in disappointment.

'Sorry. We're no further forward. Hoped some of your players might have an idea where he could have gone,' he explained.

Stevenson's answer was a deep sigh. He faced the training ground, watching the line of footballers come around to complete their first circuit, then waved a hand to bring them to a halt.

There was an immediate scramble towards a pile of cooler bags for bottles of water.

'Right, lads, Detective Chief Inspector Lorimer wants to know if you have any idea about where Donnie's gone to,' Stevenson barked out in his best sergeant major's voice.

'Is he no away hame tae Aberdeen, then?' Baz Thomson's cheeky grin stood out against the more serious expressions on the faces of the other players. 'Hus he no got a burd up there, then?'

'Naw. His burd's down here in Glesca,' someone else offered.

'An address for her would be helpful,' Lorimer suggested, his tone bordering on sarcasm, intending to show he wasn't there to be messed about.

'Ye'll find it down at the club. He signed her in last match day.'

'Aye, so he did. Shockaroonie!' Thomson laughed. 'Donnie falling for groupie number two!'

Lorimer's brow creased in puzzlement.

196

'There's a wee crowd of lassies follow us around, Chief Inspector,' Baz explained. 'We've given them numbers, put them in order of . . .' he broke off, circling his hands over a pair of huge, imaginary bosoms on his own chest as snorts of laughter erupted behind him.

'Her name and address should be in the vistors' book, Chief Inspector. Don't know why we forgot about her.' Stevenson's voice was contrite.

Lorimer nodded. 'Thanks. But if any of you have the slightest idea where Donnie might have gone, you really must tell me.' His steely blue gaze took in each one of them in turn, impressing them with the gravity of the situation. Even Baz Thomson, the class clown, fell silent under the weight of that scrutiny.

'D'you think something's happened to him?' Andy Sweeney asked, blurting out the question that was in all their minds.

Lorimer didn't answer for a moment, letting a sense of unease gather over the players. 'We don't know,' he admitted at last. But in those few seconds of silence he hoped he had sown seeds of real fear within them. If one of them did know Douglas's where-abouts his conscience might prick him into telling what he knew.

Alison Renton was the name scrawled in an untidy childish hand with an address that wasn't a million miles from Kelvin Park. Marie McPhail read out the details to the officer on the other end of the line, wondering why she felt a sudden shiver. The lassie had been a quiet wee thing, she remembered. She'd had a drink with Donnie after the match and they'd gone off together after-wards. Marie tried to recall her face as she'd stood aside for Donnie to sign her in. The girl had worn black, supporters' colours maybe, and there had been a proliferation of silver jew-ellery: bangles jingling around her wrists and several chains sweeping over large breasts. But Alison Renton's face had not imposed itself upon the receptionist's memory.

'Alison Renton?'

The woman who hovered at the half-opened door looked him up and down. 'Who's asking?' she slurred her words slowly, eyes narrowing as if Niall's manner told her all she needed to know: he was police and she didn't like that. Her eyes flicked to the man by his side.

'DC Cameron, DC Weir, Strathclyde Police. Are you Miss Renton?' Niall asked.

The woman laughed, a short, humourless sneer. 'Naw, ah'm her mither.' She pushed back the tangled mop of dyed blonde hair as if in an unconscious wish to become a younger version of herself, then turned away shouting, 'Al-ison!' in a voice that had been rendered hoarse by a lifetime of cigarettes. 'Al-ison, get yer arse doon here, it's the polis!'

A thudding of footsteps clattered behind her then the door was drawn open and a teenage girl stood, mouth gaping open at the sight of Cameron and Weir on her doorstep. She'd probably been in bed and had wrapped a grubby pink towelling-robe around her that she was still tying to one side. Her feet were bare and Niall noticed the wee designs she'd painted on every carefully-manicured toenail. The image was curiously at odds with the pale face and long, unkempt hair.

'Alison Renton?'

'Aye,' the girl answered in a monotone, but her doe-like eyes rimmed with last night's mascara showed a flicker of curiosity. .

'It's about Donnie Douglas. May we come in?'

The footballer's name was an open sesame. Mother and daughter stood back and let the tall Lewisman and his partner stride in.

'Wasn't expecting visitors. Excuse the state of the place,' Mrs Renton gabbled as she sought to plump up cushions and hide overfilled ashtrays and an empty vodka bottle, even as she steered them towards a leather sofa in an alarming shade of neon pink. Alison trailed behind her mother, her eyes on Niall, blinking as if she were still half asleep.

'Now,' Mrs Renton exclaimed, 'a wee cup of tea?'

'Thank you, that would be fine.'

Cameron waited until he was certain she was out of earshot before he began. 'Donnie Douglas: do you know where he is, Alison?'

The girl frowned at him. 'Whit d'ye mean?'

'We're investigating his whereabouts. He's been reported as a missing person,' the detective explained. 'I hoped you might be able to tell us where he could have gone,' he added, gently.

The girl curled up into her armchair as if she were trying to lose herself within the voluminous folds of pink towelling, tucking the collar up around her white, sleep-starved face. With no make-up she looked about fourteen, but the eyes that regarded him seemed as old as her mother's. Alison dropped her gaze and picked at the edge of the armchair where a piece of leather piping had worked itself loose.

'When did you last see Donnie? Alison?' Cameron bent forward, trying to catch her eye, to make her look at him, but she simply wriggled further under the dressing gown.

'Cannae mind,' she said at last. 'Mibbe Sunday?'

'*Last* Sunday?'

'Naw, day after that ref copped it. Havenae seen him since.'

'And has he been in touch? Phoned or texted you?'

'Naw.' The response was followed by a yawn and she turned her head to look blearily at them both.

Mrs Renton bustled in with a tray full of mugs. Her hair had been raked back with a clasp and her lips were a newly-painted shade of pink. 'Therr we are now. Whit's a' this aboot Donnie?'

Cameron considered the woman as she placed a mug in front of him; her tone was a forced light-heartedness but he could see panic in those narrow eyes.

'He's missing, Mrs Renton,' he said quietly, deliberately meeting her gaze. 'He's not been near the club since last weekend and his flat's empty.'

The woman sat down heavily, spilling coffee on to her bare knees. She hardly seemed to notice the brown liquid seeping into her denim skirt. Her eyes flicked between the policemen and her daughter who sat, head down, refusing to meet anybody's eyes.

'Alison! Whit d'you know aboot this!' Mrs Renton demanded, her gravelly voice harsh with suspicion.

'Nuthin.' The girl shrugged an indolent shoulder and cowered further into the cocoon of dressing gown.

'C'mon, hen, ye must know sumthin,' her mother wheedled, changing tack so quickly that Cameron guessed this was a regular routine between the pair of them. 'Did he no say if he wis goin up home?'

Alison shook her head. There was a silence broken only by DC Weir slurping the scalding coffee.

Cameron put down his mug. This was getting them nowhere fast. If Dr Brightman had been here maybe he would have seen something in the girl's behaviour. As it was, he felt she was definitely keeping something from them and so did the mother, he could see that from her expression.

'If you remember anything he said – or if you hear from him again – you will contact us immediately,' Cameron insisted, shoving a card across the narrow, ring-stained coffee table.

Alison Renton grunted in reply, leaving the card where it lay. Cameron could feel her mother's temper rising, but whether it was directed at Alison, the police or indeed Donnie Douglas himself, he could not tell.

'Let us know if you hear from him,' he repeated, this time to Mrs Renton as he prepared to leave. DC Weir put down his mug and followed Cameron out into the street where a small group of young children had gathered close to his car. He glowered at them then pulled a face, eliciting a few giggles as they backed away. It wouldn't do to foster bad feelings with even the most junior of the locals when so much effort was being put into community relations. These kids were tomorrow's citizens, one way or another.

'Okay, we drew a blank.' Cameron sighed as they drove off. 'Just wish we'd had Dr Brightman along with us. I'm sure he'd have asked the right questions.'

CHAPTER 27

'What exactly is the prognosis?' Solly asked. It was the one question he'd been longing to ask yet dreading to utter all through these last days.

Since that fateful Friday night, Rosie had been in a high-dependency unit, her airways kept functioning by machinery that Solly didn't rightly understand. All he knew was that she was deathly pale and that her vital signs were still being monitored by nurses carefully avoiding eye contact with him. Now he had summoned up enough courage to ask the consultant in charge of her case.

The Indian doctor smiled wearily at Solly and folded his hands in front of him on the desk. 'We hope she will make a full recovery, of course,' he began. 'There's a lot of damage from the impact. Normally we would expect some fractured ribs and even a punctured lung but the nature of the crash meant that Miss Fergusson sustained more internal injuries than would have been normal.'

'Why? What happened?' Solly asked, suddenly bewildered. 'I thought the lorry had crushed the windscreen . . .' He trailed off, remembering the state of Rosie's BMW: the mangled metal twisted out of shape, the chips of glass sliding around inside like an unexpected shower of giant hailstones.

'There was a metal strut that came loose from the load the lorry was carrying,' the doctor explained. 'It came through the window like a javelin and impacted against the air bag. Her injuries are mainly from that missile, Dr Brightman,' he added solemnly. 'That was why we needed to perform surgery so quickly. She needed intubation immediately and we had to set up artificial ventilation. This type of blunt chest-trauma is unusual in such a traffic accident,' he told Solly, as if that would console him some-how. 'Your fiancée has suffered severe pulmonary contusions,' the consultant continued, his tone still grave. 'We can see how these resolve from three to five days after surgery. But I'm afraid it is still too soon to give you a definite prognosis.'

'But it's four days now,' Solly pleaded.

'I know.' The doctor turned soulful eyes upon him. 'We are trying to keep her condition as stable as we can, but you must be aware that there is a risk of pneumonia setting in and of subse-quent organ failure.'

'All these tubes . . . ?'

'All these tubes,' the consultant answered gently, 'some of them are keeping her secretions cleared and others are pumping in antibiotics to prevent any possible infection.'

'Secretions?' Solly pounced on the word.

The consultant nodded again. 'Blood in the alveolar spaces pro-vides a breeding ground for infection. The tracheostomy was necessary to allow us to drain it away.'

Solly held up a hand. His stomach was trembling now with a sudden desire to expel what little breakfast he'd managed to eat. The consultant rose from behind the desk and came around, put-ting a sympathetic hand on Solly's shoulder.

'Would you like to use the lavatory?' he asked, indicating a small door to one side of the consulting room.

204

Solly made it just in time, retching over the gleaming porcelain. He groaned as he stood up, a hot flush of embarrassment sweeping over him: the man must take him for every sort of feeble wimp. But when he emerged from the toilet, the consultant came towards him and grasped his hand warmly.

'You've been through a lot, my friend,' he told Solly. 'It takes courage to do what you've been doing.'

Back in Rosie's room, Solly wondered at the doctor's words. Courage? He didn't feel as if he was doing anything at all, simply waiting by her side: waiting and hoping that she would wake up, look at him and smile that wonderful smile of hers. Then he would know that the world had not stopped turning on its axis after all and that there was more to life than this small space where they breathed the same air. He shivered suddenly despite the sunlight's warmth through the glass, imagining Rosie's breath disappearing in a moment and leaving only his own exhalations swimming through the atmosphere. She was so still, so small and still, her body functioning at the whim of all these contraptions that looked more as if they were hurting her than saving her poor damaged tissues from further attack. And if she should die? He shuddered at the thought, banishing it with a determination that surprised him. No. He would stay here and will her to live. What else was there to do?

Patrick Kennedy put down the telephone, his hand trembling with rage. How dare they? He had given a terse reply to the question from that reporter. Had it been too abrupt? Should he have tempered it with some tact? The very cheek of that man Greer had thrown him. *Where were you the night Jason White was killed?* Kennedy had sworn at him, told Greer to mind his own business.

But of course, he thought reluctantly, that sort of stuff was a hack's business, meddling in other people's private lives. It would have been better to have cut him off without a single word. Let him come to his own conclusions. But what if he already knew? The massive fists that had balled in anger now uncurled in lines of clammy perspiration.

Would Barbara remember he wasn't at home that night? Kennedy's lip curled in contempt. Of course she would. His wife knew every minute of every day: when he was home and when he was out. Her fretting over dates and timetables drove him crazy. Sometimes he wondered why he put up with it then he would look out over the green sward of Kelvin's pitch and remember. If he gave up on Barbara, with her controlling interest in the club, he'd have to give up on all of this. Once everything was sorted he'd begin divorce proceedings. But not until then. Too much still hinged on Barbara selling what looked like becoming a load of worthless shares. But there would come a time . . . Kennedy looked into the distance, imagining the future he'd so carefully planned. A thought came to him suddenly and he lifted the phone again.

'Marie? How did that journalist get my direct number?'

Back in the glass box that was the *Gazette*'s offices, Jimmy Greer took a celebratory swig from the half-bottle he kept in his desk drawer. He'd fairly rattled Pat Kennedy's cage. Maybe there was something in it after all, a wee crumb of information that he could chew on and digest. The anonymous phone call that had suggested he ask about Kennedy's movements on the night Jason White had been shot had piqued his interest. Why call him and not the CID? Should he let Lorimer know that Big Pat was unhappy to be asked his whereabouts the night his bad lad was topped? Maybe. But his story would be all the sweeter if he could find out a bit more without having Strathclyde's finest ruining it on him. Still, it would have to be handed over to the police press office eventually but the timing of that was in his own hands.

Greer imagined Lorimer's fury at not being told this latest snippet and the picture made his face break into a large grin. Serve the bastard right, he thought.

Chapter 28

The boot room was possibly the smelliest place in the whole club, Jim Christie decided, closing its door on sweat, leather and polish, then turning the key in the lock. Big Pat had stormed at him that morning about locking up, as if Jim was less than conscientious in his duties. The kitman had taken the huff. It wasn't just these wee boys running daft out there on the pitch, he'd reminded the chairman. He worked his butt off week-in, week-out so the club could turn out their teams properly.

Jim kicked the door of the boot room, adding one more scuff mark to the thousands that had accumulated over the space of several decades, then, as he spotted Wee Bert watching him, he scuttled back up the stairs.

Albert Little scowled as he rubbed the boot room door with a damp cloth. The kitman had been right out of order, kicking it like that. It just gave him more work to do, Bert grumbled to himself. When he'd first come here as assistant groundsman, there had been three of them to do the work that he had to do nowadays. Out in the open air, Bert wanted to spit on to the gravel pathway but he stopped himself; the sight of the swirling pattern that his rake had made calmed him down in a way that no soothing words could ever have achieved. He took a deep breath and scanned the grass, running his eyes across the camber and nodding in satisfaction at its perfect curve. Drainage hadn't been a problem this summer. Bert looked up into a sky that was devoid of cloud, a burning blue that claimed every speck of moisture that he showered over his precious turf. It couldn't last, this endless heat. Surely there had to be a break in this relentless sunshine? The forecast was for more sun later in the week. There were only four more days until the next game; four more days in which to cosset and cajole the pitch into a state of perfection. Bert closed his mind to Jim Christie's childish behaviour. He had better things to think about, like how long he'd leave it until setting the sprinklers to dance across his grass.

Something made him look up at the windows above the stadium. A face was peering down at him, a reminder that they were all being watched. Well, let them watch. What would they see? A middle-aged man going about his lawful business, that was what. And, thought Bert with a sudden shaft of malice, it was a damn sight more than could be said for some of them.

'We have to be careful.'

'I know,' she hissed. 'Think I'm not aware of all these journalists around the place?'

Pat Kennedy bent his head. 'Sorry. I'm just so keyed-up these days.'

'Och, I know. It's no wonder with all that's been going on.' Marie slid her narrow rump across the chairman's desk, circling one hand around his bull-like neck.

'No,' Kennedy said shortly, disengaging her hand and pushing her gently but firmly away. 'We have to be careful,' he repeated. 'Maybe I should spend a bit more time at home.'

Marie McPhail raised questioning eyebrows at him, her arms

folding across her chest, pulling her rows of chains into a golden river that fell between her cleavage.

'Life's complicated enough as it is,' he said testily. 'Maybe when this is all over—'

'Maybe what? You'll leave her? How often have I heard you say that?' Marie spat out in mock laughter.

'We could go away somewhere for a bit,' he mumbled.

'Aye? And when would that be? You wouldn't miss a match, and the fixture list's full till next May!' She shook her head at him as she left, swiping the air in disgust. 'Just don't annoy me, okay?'

Pat Kennedy bowed his head into his hands. How had all this happened? Less than two weeks ago he was on top of the world, a whole season stretching out before them, all his plans ticking along nicely. Now everything seemed to be crashing around him and even the woman who had proved adept at providing solace was no consolation.

The scream that echoed along the corridor brought the sound of running feet.

'What's wrong?' several voices seemed to be asking at once.

The boy stood, mouth open, unable to articulate his fear. They followed his pointing finger towards the end of the corridor.

'The boot room?' Andy Sweeney broke into a jog, several pairs of feet in his wake.

'My God!' The Kelvin captain slithered to a halt in front of the open door. The walls were dripping red from the huge painted words: *Kill Kennedy*. And on the floor the figure of a man in a Kelvin strip lay, face down, a blood-stained knife stuck into the middle of his shirt, intersecting the number *8*. Sweeney took one step forwards, staring at the scene, then turned to face the others.

'Is this someone's idea of a joke?' he snarled.

'Is he no deid, then?' the apprentice who'd sent them all racing to the boot room faltered.

'It wis never alive!' Sweeney kicked the body, sending a shower of sawdust into the air. Someone started to laugh but the captain turned with a furious expression on his face. 'Who did this?' he asked, killing the mirth stone-dead.

'Ah thocht ah'd seen a, a, g-ghost,' the apprentice stammered.

'Was the door locked when you went down to do the boots?' Sweeney demanded.

'Naw. It wisnae. Ah hud the key a' ready tae open it, but . . .' the boy finished miserably, trying desperately to salvage some dignity from the situation.

'Did Jim Christie give you the key?'

'Aye. He always has it ready fur me.'

'Go and find him,' Sweeney demanded. 'He's gonnae go mental when he sees this mess.' The boy hovered for a moment, uncertain. 'Go on, scram!' Sweeney told him.

The boy hared off, his boots thudding on the stone flags, leaving the rest of them staring into the boot room.

'Who d'you think it's meant to be?' asked Gudgie Carmichael, peering over their heads at the dummy dressed up in Kelvin's colours. Now that they had all seen the 'corpse' for what it really was, there was a sense of curiosity dispelling the initial shock.

'Number eight's Donnie's shirt,' Baz Thomson said, looking at each one in turn as the significance of his observation hit home. 'Someone's got a sick sense of humour.'

'We need tae tell Mr Clark. An I think he'll call the polis,' Sweeney said eventually. 'So don't any of youse touch anythin in here, right?'

*

'What about the knife?'

'Ah, strange you should ask about that. It's like the one that killed Nicko Faulkner.'

A pulse throbbed in Lorimer's head. What was the scene of crime officer trying to tell him?

'Go on,' he said.

'The injury to Faulkner was inflicted by a bread knife with a blade just like the one missing from their knife rack. The one found at Kelvin Park was a dead ringer for it. There are loads of these Kitchen Devils on the market. Every married couple seems to get at least one set as a wedding present. It could be a complete coincidence.'

Lorimer grunted as he hung up the telephone. He wasn't one to dismiss coincidences. 'There was absolutely nothing in the press about the knife,' he murmured to himself. 'I'm sure about that. So who else knew the details of Nicko Faulkner's murder?' He tapped a pencil against his teeth as he gazed out into space. Details like this were kept within the investigating team. Reports mentioning weapon types had to be filed under 'strictly confidential', especially when a court case might be in the offing.

Janis Faulkner's court case, he suddenly thought. If she'd killed her husband, was there anything stopping her from passing on details about the murder weapon? How would that work to her advantage? *If* she'd killed him, she might well be latching on to these two subsequent murders to obfuscate her own part in Nicko's death. Already Greer was dropping huge hints that all three killings were linked. Judgement by media, Lorimer thought grimly. It was happening all too often now. How the hell anyone got a fair trial these days was beyond him. He paused, one finger in the air. If Janis Faulkner's story was true, that she had left before her husband had come home – but what if she was lying?

What if she had discovered Nicko's body but not touched anything, what if she had recognised that bread knife as one of theirs? In fact, she could be experiencing flashbacks from the murder scene. And had she spoken to anyone about what she recalled? Lorimer nodded to himself. It was a feasible theory. Janis Faulkner might well be innocent of her husband's murder but was she sticking to a story that would show her up in a better light? After all, what manner of wife would leave her husband bleeding to death?

The M9 was full of rush-hour commuters as Lorimer swung the Lexus into the outside lane towards Stirling. Through the mist he caught glimpses of the castle, high upon its rocky outcrop, a fortress towering over the carse below. And there, pointing skyward, the pencil tip of the Wallace Monument. It never failed to give him the same rush of pride. Whatever William Wallace had been in his own day, he was an icon in this twenty-first century when Scotland badly needed some heroes. Lorimer smiled ruefully. They weren't likely to find many of those sporting a Scotland football jersey, despite the efforts of people like Pat Kennedy. Yet to lots of wee boys, there were heroes out on the parks every week, fighting battles for promotion or relegation.

His smile faded into a frown. What was likely to happen to Kelvin after this season? Could they possibly hope to recover from the events of these past weeks? During the summer, Kennedy had stated publicly that his team would be certain to achieve Premier League status next year. They'd just been relegated by a single point last season. And with the combination of Faulkner and White, he'd sounded confident that they were on to a winner. The twin creases between his eyes deepened as Lorimer considered the implications of these deaths. Was it too far-fetched to harbour the notion that someone was deliberately trying to sabotage Kelvin FC?

His thoughts were left in a cloud bubble as a line of traffic cones forced him to slow down and join the inside lane. Now the city was looming up through the drizzle, the parapets of Stirling Castle almost invisible in their shroud of mist. He'd asked them not to alert Janis Faulkner about his arrival: he didn't want to lose any advantage this unexpected visit might achieve.

CHAPTER 29

She didn't mean to let him see how she felt. It was as if they were both back on that quayside in Mull, his glance piercing through to a panic she wanted to suppress. *Then* she had let her guard slip, the way one does to a stranger that passes by, never to be encountered again. Yet some odd quirk of fate had placed them together. He'd towered over her as he entered the room and she found herself admiring his physique. She'd always fallen for the sporty types and Janis could swear that DCI Lorimer had been a keen sportsman in another life. But it was the look in his eyes that had undone her reserve; a mixture of pity and – what could she call it? Was it interest or curiosity? With a sudden realisation she saw that he was prepared to like her. So she'd smiled and now he was offering her his hand across the table that separated them, before bending his tall frame into the plastic prison seat.

'Thank you for agreeing to see me,' he said, still looking at her with those disconcerting light-blue eyes.

Janis pulled her hands away and hid them out of sight below the table, anxious that he would not see her fingernails digging into the soft flesh of her palms.

'That's okay,' she replied, hoping for nonchalance. But the sound coming from her lips was a strangled croak, as if she'd forgotten how to make polite conversation.

Lorimer nodded and gave a small smile of his own. She cursed inwardly. Voices were a great give-away and now he'd know that she was nervous, though she'd tried to make her handshake firm and she was still holding his gaze.

'How have you been?'

His question was so unexpected and asked in a tone of such gentleness that Janis felt the beginning of tears behind her eyelids. He wasn't supposed to be doing this. He was there to deal with her case, not to make her feel so vulnerable. For a moment she wanted him to come around that table and take her in these strong arms, to hold her and tell her that everything would be all right. But some inner sense told her that if she wasn't careful this surge of self-pity would betray her completely.

So, 'Fine,' she said, trying to inject some lightness into her tone. 'It's a real holiday camp.'

'Not spending your days stitching mail bags, then?'

'Actually it's not that bad,' she said. 'There's a good educational programme and plenty of stuff to do, really. Some of them are better off here than they are at home.'

Lorimer nodded. 'I know,' he said. 'But you're not one of them, Janis, are you?'

At last her gaze dropped and she knew he could see the struggle to maintain an outward calm.

'Tell me about finding Nicko. Was he dead when you came home that night?'

Janis sat bolt upright, feeling the colour draining from her face. She glanced to one side, making a mute appeal to the female prison officer who stood motionless by the door. But that one was staring straight ahead as if she couldn't see or hear a thing.

Janis bit her lip. It was decision time. What she said now might very well seal her fate.

'He was dead,' she replied, her voice husky.

'Tell me what you remember about his appearance.'

Janis swallowed. Was he trying to trick her into something? But a quick look from under her dampened lashes showed her that same concerned expression.

'He was lying on his back,' she began. 'There was all this blood . . .' Her voice tailed off in a whisper.

'What about the knife?'

'I – the knife?' Janis looked up. Her mouth was open but no words came. Licking her lips, she stalled for time. What had it looked like?

'God, this is a nightmare!' she said at last. 'Do I have to try to see it all again?'

His gaze told her that she did, so, closing her eyes, Janis Faulkner visualised the last time she had seen her husband.

'It was sticking out of his chest,' she began, shuddering at the memory.

I was terrified he'd get up and come for me again.

'Someone had stabbed him. I could see it was our bread knife, the one with the serrated edge.'

I just wanted to get away from there.

'I just wanted to get away from there. Can't you understand?'

'Didn't you think to feel for a pulse? Or to phone someone? Like a doctor or the police, perhaps?'

Janis opened her mouth to protest.

Does he think I'm some sort of monster?

'No. I was frightened.'

'So you ran away?'

He made it sound so reasonable. Yes, she'd run away. Who wouldn't under those circumstances?

Janis nodded. 'That's why they think I did it, isn't it?'

He didn't reply but continued to look at her as though he could understand her. Suddenly he reminded her of Lachie. She'd trusted Lachie all her life. Maybe she could trust this man too?

'It must have been some lunatic,' she insisted. 'Look at these other deaths. It's obviously the work of some mad person.'

'Did you tell anybody about the knife?'

Janis frowned, puzzled. What was he harping on about the knife for? Why wasn't he listening to her?

'What d'you mean?'

'Have you described the murder weapon to anybody?'

'No, of course not. I mean, I only just told you I was there after he died . . .'

'Tell me again. Where had you been that night?'

'I – out at the gym. I came home and found him in the kitchen . . .'

Where is he going with this?

'You told your solicitor you'd left the house earlier after a quarrel with your husband. That he'd given you one beating too many and you decided to leave him.'

The voice was more matter-of-fact now, less cosy. She chewed on her lower lip, considering.

'That seemed to be the best thing to say,' she said slowly, watching as he nodded. 'I didn't want to seem a heartless bitch. And anyway, I *was* going to leave him.'

'After all the terrible things he'd done to you,' Lorimer agreed, still nodding his head.

'I didn't kill him,' she said suddenly. 'And there's no proof that I did.'

There's no forensic trace to link you with the murder, Marion Peters had told her.

220

'A jury would understand the provocation that might drive a woman to kill her husband,' Lorimer suggested.

Janis shook her head. She wasn't going down that road, not now and not ever.

'So, up until now nobody knows that you recognised the murder weapon?'

What was it with the knife? Why was it so important?

'No.' Yet even as she spoke, Janis felt the sweat break out on her palms. Had she heard Marion Peters discuss the murder weapon? And what exactly had she told that reporter? For an instant she was about to mention Jimmy Greer but something stopped her.

The DCI was leaning back in his seat, hands stroking his chin as he considered her. Janis froze. Had it all been a game? Could he see through her story and its shreds of truth and lies? Now he was on his feet and she stood up too.

'Thank you for seeing me today,' he was saying. She felt the warmth of his fingers clasp her own, then, giving a small smile and a nod to the prison officer, he was gone.

For the first time since coming into Cornton Vale, Janis Faulkner felt utterly bereft.

CHAPTER 30

'I think you ought to go and see your client,' Lorimer told Marion Peters. 'She's just told me that she was in the kitchen after her husband was killed.'

'What?'

Lorimer could imagine the lawyer's expression of disbelief. In the ensuing conversation he tried to maintain a neutral tone but he feared his excitement was palpable. Janis Faulkner's story could be true. Maybe she had come upon her husband's body like she'd said. But if she had, why scarper like that? Unless she'd worried that she'd be fingered for the crime. He'd seen other cases where perfectly innocent people had reacted in a panic, only to plunge themselves into a bad light. It happened. But even as Lorimer tried to visualise the scene in that kitchen he wondered how the woman had felt. Hadn't she realised that her dead husband couldn't harm her ever again?

Maybe there had been occasions when Janis Faulkner had considered plunging that knife into Nicko's chest. And maybe she had reacted once she'd seen the visible result of all her guilty thoughts.

He sighed. That was something for her lawyer to deal with now. He steepled his fingers against his chin, wondering yet again at how much truth had been in the woman's words. Had she told anyone about that knife? Or was it simply a bizarre coincidence that an identical one had been plunged into Donnie Douglas's shirt?

Not for the first time DCI Lorimer wished he could talk things over with Dr Solomon Brightman.

Donnie slumped down beside the riverbank, his trainers sending up small puffs of dust as their heels skidded against the dried ground.

What had he done?

He recalled the way he had stormed around his room, smashing stuff in a fit of rage. It was like his old man all over again. *He*'d smashed faces into walls, irrespective of whether they belonged to friend or foe. Even his family had come in for that sort of treatment. And violence had bred violence. That's why he'd got out. Not just because the old man was in the nick. That was bad enough. But to stay, tainted with the name of being 'one of those Douglas boys' was more than he could stand.

He'd never minded that they called him the quiet one, the baby of the family; he'd been lucky, indulged as he was by his older brothers and protected from the worse excesses of their brutish father. They'd been proud of the way he'd shown talent from an early age, kicking a ball about the playground then being chosen for the school team. None of the Douglas boys had bothered with school except Donnie and it was the footie that had kept him there until the day a scout from Inverness Calley Thistle had spotted him in a schoolboys' league cup-final. That had been his ticket to better days and he'd taken it without a backward glance. Being transferred to Kelvin had been a dream. Not only had it taken him away from the residual influence of his family, but it had been a new start of a different sort: nobody down here had known who he was. His teammates just thought of him as Donnie, the number eight mid-fielder. And if his accent wasn't pure Glasgow, what did that matter? There were English boys and others from farther afield, like Leo. He'd been accepted for what he was and so far nothing but the game had really mattered.

Donnie heard a sound and lifted his head, suddenly aware that it was a groan escaping from his own lips. What had he done? He shook his head as if the memories could be as easily shaken from his mind. He'd run away from it all, terrified of the consequences, imagining the disgust on the faces of his mates when they found out.

And he'd compounded his sin by absenting himself from the squad. Mr Clark would never take him back. He'd ruined everything now. What was it they called it in the army? Going AWOL. That's what he'd done.

He lifted his head at the sudden thought. Maybe he should join up? That's what blokes did in this situation. They joined the French Foreign Legion. Or maybe he could simply disappear.

He looked up and down the riverbank. Masses of rosebay willow herb stained the slopes a bright pink and butterflies were dotting their way from bloom to bloom like drunken men on a pub crawl. Donnie envied the easy way they swayed from one flower to the next. He wouldn't mind coming back as a butterfly if all that stuff about reincarnation were true.

Shading his eyes from the sun, he gazed at the shapes of houses on the southern bank of the river. There were rows and rows of white houses with dark sloping roofs and, here and there, a patch of grass between. People were going about their lives over there doing normal things. How did it feel to belong to one of those houses: to close your door knowing the next day you'd open it again and be able to go out, free as a bird without a care in the world? He'd been sleeping rough for several nights now, making his way steadily downriver with no clear idea of his eventual destination, just following the instinct that had told him to get away.

Donnie felt a lump gather in his throat. He missed his wee flat. It had been the first real place he'd had of his own. What he'd done had cost him that and so much more. He couldn't go home. And he sure as hell couldn't go back to Glasgow. So where on earth was he going to go?

CHAPTER 31

SHOCK DISCOVERY AT KELVIN FC

The body of a dead footballer was what they saw on arrival at Kelvin Park this morning. But closer inspection revealed it to be a dummy figure dressed in the number eight strip, the one usually worn by missing player Donnie Douglas. Players and staff at the club are still recovering from shock at the discovery.

A large kitchen knife had been stuck into the 'body', a macabre reconstruction of the death of player Nicko Faulkner. The words 'KILL KENNEDY' were scrawled in red paint on the boot room wall. Douglas is still officially listed as a missing person and now there must be real concerns for his safety. It has also emerged that there have been other threats to Kelvin chairman Kennedy in recent days.

Sources close to the Gazette have been informed that Strathclyde Police are treating this as merely some sort of hoax. A possible reason for this is that the football team's boot room is the source of alleged sightings of football legend Ronnie Rankin, or what some folk believe to be his ghost. Only last week one of the apprentices had to be taken off boot room duties after a scare.

'It's terrible that someone is trying to upset the team at a time when they are still struggling to get over the shock of the recent murder of their two teammates and the referee Norrie Cartwright,' said manager Ron Clark.

Whether or not this is the work of the triple killer has been the question uppermost in players' minds. And what Gazette readers must be wondering is what sort of sick mind is behind this latest development and how long it will take for an arrest to be made.

Jimmy Greer

The reporter leaned back, a small laugh escaping from his thin lips. Sick mind? Aye, well, he supposed that was true enough. Inventive, though. Surely they'd grant him that. He'd love to have been a fly on the wall when they'd found the dummy. Pity there was no chance of a photo, but, hey, you couldn't have everything. At least this kept the story alive for a bit longer, just what his editor wanted. The public would lap this up like a cat drinking cream; they just loved sensation and Jimmy Greer was the wee boy to give it to them. He put his hands behind his head, chuckling to himself. This one would run and run. Janis Faulkner's case would see to that. In a way, he told himself, it was no bad thing they hadn't caught the killer yet. Speculation sold more papers. And he could take the occasional dig at DCI flamin' Lorimer so long as the SIO was still apparently clueless. Sick mind? They didnae know the half of it!

Albert Little folded up the newspaper, heart thumping. Kelvin FC was looking like a laughing stock, now. There were all sorts of rumours flying around about one of the boys doing it as a joke. Clark and Stevenson had hauled them all up but not one of them had confessed to the mess in the boot room. He'd wanted to clean it up right away and had been horrified to find police photographers and forensic technicians crawling all over the place. Eventually, after much grumbling, he was being allowed to whitewash over the lurid red letters. For the first time since all those incidents, the groundsman felt a sense of unease as he filled the brush and swept it over the offending graffiti. He turned around more than once, the hairs on the back of his neck prickling, but there was nobody there, just a feeling of intense cold and the sense of being watched.

'I don't know. Either there's a sick-minded bastard out there and he's somehow been able to access the grounds, or there's somebody in the club behind all of this,' Lorimer growled, unconsciously echoing Greer's own words. The tight security measures already in place would point to the latter. 'Only someone from the club could get into the boot room.'

'But do you think it's necessarily the killer who's done this?'

Lorimer was silent. That was the real question, wasn't it? Niall Cameron hadn't been afraid to ask it, either, he thought, appraising the tall Detective Constable loping along at his side. Cameron had fairly put in the hours on this case. He'd scoured the city for any sighting of Donnie Douglas and had begun to put out feelers further afield in the hope that someone would find the missing player.

'D'you think we'll find Donnie Douglas alive?'

'God, I hope so.' Lorimer sighed. 'I'm beginning to believe the newspapers' insistence that we've got some grade-A serial killer out there on the loose.'

'Is Doctor Brightman . . .' Cameron left his sentence unfinished. They both knew what he'd wanted to say. If Solly Brightman had been able to provide some sort of profile then at least that would have given them a direction. But Solly was still at Rosie's bedside and nothing could prevail on Lorimer to try to prise him away from her.

'We have to find Douglas.' Lorimer stopped and turned to Cameron. 'We should put something out on national television. Maybe that'll flush him into the open. If he's still with us,' he added with a sour twist to his mouth.

News-stands around the city were enjoying a roaring trade, their vendors bawling out the *Gazette*'s latest lurid headlines. The whole world and his wife seemed caught up in the Kelvin story, this latest bizarre twist serving to shock and amaze. By the time commuters had reached home, the affairs at Kelvin FC were on everybody's lips. So it was no great surprise when the face of Chief Inspector William Lorimer appeared on their evening television screens.

Maggie Lorimer, hastily forewarned, was sitting staring at her TV, waiting for the news item that would bring her husband into their front room. It wasn't the first time he'd appeared on television and probably wouldn't be the last. Sometimes the job demanded a lot of public support and what better way to reach the masses than this.

There was a news item about the latest atrocities in the Middle East, then the newsreader turned towards a screen behind him. There he was. Maggie's heart gave a little flutter seeing her husband standing at the entrance to Kelvin Park. He was frowning into the camera as the questions began.

'Chief Inspector, rumours have been flying about, regarding

this incident in Kelvin's boot room. What is the official police opinion on this?'

Lorimer shifted from one foot to the other as he replied, making him seem uneasy. It was simply his restless nature, Maggie knew, but viewers might interpret his manner otherwise. Stay still, will you, she urged his image on the TV screen.

'Strathclyde Police treats every incident surrounding these recent deaths very seriously indeed. Whether the reconstruction of a player's murder was a hoax or not, still remains to be seen. Several forensic experts have examined the scene and so far there is nothing to suggest that anyone from outside the club was involved.'

'This could be someone's idea of a joke, then?' The newsreader's eyebrows went up and his voice sounded sceptical.

'We can't say anything for certain at this stage of our investigation, certainly not while we still have a missing person.'

'Donnie Douglas, the Kelvin mid-fielder. Is he a suspect in these murder cases?'

'That's something I'm not at liberty to answer, I'm afraid,' Lorimer replied, his mouth a thin line of disapproval.

'Do you think there might be someone stalking the players?'

'Conjecture isn't very helpful—'

'But surely the threats against Chairman Patrick Kennedy must be taken seriously?' the man interrupted.

Maggie made a face at the screen. The interviewer was making it look as though the police were doing sod all, whereas the opposite was true. Lorimer's team had been working flat out on this case.

'As I've already said, we are taking everything seriously. Three people have lost their lives in the last few weeks. There have been extensive procedures undertaken, most of which I cannot discuss lest it jeopardise our investigation. Let me say, however,' and now Maggie saw her husband turn to face the camera, 'any person who has information that might help to find the perpetrator of the recent killings or who knows the whereabouts of Donnie Douglas should contact us immediately. No matter how insignificant you might think your information is, we need you to come forward. Anything you tell us will be treated in the strictest confidence.'

The Chief Inspector's blue eyes glinted with determination, though his voice was quietly persuasive. Even the newsreader seemed impressed as he read out the number to call.

Then suddenly it was over. The screen behind him went blank as the man continued with other news stories. Maggie sank back, wiping her hands on her linen skirt. He'd not shown a bit of nervousness yet here she was, a total wreck just watching him. What would he be doing now? Was his working day over or would she have to console herself with the ginger cat for company once more? As if on cue, Chancer jumped up on to Maggie's lap, purring, his face rubbing against her cheek. She smiled and cuddled him close, warmed by the animal's spontaneous affection. It was okay. She'd hear all about it come bedtime.

'I really don't know, Chief Inspector,' Pat Kennedy said slowly. 'Enemies? That's a strong word to use, surely? I mean, in the world of football you make friends and you fall out with others. Players have to be disciplined and sometimes dropped but that's just the way it is. Nobody's going to make a great scene about it.'

'What about fans?'

'Oh.' For a moment the chairman was silent, tapping his huge fingers against the side of his seat. They had chosen to sit out on the terracing, away from prying eyes and ears. The evening sun was still high in the sky but deep shadows were cast by the overhanging roof on this side, providing a relief from the heat.

'We have had a few problems,' Kennedy began. 'There are always some who take things to extremes. Bad-mouthing opposing fans is the norm, but sometimes there are fans who act . . . well, violently, I suppose I have to say.'

'But surely the police officers at matches deal with that?'

Kennedy shrugged. 'You've seen the reports from last year's matches. Nothing to write home about, maybe. A few yobs who'd been drinking too much before games. No,' he hesitated then turned to look Lorimer straight in the eye. 'I was thinking about Big Jock.'

'Who?'

Kennedy looked away again, shaking his head slightly. 'Och, maybe I'm clutching at straws here. Big Jock's a nutcase. Appears at home games and makes a bit of a fool of himself. But he's funny, you know, really a comedian. Not right in the head, though. Says daft things, writes mad letters to the club.'

'Why haven't you said anything about him before now?' Lorimer's frown was etched on his forehead.

'He's a harmless big soul,' Kennedy protested. 'At least—'

'At least you thought he was before all this began.' Lorimer finished the sentence for him. 'Better give me any details you have about this character, okay?'

'You don't really think anyone's got it in for me, do you, Chief Inspector?'

Lorimer looked across at the chairman. He was a different man this evening, a troubled man whose arrogance had vanished under the weight of this latest incident. Was he afraid? It was hard to

233

imagine the blustering Kennedy having any fears at all, but perhaps the sight of these blood-red painted words had finally unmanned him.

'I think,' Lorimer answered slowly, 'someone is trying to frighten you. Whether your life is in any danger is another matter. But we'll set up a CCTV system at your home if you want it.'

Kennedy gave a huge sigh and then shook his head. 'No. You've done enough.' He bit his lip as if to stop any more words issuing from his mouth, a gesture that made Lorimer curious. What else had he been about to say?

'The press are having a field day,' Lorimer remarked as they stood to go inside. 'Are you going to restrict entry to the press box for this Saturday's game?'

'No. Let them come. We're going to show them a good football match this week. And I want everyone to see us out there. Ron Clark's doing a magnificent job bolstering the boys' morale. We've got a great chance against the Pars. Let them see that nothing's going to stop us playing our best. And winning,' he added, shooting a defiant look at Lorimer.

The DCI simply nodded as they walked back down the steps. This was more like the Kennedy he'd come to know: a strong, determined bear of a man. He glanced behind him as if the other Kennedy, the one he'd glimpsed back there on the shadowy terracing, might still be sitting, head in hands, fearful of what lay ahead.

'So? What happened after that?' Maggie snuggled closer to her husband's shoulder, luxuriating in the feel of his skin against her breasts.

'It was a bit shambolic, really. Trying to round up everyone for fingerprinting. Can you imagine it? There are loads of staff employed in that place. Anyway, we got it over with and telephoned the players who weren't at the club.'

'Oh? Anyone suspicious?'

'Not so's you'd notice. There are a few lads who live way out of the area. They'd already gone home.'

'When will you get a result on the prints?'

'When the Scottish Criminal Record Office boys and girls see fit to tell us. That's a huge assignment for them.' Lorimer rolled over and sighed. 'Just one print that's different from all of the ones we've done today. That's all it takes. And the rest can be eliminated. At least that's what we're telling them.' He grinned. 'Anyway, I thought my work was done for the day, woman.'

Maggie giggled as his hand slid under her thigh, touching a ticklish spot. Then the laughter turned to an indrawn breath as he began to kiss her neck. A shiver ran through her and she drew the sheet over them, clutching it tightly in one damp fist. Thoughts of footballers and fingerprints dissolved into nothingness as she closed her eyes, letting her other senses take control.

It was that time between light and darkness when the sky becomes a deep shade of electric blue, the invisible sun sending vivid echoes of colour above the earth's black rim. A few stars winked blearily from their long daylight sleep, waiting for the dark to uncover their naked brightness. Sitting alone on the topmost row of the East stand a figure sat, staring at the horizon, breathing in the cool air like draughts of wine. The sight of every spire and rooftop was comforting in its familiarity, like coming home after an enforced exile.

That's what it had been like, he thought. Those years away had been an exile from his true love, this football club. No woman would ever understand just what that meant to him. He belonged here and the place belonged to him. It was as simple as that. Nobody was going to take that away. He stroked the bulge under the thin material of his jacket, feeling the solid shape of the gun. A small sigh escaped him. But it was a sigh of pleasure and a smile creased his face. Everything would be all right now.

CHAPTER 32

'There's one thing that makes it different,' Lorimer told the assembled team. 'Faulkner was stabbed in the chest, and here,' he pointed to the image on the screen, 'is a faked dead body with a knife stuck into its back. Okay, maybe the idea was to highlight the number eight, Donnie Douglas's number, but that difference in the MO tells me this was not done by the same hand that killed Faulkner.'

'I thought the wife was pretty well in the frame for that,' a voice commented from the back of the room.

Lorimer looked up. DI Jo Grant was looking at him quizzically, her arms folded across her chest. Jo was a tough cookie and Lorimer had a lot of respect for an officer whose CV included undercover work. He nodded slowly as he replied. 'It all points to her, certainly. If we had a wee bit of forensic evidence then we could wrap that up happily enough. Changing her story has probably weakened her defence.'

'Why doesn't she confess, then? Her sentence would be all the shorter for a guilty plea,' Jo grumbled. A small murmur of agreement rippled among the team.

'And a confession would make all our lives easier, right?' Lorimer replied, but his tone had that edge of quiet anger that they all knew so well and Jo Grant simply shrugged and kept silent. 'I've seen her,' Lorimer continued, 'I've tried to persuade her to come clean but she persists in maintaining her innocence. But so have hundreds of guilty killers before her. We must remember that. And, besides, her defence lawyer will insist on the burden of proof being demonstrated by the prosecution.'

'But someone knew about the weapon,' Niall Cameron piped up. 'That's not coincidence, surely?'

Lorimer gritted his teeth. This was a factor that had kept him awake long after Maggie's breathing had become heavy and shallow, her head nestled against his chest. 'Janis Faulkner may have told somebody. She says she didn't. But she denied being in the house with her husband's dead body and then changed that story. So why should we believe her over this?'

'Jimmy Greer.' DS Wilson nodded his head as he uttered the name. 'That's who she's told. Bet you any money you like that wee toerag's got a hold of her story. We know he telephoned her several times at Cornton Vale, thanks to our ever-efficient prison officers. Who's to say he didn't weasel that little titbit out of her?'

Lorimer was silent for a moment. The image of Janis Faulkner came to him: her fair hair over that child-like face, her vulnerability almost tangible. For a hardened hack such as Greer to have succeeded where he himself had failed left a sour taste in his mouth. But then, he reasoned, Greer represented the media and all its power to sway public opinion; DCI Lorimer and all those officers standing before him represented the forces of the law. And if the footballer's wife had really crossed that deadly line then maybe she had found it easier to throw in her lot with a sleazy journalist who promised her some form of redemption.

'Aye, you could be spot on, Wilson. Want to see what Greer's been up to lately?'

*

When the doorbell rang, Jimmy Greer rolled over on to his side with a groan. His eyes opened to the sight of an empty bottle of whisky on the table. Hell, surely he hadn't fallen asleep? The bell persisted in drilling a hole into his skull and he tried to sit upright on the settee. If he ignored it they'd go away. But the sound continued as if the person behind the door had put his finger on the bell push and wasn't going to let up.

'Aw, shut yer face!' Greer called as he shambled down the hallway. He yanked the door open, a belligerent scowl pasted on his thin features, ready to blast whoever had woken him up. But his expression changed in an instant when he saw the policemen standing on his doormat.

'DS Wilson, DC Cameron,' they told him, waving their warrant cards at his bloodshot eyes. Greer stood aside automatically, letting the CID officers into his flat.

The journalist followed them into the wreck of his living room. The smell of whisky mingled with the remains of a curry that lay in a foil container on the floor beside the television. Greer looked at it stupidly. Had he eaten that last night? He couldn't even remember going into his local Asian takeaway.

'Mind if I get a drink?' he asked, heading towards the kitchen. A tumbler of water would help him to see straight, to think fast.

'Looks like you had a skinful already. Good party, was it?' Wilson asked.

Greer made a noise that was midway between a grunt and a mutter as he left the room.

'Mind if we open a window?' Wilson called out as loudly as he could. He grinned to himself, imagining the pain throbbing in the man's skull.

'He's in a bad way,' Cameron remarked.

'Ach, don't waste any sympathy on that one. Besides, it's self-inflicted. Wonder what he was celebrating?' he added.

Greer came back into the room, a half-empty tumbler of water clutched in one hand. 'Right, what do you want at this time in the morning?'

'My goodness, Jimmy.' Wilson folded his arms and grinned. 'Do you not see it's nearly eleven o'clock? Must be nearly time for your midday snifter, eh?'

'What?' The journalist's jaw dropped and he pulled up a shirt cuff to peer at his watch. 'Bloody hell,' he muttered.

'Should have been somewhere by now, maybe?' Wilson suggested. The Detective Sergeant was clearly enjoying Greer's discomfiture.

'Aye, well, you're here now, so I suppose I can say I was on official business,' the journalist replied, his usual cockiness reasserting itself.

'Can we sit down?'

'Go ahead,' Greer said, plonking himself into the nearest seat, an ancient leather armchair that did not match any other furniture in the room. 'What's all this about?'

Wilson nodded briefly at Niall Cameron who sat forward, fixing Greer with what he hoped was his best imitation of DCI Lorimer's famous stare.

'We're investigating certain matters surrounding the Nicko Faulkner murder,' Cameron began. 'We believe you have been in communication with Janis Faulkner.'

'No me, son,' Greer blustered.

'That's not what the officers in Cornton Vale have been telling us, sir,' Cameron replied stiffly, never once taking his eyes off the journalist.

'Aye, well.' He shifted uneasily in his chair. 'Maybe I did give her a wee phone call.'

'Maybe you gave her more than one,' Wilson chipped in, his words eliciting a scowl from Greer.

'We would like to know the nature of your conversations with Mrs Faulkner,' Cameron continued.

'Ah, classified information,' Greer sneered. 'Cannae divulge that.'

'If you don't divulge what was said between you then a court would likely find you guilty of obstructing the course of justice, Mr Greer,' Cameron said mildly.

For a moment the journalist looked from one officer to the other, searching their expressions as if to gauge the seriousness of this threat.

'And what if I cannae remember what we said?'

'I'm sure you'll have written notes transcribed from tape,' Cameron suggested encouragingly. 'Isn't that the norm in your profession?'

Greer licked his lips then took a gulp of water from his glass. Wiping the drops from his moustache, he gave a resigned sigh. 'Okay, what exactly is it you're after?'

'What did Janis Faulkner tell you about Nicko's murder?' Wilson asked.

'She didn't do it.'

'That's not what we want to know. Did she give you any details about the murder scene?'

'Like what?'

'Like the MO.' Wilson nodded grimly.

'He was stabbed, wasn't he?' Greer was evidently trying to play for time as his eyes flicked from Wilson to Cameron and back again.

'And the murder weapon?'

Greer stayed silent but the beads of sweat that were gathering on his brow were nothing to do with the heat in the room.

'She told you what it was,' Wilson persisted. 'Didn't she?'

'Cannae mind,' the journalist muttered.

'Oh, come off it, Greer, that's one juicy bit of info you wouldn't forget in a hurry.'

'All right then, she says it was one of these Kitchen Devils. A big bread knife.'

'And you told how many people?' Wilson shot back.

'Don't know. Can't remember. Maybe I didn't tell anybody,' he said, running a hand over his head with a groan. 'Haven't used it in the paper. You lot would have had my guts for garters.'

'Well you should think very carefully, Mr Greer. Try to remember exactly who else might have this information,' Cameron warned him.

'Aye, well I'll let you know. If I remember,' he mumbled. There was a silence that made him look up in time to see the two men exchanging a glance.

'Is that it, then?'

'For now,' Wilson replied, standing up, ready to leave. 'Oh, there's just one more thing,' he added, looking back before he and Cameron left the room. 'You need to come down to HQ to have your fingerprints taken.'

'What for?'

'Process of elimination,' Cameron told him blandly, then followed his colleague out into the fresher air of the Glasgow streets.

'He's not my idea of what a senior newspaper reporter would be,' Cameron remarked as they set off in Wilson's car.

'Och, don't let him fool you. He's not so daft, that one, believe me,' Wilson chuckled. 'Anyway, we got what we wanted. Now let's see if Greer has had dealings with any of the Kelvin players.'

*

Back in his flat, Jimmy Greer looked vacantly into the empty tumbler. What if he'd left a trace? What if they really had a print? He examined his hands, first one then the other, watching each of them shake. And for the first time in a long time he wondered if what he had done in the name of capturing a good story would come back to haunt him.

CHAPTER 33

The prison officer walked past the flower beds, admiring the neat rows of annuals that the girls had planted. They'd excelled themselves this year. The prisoner who'd brought them all on from seed was there every day, tending to her beds with a devotion that had surprised the prison staff. She had been found guilty of assault to severe injury and would be here for several more years, able to take at least a small pleasure from the changing seasons and what they might bring. Anyone looking at her, absorbed in her work, would never dream that she'd left her partner fighting for his life and permanently disfigured after her rampage with a baseball bat. She'd meant to kill him and had almost succeeded. Maybe, just maybe, this ability to care for living things would rub off when the time came for her release.

The thought of gardens was quickly banished as the officer unlocked the blue door and closed it behind her. Some duties were harder than others and this was one she didn't relish at all. Telling a prisoner bad news could provoke all sorts of behaviour: some went quite loopy, smashing stuff and howling hysterically; others merely shrugged, used as they were to life's hard knocks. How this one would react was anybody's guess.

She was sitting in the main recreation room, flicking through a magazine that someone had brought in for one of the other girls. The officer sat down opposite her, saw the prisoner glance up then look back at the article she'd been reading as if wishing to ignore this unexpected visitor.

'Janis,' the officer began, leaning forward so that only the prisoner could hear her.

Janis Faulkner looked up, then, seeing the expression of the other woman's face, she let the magazine fall from her hands. 'What is it?' she whispered.

'They're not letting you out on bail,' the officer told her.

'Why not?' she asked. The question burst from her lips.

'Don't know. Your solicitor can probably tell you more.' Then, watching the blood drain from Janis's face she reached out a hand and touched the prisoner's shoulder. 'You okay? Want a drink of water or something?'

Janis Faulkner shook her head, staring at the prison officer as if seeing her for the first time. 'No,' she said at last. 'I'm fine. Really.'

The woman gave Janis another quizzical look as if to reassure herself that her news was not going to precipitate an incident. 'Well, if you're sure . . .'

'It's okay, just a bit disappointing, that's all.' Janis looked as if she was forcing the smile on to her face. The officer took the hint. She'd want to be alone for a bit right now and was probably willing this messenger of bad news to get up and go away. She stood up, nodding her understanding and smiling back at Janis with an expression of relief.

'I think she'll be all right,' she told the duty officer downstairs. 'Just keep an eye on her, though. You know what can happen,' she added, raising her eyebrows significantly.

*

It couldn't be true. Marion Peters had as good as promised that she'd be granted bail pending an appeal. For days now she'd dreamed of having a proper shower or a bath. Putting on clean clothes and walking along a street where nobody would be looking at her, watching her every move. Now all these thoughts were crumbling into dust. Janis clasped her hands together tightly, willing herself not to cry. How long had she been in here already? And how long would it be till her case came to court? Lips trembling, she made the calculation. God! She might still be here at Christmas. The idea was unbearable. And if they found her guilty? Janis tried to stand up but her knees were weak beneath her and she sank back on to the chair, letting her hair cover her face so nobody could see the tears that weren't too far away.

Images of Nicko came into her mind then, his laughing face and the memory of his arms holding her hard against their bed. And in that moment Janis Faulkner knew such hatred that it made her gasp. *He* was the guilty one, not her. *His* life had been full of brightness, charm, success and power. Now what was she to have? Punishment? But hadn't she been punished enough already? She'd been at his mercy when he was alive and she was still suffering now that he was dead.

CHAPTER 34

Lorimer put down the telephone and leaned back, staring into space. So, only two sets of prints had been found on the dummy and none on the knife. There had been plenty of partials and a few whole prints inside the boot room itself but since people went in and out of there every day these were not of any significance. The players had been subdued when they'd had their prints taken, still shocked, no doubt, from the macabre discovery. But not one of their prints matched up with the ones that held most significance. Nor had they matched with any of the club's personnel. It was frustrating. How had someone managed to slip past the police presence and into the boot room in broad daylight? Albert Little had been beside himself with fury when he'd seen the mess, Baz Thomson had confided in the DCI. And how somebody had unlocked the room without his knowledge or Jim Christie's was a sheer mystery. 'Maybe it was Ronnie Rankin's ghost,' Baz had joked, making Lorimer wonder if the striker had in fact had some hand in the incident. But that was just Baz. He couldn't resist a cheeky comment even when faced with the presence of Strathclyde's finest.

Still, it wasn't over yet. They had more results to come in from those players who had left early and from the *Gazette*'s senior reporter. Meantime there was plenty for the team to do. The TV

249

appeal had produced a good response and officers were collating information and following it all up. There had even been a possible sighting of Donnie Douglas. DC Cameron had tracked down the man who had been spotted but it turned out to be a false alarm. Lorimer pursed his lips. He didn't like to appear heavy-handed with his officers but maybe having Alison Renton in for questioning in a police environment might elicit a better response than Cameron and Weir had received. He would put it to the Detective Constables as tactfully as possible.

The girl sat in the interview room, her dark hair smoothed back from her face with a shiny butterfly-shaped clip. It glinted in the sunlight as she turned her face towards Lorimer.

'Alison Renton?'

The girl nodded as he put out his hand. The soft, warm clasp of her fingers in his reminded him just how young she was. But the expression on her face lacked the innocence of that brief touch. This one had been around a bit, he thought, seeing the frank appraisal that swept over the men in the room. *Groupie number two*, the footballers' words came back to him just then and Lorimer wondered what sort of young girl followed in the wake of these sportsmen, hoping for cheap thrills. Yet she'd dressed nicely for this interview, a short-sleeved white blouse billowing out over a neat black skirt. Had this been her school uniform not so long ago?

'Donnie Douglas,' Lorimer began. 'We wondered if you'd had time to think where he might have gone. Or,' he added, keeping the girl's eyes fixed on his, 'why he left his flat so suddenly.'

Alison Renton looked away from him towards the uniformed officer at the door then back to Lorimer. She bit her lip then, leaning forward, she whispered, 'Does he have to be in here? Can I no speak to you on my own?'

Lorimer cocked his head to one side. What was this all about?

'Afraid not. Security regulations demand that you have the protection of other officers present.' His voice sounded suddenly stuffy to his own ears and so he grinned and whispered back, 'I might eat a wee girl like you for my dinner.'

Alison sniggered, her face changing in an instant to the young lassie she really was underneath the layers of cheap make-up. She wasn't as streetwise as she liked to make out, Lorimer decided.

'Anyway, why would you want to talk to me on my own?'

Her gaze fell and she mumbled something into her swelling bosoms.

'What's that?'

'Don't want everyone to know,' she repeated.

Lorimer leaned back, smiling encouragement. 'This meeting is taking place in the strictest confidence,' he told her. 'Not a soul outside these four walls will be allowed to divulge what you say unless I let them.' He tried to look both grim and encouraging. It must have worked because the girl heaved a sigh that could only be relief.

'I havenae told my maw,' she began. Then she looked down at her lap again and Lorimer could see her twisting the ends of her white shirt. She risked a glance up at him again. 'It's why Donnie left,' she said at last.

Lorimer nodded, letting her continue without interruption.

'We had a big fall out,' she admitted, 'Donnie was mad at me cos . . .' She fell silent, biting her lower lip again, fingers still working nervously at her blouse. 'Cos I wouldnae do things his way,' she added lamely.

Lorimer let the silence grow between them, watching the girl begin to rock back and forth, torn between keeping her secret and revealing it to this policeman who kept staring at her.

251

'Why did Donnie leave, Alison?' he asked at last, his voice quiet and reassuring, inviting her confidence.

She put both hands up to her face, covering her mouth as though to stop herself from bursting into tears. Then, shaking her head as if an inevitable moment had come, Alison Renton gave a strangled sob.

'I'm pregnant,' she said.

Maggie turned from the kitchen sink, her face lighting up as she saw her husband coming towards her.

'Hey, give me time to take these off,' she said, waving her rubber-gloved hands in the air.

Lorimer stepped back, watching his wife pull off the yellow gloves and throw them to one side. Then she was in his arms, her head tucked against his shoulder. It was the best time of the day, this sweet moment of coming home, he told himself, hugging her closer.

'You're gorgeous,' he murmured into her hair.

'Mm,' came the reply, then she slipped from his grasp and turned back towards the sink. 'Lobster salad,' she said, indicating the array of foodstuffs she'd been preparing.

'Oh? Any special reason?' Lorimer asked, brow furrowed. Had he missed some anniversary? But Maggie was smiling and shaking her head.

'No. Saw it on special offer and decided you and I needed a wee reminder of Mull.'

'Good thinking.'

'So, let me finish this while you open that nice Chablis I stuck in the fridge. Okay?'

'Sounds great.'

*

Lorimer gave a sigh of satisfaction, 'That,' he said, raising his glass in salute, 'was magnificent.'

'Och, you deserve a treat. What with the hours you've been working.'

'Does it bother you?'

Maggie shook her head. 'Not really. Anyway, what's new with this horrible murder case? No more bodies, real or otherwise, I hope?'

'No.' He paused, swirling the straw-coloured wine round his glass thoughtfully. 'But I did have somebody in to see me today that would interest you.'

'Oh?'

'Strictly confidential, of course.' He smiled. Maggie could be relied upon to keep his news to herself, but after his promises to Alison Renton he felt obliged to underline this.

'Maybe you shouldn't tell me, then,' she retorted, with a shake of her dark curls.

'Donnie Douglas: you know, the footballer who's disappeared . . . well, his girlfriend came in to see me at our request.'

'Hadn't Niall and that new fellow visited her already?'

Lorimer nodded. 'Thought a new face might impress her sufficiently to winkle out some information. Niall felt she was holding something back when her mother was there. And he was right.' He took a swig of wine as Maggie watched him, her interest piqued. 'She finally let on that she was expecting Douglas's child.'

'Wow. So, what . . . ?'

'They'd had a huge row about it. She wouldn't tell her mother. Didn't want anyone to know. Said she wanted money from him, to have an abortion. Douglas went ballistic. Screamed the place down, according to the girl. Said he wasn't having any of it, that he'd marry her and they'd bring up the baby together.'

'So, what was her problem?'

Lorimer sighed. 'You'd have to see her. She's just a wee lassie, probably ages with some of your sixth years. She just wanted to have a good time, hang around the footballers, get off with as many of them as she could.'

'Sounds a right wee slapper to me,' Maggie replied.

'Hold on, though. She's also a calculating young woman. According to her, she told Donnie Douglas that if he didn't get her the money for an abortion she was going to contact the club and tell them everything.'

'And she told you this of her own volition?' Maggie's tone was sceptical.

'Aye, but guess what? She'd changed her mind. Typical woman.' He laughed as Maggie made a face at him. 'No sooner does Douglas do a runner and she can't contact him on his mobile, but she decides she wants the baby after all.'

'A case of "you don't know what you've got till it's gone",' Maggie sang the Joni Mitchell lyric lightly.

'That about sums it up. Poor bloke's off somewhere thinking he's being blackmailed by a girl he really cared about and he's worried, no doubt, about all the flak waiting for him back at the club.'

'Why should the other players give him a hard time? Surely they'd be sympathetic?'

Lorimer shook his head. 'Think of your kids in the playground, Mags. The ones who make life misery for a few of their mates; it's like that. Imagine a crowd of daft lassies following the players around, making themselves available, let's say. Well, the boys had them sussed. Gave them names like "groupie number one" and so on.' He paused, deciding to leave out the more lurid details. 'Anyway, Alison Renton was one of this crowd and Donnie Douglas fell for her. Simple as that.'

'So,' Maggie asked slowly, 'do you think she had anything to do with the dummy incident?'

Lorimer shook his head. 'No, I don't. Had her prints taken, though. She was actually rather good about that, said she hoped it would help to find Donnie. No, I think whoever did this wanted to draw attention to something else. Using the number eight shirt was maybe just something to spice up the scene.'

'Go on.'

'I'm wondering if the real reason somebody broke into the boot room was to paint that stuff on the wall.'

'*Kill Kennedy*?'

'That's what I think. There's something odd about the man. Something that doesn't feel right . . .' He tailed off, eyes looking beyond his wife to a place only he could see.

Maggie Lorimer, knowing that look of old, slipped away quietly. She'd make some coffee, have it outside in the garden. He'd come and join her eventually, but right now her husband was back at work even while he sat at his own table, oblivious to everything around him.

CHAPTER 35

Rosie dreamed that she was in a white room. Everything was white: walls, floor, furniture, even her clothes were made from some thin white stuff. She could feel the fabric cool under her fingers, the garment floating loose around her naked body.

But she was not alone in this room. There was a tall man dressed in a pale uniform who seemed to be waiting for her by an open door. He stood very still and Rosie thought to herself that he had a military sort of bearing; this seemed to be confirmed by the peaked hat tucked beneath the crook of his elbow and the clipboard full of papers he was consulting. She felt herself move towards him, curious to know what the papers contained. They were to do with what was to become of her, she knew that instinctively without having to be told.

'You'll go through there,' he said, pointing to the doorway. Rosie looked up, prepared to smile, but his face was so grave that she looked beyond his outstretched hand to see where the door might lead. She didn't want to leave this familiar whiteness behind but the man's face told her that she had no option, so she moved through the doorway, shivering as she entered into a shadowy corridor. Blank walls on either side curved overhead to form an arch all the way along, so it was more like a tunnel than a corridor. The darkness did not intensify, rather the quality of twilight remained the same even when the white room was left far behind. On and on she walked until all sense of time had vanished. She never stopped travelling forwards, only hesitating sometimes to rub her eyes and blink in the dim light. Rosie felt no fear, only a growing curiosity as to where the tunnel would lead and what she might find at the other end. At last the stifling greyness gave way as pale light shone against a curve on the wall and she stepped out into a brightness so intense and dazzling that she had to close her eyes tightly and cover them with her hands.

A sudden babble of voices filled her ears, so loud that Rosie wanted to scream. The sound of her own voice came to her then, a high, thin sound like an infant's mewling, and she felt helpless against the hands that lifted her up and away from the ground. For a moment she felt safe – these hands were strong – though they held her body in a vice-like grip. I'm just tired, she told herself. My body is weak, that's all. But then the dream took on nightmarish proportions as everything happened at once. A hand pushed her down, hard, and her body was forced into a small cage. Rosie felt sharp edges graze her arms and something cold strike her bare feet. The snap as a lid was shut above her echoed all around, mingling with screams and curses. Before she knew what was happening, the world tilted sideways and then her whole body jarred as the cage came to earth with a thud. She tried to speak, but no sound came from her lips. Her neck was twisted into an awkward angle and then she felt her head thump against the side of the cage as if it were being pulled over rough ground.

The motion stopped and Rosie opened her eyes to see stars wheeling above her in a night sky; not twinkling sparks of diamond light but blood-red like carrion waiting for the ripeness of her flesh.

'She's here,' a voice said and Rosie tried moving her head to see who had spoken.

Then Solly was there by her side, his face wet with tears. Rosie wanted to reach out her hand, to touch him. But at that very moment the pain intensified, filling her body, and she felt herself being lifted away into the blackness even as she tried to say his name.

CHAPTER 36

Solly was sitting outside Rosie's room, head bowed into his arms, when Lorimer came around the corner of the hospital corridor. The tall policeman paused, uncertain. Had the worst really happened?

He sat down next to the psychologist and placed an arm around his shoulders. For a while they said nothing then Solly looked up, his face blotched with recent weeping. Lorimer swallowed hard, not trusting himself to ask the question, fearful of its response.

Then Solly shook his head and gave a shuddering sigh. 'They think she's going to be all right. There were a few bad hours early on this morning, when they thought her lungs were filling up, but she's over that now. Sleeping peacefully.' Dr Solomon Brightman lifted his haggard face and the policeman saw fresh tears coursing down his cheeks. But they were tears of relief and in one swift movement Lorimer had him in his arms, holding him as he sobbed like a child.

A decent meal and a couple of glasses of milk had worked wonders for him, thought Lorimer, looking at his friend across the table. When had he last eaten? Days spent moving between Rosie's room and the coffee machine had taken their toll on the psychologist. His usually benign face had lost its rounded contours, the cheekbones showing sharply beneath the pallid flesh.

'Come on, let's get you home,' Lorimer began.

'No! I couldn't possibly leave now.'

Lorimer made a face. 'Think you could do with a shower and a fresh change of clothes, pal. Surely you don't want Rosie to wake up seeing you like this?'

As Solly looked down at his sweat-soaked T-shirt, Lorimer hid a smile. The psychologist was the least vain man he knew, totally unaware of his appearance, but his expression of amazement at his unkempt state was almost comical.

Leaving the hospital canteen, they strolled out into the morning sunshine towards the car park.

Solly lifted his face to the warmth of the sun and spread out his hands. 'What a beautiful day,' he said simply.

'Any chance you might want to come into the station later on? We could do with your help,' Lorimer suggested lightly as the Lexus drew up outside the West End flat.

Solomon Brightman looked serious for a moment. 'I've let you down, haven't I?'

'No. There was no way on God's earth you could have done anything else.' Lorimer grinned. 'We've just had to manage without you for a bit. Besides, it would've been a hassle to get anyone else of your calibre during the holiday period.'

'Can you give me an outline of what's been happening since . . .' Solly broke off, unable to refer to Rosie's accident.

'Funny you should ask.' Lorimer pulled a file from the back seat of the Lexus. 'See what you make of that and we'll see you around five-thirty. Okay?'

Solly raised his bushy eyebrows. 'You were quite sure I'd come back to the case, then?'

'Oh, yes,' Lorimer smiled.

The first things she saw when she opened her eyes were the yellow roses. There were masses of them crammed into cut-glass and crystal vases, the refracted sunbeams filling the room with shards of rainbow-coloured light. Rosie blinked to see if this was another dream or if she was indeed awake. A slight breeze came from her side and Rosie glanced at the fan whirring around on her bedside cabinet. That, more than anything, told her she was in a hospital bed. Gradually she became aware of the tubes taped to the back of her wrist and the drip that was positioned slightly behind the bank of pillows so that she caught only a glimpse of chrome. There was no pain so she must be receiving a fair quantity of morphine, Rosie thought. For a time she took in her position dispassionately as only a trained doctor can do. Of the accident she remembered nothing at all, but there could be no doubt that something frightful had happened to make her land in hospital. Trying to recall the events met with a blank and she feebly raised her eyebrows in a gesture of capitulation. Someone would tell her about it. Closing her eyes again, Rosie felt a peace that was borne of the simple knowledge of being alive.

'She's okay!' Lorimer shouted down the phone. 'Rosie's going to be okay!'

Maggie sank down on to the floor by the telephone, her throat constricted by an overwhelming need to weep.

'Can you hear me, Maggie? She's going to be fine.'

'Yes,' she whispered back. 'I hear you. Oh, thank God!'

Replacing the handset, Maggie Lorimer leaned back against the wall and shivered. The days spent waiting for these words had been so long, so drawn out, that she felt totally spent of all emotion. As if from nowhere, a warm ginger head ducked under her hand, demanding a caress, and she buried her face into Chancer's soft fur, her heart suddenly gladdened by his insistent purr. But in that moment it occurred to her that her pact with God might really come about and that she might have to relinquish the comfort of this little creature.

'I love you, little one,' she told the cat, 'but Solly loves her more.'

That afternoon's meeting in divisional headquarters had a light-heartedness about it that belied the discussion of a triple murder case: the news about Dr Rosie Fergusson had spread around. Even Lorimer couldn't keep a grin off his face as he reintroduced Dr Brightman to their team. A spontaneous round of applause broke out that made the psychologist blush to the roots of his beard.

'I'm so sorry to have abandoned you all,' he began but his words were drowned out by exclamations of support from various members of the team who knew and respected the forensic pathologist.

'I did have the beginnings of a profile before Rosie's car crash,' he told them, 'and in the light of subsequent events I think I can give some indication of the man we are looking for.'

The atmosphere changed abruptly at his words and all eyes turned to see the psychologist's solemn face regarding them.

'The murders of Mr White and Mr Cartwright have several similarities and show that an organised mind is behind them.

These killings were not random. We are not, I suggest, looking for someone who acts on impulse but for a man who is quite in control of his own mind and who has an agenda.'

'So you think Pat Kennedy could be a target?' DI Grant piped up.

'Indeed I do. There seems to be just a little too much focus on Mr Kennedy for this to be all bluff. From the bogus email and the website threat, to the painted words daubed on the wall of Kelvin's boot room, it seems to me as if our man is taking more risks as he becomes secure in the knowledge that he has already got away with a double murder.' Solly paused to look around the room, wishing to see the effect of his words. As his glance fell on the SIO he could see that Lorimer had one hand upon his chin, considering what had been said. That was something of a relief. His insistence that the same person had taken the lives of White and Cartwright was not being disputed. Of Nicko Faulkner's murder he made no mention; a deliberate omission to emphasise his point.

'So,' Jo Grant came back again, 'you think it's someone inside the club?'

'Indubitably, DI Grant,' Solly replied, inclining his head towards her. 'Which should make your lives a lot easier,' he added with a sudden grin.

Lorimer watched his friend scurrying towards the taxi that would take him back to Rosie's bedside, then turned away from the window. Things looked brighter now, especially as the team had done some serious work trawling the local internet cafes in and around Glasgow. Cafe Source, a twenty-four-hour establishment in Glasgow's West End, had been located as the most likely origin of both the website threat and the bogus email to

Tam Baillie. But it was unlikely that any of its staff would be able to identify one out of their numerous casual customers. If he had a suspect then they could at least show a photograph. Lorimer clenched his jaw. Pat Kennedy had come to the top of his list more than once, though what his motivation would be for killing these two men was something that gave him pause. It was just the man's manner, the belligerent, bullying arrogance that seemed to suggest he was capable if not of murder then of having it arranged. An organised mind, Solly had said to them. But did the organised mind belong to the person who had pulled these triggers or to someone who was organised enough to have a professional hit man?

Lorimer considered the reports lying on his desk, the results of today's actions. They'd begun to look at the football club's financial background. Was there something in this pile that might help to heave the case out of this slough of despond? Lorimer flicked through the papers until he found what he wanted. Yes. Here it was. Not just a list of the club's directors, who included a well-known Glasgow solicitor and a property developer, but the major shareholders as well. He sat back and held the page out at arm's length, emitting a low whistle. So, Barbara Kennedy was one of the directors and held the club's controlling interest. He cast his mind back to the red-haired woman at Kelvin Park. His policeman's nose told him that there was some amorous entanglement going on behind Mrs Kennedy's back. Kennedy was a fool to risk his wife's ire if she really held the club's purse strings. But maybe taking risks was part of the attraction. He remembered the scrawny woman behind that glass-fronted office. She wasn't exactly a beauty. But perhaps she had other attributes.

A knock on his door ended that particular train of thought and he saw that DC John Weir, the latest addition to the team, stood uncertainly on the threshold.

'Sir?' His eyebrows were raised in supplication.

'Come in, Weir, what is it?'

Encouraged, the DC entered the room and handed a file to Lorimer. 'I didn't manage to finish it in time, sir. Had to wait for the bank to get back to me with details.'

Lorimer noticed a tinge of pink flushing the young man's cheeks. He was certainly excited about something.

'It's the report into Norman Cartwright's financial affairs, sir. That's it all there,' Weir added unnecessarily.

Lorimer skimmed through the report, turning over the yellow Post-It notes that were obviously the Detective Constable's preferred way of highlighting something of significance.

'Hm!' Lorimer's eyes widened as he came upon the reason why Weir had emphasised one particular yellow sticker with a double asterisk and an arrow. There, in a long line of figures, was a sum of money far exceeding any other deposit in the late Norman Cartwright's bank account. 'Any idea where the money came from?' Lorimer asked.

'No, sir, but I found out that it was paid in cash.'

'Twenty thousand pounds in *cash*?'

'We think it might be a win on the horses, sir. He had an account with Ladbrokes.'

Weir came alongside Lorimer. 'If you look back a couple of pages – there.' He pointed to another highlighted figure.

'That's exactly—'

'—the sum he was overdrawn, six weeks previous to his death,' Weir finished dramatically.

Lorimer scowled at him. Finishing a senior officer's sentences wasn't good form and Weir had better learn that fast. Still, the new recruit to CID seemed to have turned up a few interesting facts about the referee.

'And he managed to find enough cash to balance his account just days before his murder.'

'What if . . . ?' Weir began then stopped, unsure if he had already allowed his enthusiasm to run away with him.

'Let's hear it,' Lorimer told him, though his own mind had already leapt to a somewhat unsavoury conclusion.

Weir sat down in the vacant chair opposite his DCI. 'Well, what if he'd been bribed to throw the match?'

'By Queen of the South?' Lorimer laughed. 'I don't think so.'

'No, by someone who's been trying to bring down the club. D'you not remember how they finished at the end of last season? Baz Thomson just gave away that penalty,' Weir protested with a vehemence that betokened the true football supporter.

Lorimer nodded. It had been a strange end to a season full of surprises, not least Kelvin's relegation. Gretna's meteoric rise into the Scottish Premier League had only been eclipsed by Saint Mirren winning the Scottish Cup in extra time after a battle against Inverness Caledonian Thistle. That the Old Firm of Rangers and Celtic had suddenly lost their stranglehold on Scottish football was a favourite topic among sports pundits; Kelvin's demise from top-level Scottish football was a nine-day wonder in comparison.

'D'you think Thomson could have thrown the game, sir?' Weir asked, meeting Lorimer's gaze.

'Well, that's something we'll just have to find out, won't we?' Lorimer replied drily. 'Why don't you follow this one up yourself? Bring him in for questioning.'

Weir's eyes lit up. 'Me?' he asked, an expression of astonished delight on his face.

'Aye, you, Detective Constable Weir,' Lorimer answered, trying hard not to smile.

The young man was obviously eager to show his promotion out of uniform had been justified and there was something about this new recruit that reminded Lorimer of himself at that age. 'Just remember all those interview techniques they taught you at Tulliallan.'

CHAPTER 37

'That's him!'

The police patrol car changed lanes swiftly and turned left into the housing estate, following the progress of a young man dressed in a shabby tracksuit.

Turning his head, Donnie Douglas saw the two officers staring at him from the car; one had his arm out of the open window and was signalling at him to come over to them. For a moment Donnie hesitated. His instinct was to make a run for it through the maze of council houses and try to lose the police car. But something stopped him. He was tired of running. Tired of fearing the consequences of his actions. And somehow, these two faces looking up at him from the car were less intimidating than he had expected, in fact the one beckoning him over was smiling in an encouraging way. With a sigh, Donnie turned around and headed towards the car.

'Want a lift back to Glasgow?' the smiling one asked.

'Aye, why not,' Donnie replied and with a shrug meant to convey his indifference, he heaved his knapsack into the back seat and slung himself in beside it.

Lorimer unwrapped a second sherbet lemon and popped it into his mouth. It felt like a reward for a job well done, though truthfully DC Cameron's long hours had been behind this success. The young Lewisman was straightening his tie and looking determined as he headed towards the interview room where the Kelvin footballer sat sweating in the afternoon sunshine. He'd been picked up in a housing scheme in Garelochhead, not far from the Ministry of Defence's nuclear naval base. Watching Niall Cameron walk purposefully out of sight, Lorimer mentally wished him luck.

When he entered the room with Detective Inspector Grant, Cameron knew what was expected of him. The DI had chosen to let Cameron begin the interview, not just deferring to his extensive knowledge of football but because he had put in so much effort at finding the errant player.

Donnie Douglas sat behind the table with his hands clasped in front of him, looking nervously from one officer to another.

'Detective Constable Cameron, Detective Inspector Grant.' Cameron introduced them and was surprised when the footballer leaned across to shake their hands. Well, that was a good beginning, he thought. 'Time of interview, two-thirty p.m.'

'You're not from around here, are you?' Donnie asked suddenly.

Cameron's eyebrows shot up. *He* was supposed to be asking the questions, not the other way around. 'Not originally, no,' he admitted, though his Lewis lilt was a clear giveaway. He cast a glance at Jo Grant. Her face gave nothing away. If she was laughing at this odd beginning to an interview, she had the grace to hide it well.

Suddenly all his carefully prepared questions seemed to go out of the window and he pushed his notes along the table and leaned in towards the Kelvin player.

'D'you know the amount of worry that you've caused everyone?'

272

he said, adopting the tone of voice he'd heard many a Lewis parent use to chastise their child.

Donnie Douglas looked aside sheepishly, not wanting to be held in the DC's penetrating gaze.

'We've had half of Strathclyde's police out looking for you!' Cameron scolded, though that was something of an exaggeration.

'I'm sorry,' Donnie replied, biting his lip.

Niall Cameron tried to continue his stern demeanour even though he wanted to ask the forbidden question: why. Why did you kill your wife? Why did you rob that store? Why did you run away from Glasgow? All these were questions that could be simply defeated by a shrug or a dunno in reply. He'd learned already that it was better to come to such things more obliquely if he were to have any sort of success.

'Mr Clark was frantic,' the DC continued. 'He was hoping to field you for this Saturday's game.'

'Against Dunfermline? Against the Pars?' Donnie sat up, a new light in his eyes.

'Aye.' Cameron nodded. 'It's an important fixture. How fit d'you think you are?'

Donnie looked down at himself, a sudden doubt casting a cloud over his features. He'd walked for miles these past few days but hadn't eaten a hell of a lot, misery having robbed his appetite.

'If I had a decent meal . . .' the young man began.

'You think you could make it?'

'Is he no mad at me?' Donnie asked, looking doubtful once more.

'Why should he be mad at you?' Cameron countered, wondering at the reply he was going to get.

'Left them in the lurch, didn't I? As bad as Jason White getting banged up for being in that fight.'

The Lewisman said nothing, hoping that Donnie would fill the silence for them.

The footballer gave a huge sigh. 'I suppose it was stupid,' he began, 'but I couldn't think what else to do. You see—' He broke off nervously, eyeing Jo Grant with a wariness that suddenly made Cameron wish he did not have a female officer there at his side.

'I had a problem with my girlfriend,' Donnie dropped his voice to a conspiratorial whisper.

'Alison Renton?' the DC asked, with an encouraging smile.

'How do you know?'

'I've met her. We went to see if she could help find you,' Cameron said simply.

'So do you know . . . ?' He left the rest of the question hanging in the air.

'Please speak up for the tape,' Jo Grant's voice suddenly broke in.

Donnie gave a start, then nodded. 'Do you know that Alison is expecting our baby?'

'We do. She's been in to see us. I don't think she'll be sorry that you've been found safe and well,' he added.

Donnie frowned. 'What d'you mean?' Then his expression changed to one of horror. 'You didn't think anything had happened to me, did you?'

There was another silence this time broken by DI Grant. 'There has been the little matter of murder, you know,' she began conversationally, though there was no hiding the sarcasm in her tone. 'Remember that, do you, Mr Douglas? The two Kelvin players and the senior referee?'

Donnie Douglas blushed to the roots of his hair. 'You never thought I'd been killed, surely? I mean . . .' His face changed colour again as he realised that was exactly what people had been thinking.

'Wait till you read the back issues of the *Gazette*.' Jo Grant smirked at him as if she were enjoying his discomfiture. 'And of course there was that television appeal, wasn't there, DC Cameron?' she said, turning towards him as if for confirmation.

'My God, I didn't mean to cause all that trouble. Really I didn't.' Donnie Douglas looked truly appalled.

'Well,' the DI straightened up and began smiling properly at him, 'maybe you can help us with our inquiries to make up for that.'

Niall Cameron looked across at his colleague with admiration. She'd handled that one brilliantly. Now Donnie Douglas was eating out of their hands, a mixture of relief and embarrassment making him only too willing to tell them anything they wanted to know.

It was after four o'clock by the time they shook hands again, the footballer more relaxed with the two officers, even smiling as he was escorted from the interview room. Niall Cameron walked out into the public area with him, knowing the footballer was in for a surprise. There, sat in the foyer, was Alison Renton. As they approached, her face lit up and then all Cameron saw was the two of them clasped in an embrace. Turning away to sign him out, the DC missed the expression on Alison Renton's face but he could not mistake the proprietorial tone in her voice. 'Don't you *ever* do anything like that again. D'ye hear me?'

'Douglas is back.' Ron Clark stood at the door of the chairman's office, arms folded.

'Good God!' Kennedy appeared startled, then he gave a slight shake of his head. 'Is he all right?'

275

'Aye, tail between his legs but he's okay. I can put him on Saturday's team sheet.'

'What the hell happened?'

'Woman trouble,' Clark said shortly. 'Nothing to do with what's been going on here.'

Pat Kennedy's jaw dropped and for once Ron Clark had the advantage of seeing the Kelvin chairman speechless.

'His girlfriend's in the family way. But there was more to it than that. Anyway, can we just forget it and get on with the business of me running this football team?' Clark nodded sourly at his boss, hardly noticing the expression of surprise and admiration he received in return.

Ron Clark took the steps two at a time. He would give the boys a real talking to before Donnie's return, he thought, DCI Lorimer's words of wisdom still ringing in his ears. Donnie and Alison's relationship was none of their business. Giving the boy their utmost support was of far greater importance both for Donnie's peace of mind and for the greater good of Kelvin FC.

As Clark headed towards the gymnasium he considered the forthcoming league match against Dunfermline. He had two more days to pull off this victory. And suddenly he was confident that he could.

CHAPTER 38

It was the kind of morning you just die for, thought Jimmy Greer, opening the curtains onto a vista of cloudless blue skies over the Glasgow rooftops. He'd not taken any of his annual leave yet, and wasn't sorry. Not only had he been able to make capital out of the fracas surrounding Kelvin FC but he'd spent it in a city basking in brilliant sunshine. As he looked at the tenement flats across the street from his own he could see windows pushed wide open to let in the fresh morning air. The journalist gave his own window frame a shove and leaned out, breathing deeply. Life had been pretty good to him these past few weeks and if he didn't have this nonsense from Strathclyde Police hanging over him things would be just perfect. Jimmy reached into his trouser pocket and pulled out a packet of cigarettes. Soon he was replacing the quality of fresh air in his lungs with something he reckoned was even more satisfying. Yes, life was no too bad, he told himself again.

Jimmy's perfect moment was interrupted by the telephone's strident ring.

'Greer,' he said, taking the fag from his lips. His face stiffened as he recognised the voice on the other end of the line. 'Oh, aye, what do you want, then?' He moved across the room, cordless phone against his ear, then back towards the window to flick out his cigarette ash. Biting his lip, Greer listened to his caller. Anybody seeing the journalist would have noted the seriousness creep into his expression followed by a certain anxiety.

'Are you sure about that?' he said eventually. 'You know I'll be in deep shit if you're wrong.' Greer turned away from the window, nodding to himself as he heard the caller's reply. 'When?' Greer asked shortly, then 'Where?', followed by a belligerent 'Why there?' His face twisted into a grimace of displeasure then, looking at his watch, he said, 'Aye, in about an hour, then. Okay. See you.' Switching the phone off, Greer examined the end of his cigarette thoughtfully before taking one last draw and then tossing it out of the window. The butt described an arc, its glowing tip like the cone of a rocket, before coming to earth on the pavement below.

Woodlands Road on that particular morning was full of people going about their particular business. Had he been interested, the journalist would have been able to say that this little part of Glasgow had a distinctly Eastern flavour, especially given the pungent scents of spices drifting out of the Asian grocery shops. But Greer seemed oblivious to the delights of the street and its colourful fruit and vegetable stalls spilling on to the pavements. Head down, he walked purposefully towards the pub where he had agreed to a rendezvous.

Just before he reached its door, a sudden loud crack from across the street made him look up. But when he tried to see where the noise had come from, Greer found himself blinded by a flash of sunlight so strong that he put his hand up to shield his eyes.

In that moment the world stopped turning on its axis. For, instead of being able to peer up at the scrubby copse of trees across the busy road, Jimmy Greer felt a pain in his head that blinded him to everything.

He was aware of his legs giving way and voices around him shouting, but the last thing he ever noticed was the feel of the warm pavement under the palm of his outstretched hand, before the blackness overwhelmed him.

'Jimmy Greer's been shot.' DS Wilson burst into Lorimer's office with the news.

'Good grief! Is he hurt?'

'He's dead,' Alistair Wilson replied tersely. 'Someone took a shot at him outside the Uisge Beatha on Woodlands Road.

'Any witnesses?'

'We've got a couple of officers over there now taking statements. A crime scene's been set up and the SOCOs are doing their best under quite difficult circumstances, as you can imagine.'

'My God!' Lorimer sat back heavily. 'In broad daylight! I can't believe it.'

'It was busy enough over there. Surely someone will have seen something,' Wilson said hopefully. 'If it's our man then he's taking big risks killing someone in such a public place.'

'But why Greer?' Lorimer shook his head, still trying to take it in.

'Maybe someone was trying to shut him up,' Wilson suggested.

'Aye, that would come as no surprise,' the DCI countered, not trying to disguise the sarcasm in his tone. There would be plenty of folk with things to hide who would not mourn the journalist's passing, though he was surprised to note that he did not number himself among them. Jimmy Greer may have been known as a scandal-mongering hack who delighted in the more salacious aspects of his stories, but Lorimer still felt a sense of outrage against anyone who had robbed another man of his life.

'When will he be over at the mortuary?' Lorimer asked suddenly.

'Don't know but I can find out. Why?'

'Perhaps I might go over there myself,' Lorimer told him. 'They'll need someone to ID the body, won't they?'

That night the Uisge Beatha would do a roaring trade, but now what few clientele remained had been lined up as witnesses to Greer's murder. Those passers-by who had given information to the police officers had also been herded into the pub which was being used, meantime, as an incident room. Members of Lorimer's team, their resources already stretched to breaking point, were busy taking statements from anyone who could offer the slightest bit of information.

DC Niall Cameron had never set foot inside this particular hostelry and his eyes kept straying in the gloomy half-light to various objects around the room. From his position in one corner of the booth, Cameron could see heads of various moth-eaten animals (mainly stags) that were mounted on the walls, but one curious addition to this form of interior decoration drew his eye. High in the corner, diagonally across from where he sat, the bust of a well-known politician jutted out from the wall. Yes, there was no mistaking, it was Margaret Thatcher, but not as he had ever seen her. Some waggish sculptor had designed a caricature of the former prime minister as though she were hanging (literally) from a red rope around her neck. What could be seen of her frock was blue, matching the colour of her cheeks; this was meant not so much to show her political leanings but her last few breaths. The artist's satirical humour showed through as much as his obvious political dislike of his subject, thought Cameron. He gave a shudder. It was eerie given that a man had been shot dead only a couple of strides from where that object was hanging.

They had set themselves up in the three separate drinking booths that were conveniently located in the main bar, and statements were being taken from all who claimed to have either seen Jimmy Greer, heard the shots or caught a glimpse of his assailant escaping. Cameron sank back against the wooden-framed booth, waiting for the next witness. It was dark in here and so the lamps were lit despite the bright daylight outside. The deeply recessed double doors to the pub's interior did not allow for much natural light. On the scarred table in front of him, a tallow candle had been pushed into a wax-spattered green glass bottle that had once held Tullibardine whisky. No doubt this and other candles scattered around the pub would be lit every night, there would certainly never be a shortage of bottles to contain them. Cameron had clocked the double row of whiskies shelved high above the main bar as he'd come in; Uisge Beatha, translated from the Gaelic as *the water of life* by some (or simply as whisky by others) certainly was an appropriate name for this particular establishment. It was strange seeing the name glowing there in neon green and suddenly Niall Cameron felt the tug of home in a way he had not done for a very long time.

'Hello, please take a seat. I'm Detective Constable Cameron.' The Lewisman was on his feet the moment the man appeared in front of him.

'Donald McIntyre,' the man replied, fitting his huge shape between the two carved wings that formed a chair within the booth.

'Mr McIntyre, thank you for waiting so long. If you wouldn't mind just writing your name, address and date of birth here.' Cameron indicated the top of his hastily acquired A4 pad. 'Thanks,' he added, pulling the knot of his tie a little looser. It was hot in here and they had had to keep both sets of glass doors closed so their only source of air was supplied by that single fan whirring lazily from the ceiling.

'Now,' Cameron began, 'what can you tell me about this incident?'

Donald McIntyre looked back solemnly at the Detective Constable. He was a man, probably in his early forties, whose large physique owed more to his dedication at the Uisge Beatha's bar than anything else. He had placed both hands flat upon the table as though in readiness for some serious business but Cameron found the gesture oddly distracting.

'I wis there when the man wis shot,' McIntyre stated. 'He fell right down, crashed his heid aff the pavement, so he did.'

'Did you see him before he was shot?'

'Aye. Ah wis jist coming alang the road when ah hear this bang then seen this flash.'

Cameron frowned. None of the other witnesses had mentioned this before.

'Could you describe it for me?'

'It wis like someone shinin stuff intae yer eyes. Like when somethin's reflected.' He paused, looking distractedly around him as if for inspiration. 'See when ye're drivin an ye cannae see fur the sun comin' aff the puddles?'

Cameron nodded. 'Go on.'

'Well it wis like that. Jist wan great flash and then anither bang.'

Cameron nodded again. They already had statements that two shots had rung out and the SOCOs were still trying to locate the missing bullet from the first shot that must have missed Jimmy Greer.

'What direction did this flash come from?'

'Ower there, right by the bowling green.' McIntyre pointed to a spot in the wall as though he could actually see through it. 'See where the railings end?'

Cameron couldn't, but he'd check it out later, so he just nodded encouragement again and let the man go on with his story.

'There's a wee lane that goes frae Woodlands Road up the hill. The flash came from there.'

'And did you see anyone in the lane?' Cameron asked, regarding McIntyre carefully.

The big man looked even more solemn as he nodded his head. 'Aye. There was a man. He wis running away.'

'And did you see him carrying anything?'

A grim sort of smile spread across Donald McIntyre's face. 'Aye, something long and thin and it wisnae a fishin rod. Know whit ah'm sayin?'

Detective Constable Cameron knew exactly what he was saying and his heart beat that little bit faster as he pressed the witness for a description of the man who had killed Jimmy Greer.

DCI Lorimer watched dispassionately as the mortuary attendant rolled out the remains of Jimmy Greer from the refrigerated wall of corpses. In death, the journalist appeared older than his forty-eight years. His wispy grey hair was matted with blood from the single gunshot wound to his forehead. Lorimer's jaw tightened: that blackened hole, right in the centre of his brow, made it looked typical of an execution killing. The man's mouth was open, showing a set of stained and broken teeth. Had he been a stranger, Lorimer would have doubted anyone could have identified him from dental records: these discoloured teeth looked as though they'd never been seen by a dentist. Lorimer was used to seeing dead bodies and knew how a corpse's features could collapse, but, staring at Greer, he saw an old wizened man, bits of skin sagging from his stubbled cheeks. The journalist had made life difficult for him at times but he felt no recrimination now, just a kind of pity for a life cut short.

'Aye, that's him,' he told her, then he held his hand up. 'See if you could do something for me?' he began as she lifted a sheet to cover up the body.

The girl looked at him questioningly.

'Could you take a set of his fingerprints? He was meant to come in to have them taken, but . . . well, looks like he got distracted, doesn't it?'

The girl grinned back at him. They were used to graveyard humour here, it was part of the atmosphere, though all of them were well trained to treat the actual bodies with dignity and respect. 'Sure. I'll make up a set myself and have them sent over to you later today.'

Lorimer's last sight of Greer was that gaping maw and a pair of yellowing upturned toes. As he turned away he muttered to himself, 'Who did this to you, eh, Jimmy?' Unbidden, some words of Burns came to him: 'Wi' usquebae, we'll face the Devil!' What devil had Jimmy Greer faced? And was it the same one that had already taken two men's lives in this city?

The papers were full of it. Every headline screamed the journalist's untimely death and several of his rivals in the reporting fraternity had already composed an obituary, much of which had been written with creativity rather than an eye for the unvarnished truth. So the columns that Janis Faulkner was scanning told her of the man to whom she had spoken but had never seen. He appeared to have been a friendly sort of fellow and a more than adequate journalist. His early career even spoke of an award he had received for investigative work into a drugs ring.

Janis looked hard at the photograph. The dark hair was slicked back in an old-fashioned style so she supposed it had been taken some years ago, but these narrow eyes grinning at her looked full of fun. Fun? No, she decided, more like mischief. With a sigh, she put down the newspaper. Had Jimmy Greer made mischief or merely enjoyed it? Janis bit her lip. She had given him a description of Nicko's body, whispered over the telephone. And she knew, contrary to what she had told DCI Lorimer, that the journalist was perfectly aware just what the murder weapon had been.

The news reports all suggested that the journalist had been gunned down, execution-style, for his inside knowledge of the Kelvin Killings, as they were calling them. Janis shivered. Greer had promised the footballer's widow a chance to tell her side of the story once she was out on bail. But that had never happened. And now he was dead.

Janis felt a trickle as the first tear coursed down her cheek. She brushed it away angrily, knowing that she was not weeping for the passing of a man she had never met but for herself, yet still the tears kept coming.

CHAPTER 39

'Oh, it's great to see you!' Maggie's lip trembled and she dashed away a tear as she looked down at Rosie.

'It's great to see you too,' Rosie Fergusson replied.

Maggie opened her mouth to exclaim at the weak, wee voice that spoke these words, then thought better of it. Rosie had been through a hell of a lot and although she was out of any danger she was still a sick woman.

'Oh, Rosie,' she said instead then bent down and planted a sudden kiss upon her friend's brow. 'There now, kissed it all better,' she declared.

Rosie smiled at her. Maggie Lorimer would have made a brilliant mother. Some things just weren't fair.

In the hours that had passed since she had woken up, Rosie had been told different versions of what had actually happened to her. She'd had the dispassionate one from the consultant, doctor-to-doctor, about her condition and its prognosis. Thankfully there was no long-term damage but she would be off work for up to three months recovering from the delicate surgery that had saved her life. In her present weakened state, Rosie was pretty sanguine about that, but she knew it would become harder to stay at home as she regained her strength. Solly could postpone his return to work until the end of September and the flat was in easy walking distance from the University, anyway. She wouldn't be lonely, but she might be bored. Solly's own version of events began with a police visit to the flat and went on to give only short descriptions of how she had appeared, punctuated with frequent repetitions of how terrified he had been at the thought of losing her. Bit by bit, Rosie had pieced all the events together so that she was now aware of how the crash had happened and what the physical consequences had been thereafter.

'How's the football case getting on? That husband of yours got anyone in the frame yet?' Rosie asked.

'He said I wasn't to talk to you about it. Said you needed to think of nicer things.'

'Aye?' Rosie said drily. 'Like pink fluffy bunnies? Come off it, Mags, I never was a pink-fluffy-bunny type of girl!'

Both women laughed aloud, then Maggie's face changed as Rosie began to cough.

'It's okay,' she gasped, 'just a bit fragile in the old thoracic department. Don't worry,' she said, seeing her friend look down at her anxiously. 'Now, if you want me to shut up and not cough, you'd better do all the talking. Starting with a résumé of the case,' she added, a glint in her eye.

Maggie Lorimer knew when she was beaten, so she leaned forward and began to tell the pathologist everything that had happened at Kelvin Park since the afternoon of Rosie's accident.

The DCI's wife had been a lot more forthcoming than Solly, who had point-blank refused to discuss the murder case with his fiancée. The fact that Rosie had conducted the post-mortems of Faulkner, Cartwright and White made absolutely no difference to Solly. She could sigh all she liked, he told her, there were better things to talk about. He'd been so sweet, even bringing her some wedding magazines to look at. They still planned a Christmastime wedding and by then, Rosie knew, she'd be back to her old self. So it had fallen to Maggie Lorimer to fill her in on the latest murder and the deceased's part in the affair. Rosie's eyes had widened as she learned about Greer's death. Another shooting? She wondered who had done the man's post-mortem and what type of bullet had been removed from his skull.

Rosie closed her eyes. Maggie's visit had been good but now she was tired. Thinking made her head hurt and she welcomed the sensation of sleepiness that overwhelmed her.

'Well, we know who it was now,' Lorimer exclaimed, waving the sheet of prints in the air. 'Jimmy Greer was at Kelvin Park and had somehow gained access into the grounds. His prints match up with those found on the dummy, so I think we can conclude our erstwhile reporter had set up the entire thing himself.'

'As a hoax?' someone asked.

'As a way to sell newspapers, more like,' Alistair Wilson responded drily. 'What's his editor saying?'

'Claims to know nothing about it. Surprise, surprise.'

'Somebody must have let him into the grounds.'

'And to the boot room. Wasn't it supposed to be kept locked?'

'Maybe it was the ghost.'

Lorimer held up his hand again to silence the suggestions that were beginning to fly around the room. 'We'll stick to facts, if you don't mind. Now, I know it's a bit late in the day, but do I have any volunteers to interview Jim Christie and Albert Little? They are the only ones we know of that have keys to the boot room. Oh, and somebody better see the apprentice who found the dummy.'

Several hands went up. Lorimer calculated the amount of leg-work that had been done on this case already. Niall Cameron deserved to benefit from this. He had a good chance of making Detective Sergeant, Lorimer reckoned, and he wanted to encourage him.

'Right – Grant, you and Weir see the young lad, Wilson and Cameron can find out Christie's and Little's home addresses and see them. I'll expect a full report by the morning.'

They'd drawn a blank at Albert Little's flat but Jim Christie, the kitman, answered the door of his terraced cottage to the two CID officers. Christie was a small man of about fifty, his tonsure of white hair around a shining bald pate making him seem more like a priest than a man who looked after football kit. His benign smile added to this impression as DS Wilson made the introductions.

'Come in, gentlemen,' he said, opening the door wide. 'Mary, we've got visitors,' he called out to someone behind him. A small middle-aged woman appeared by his side, wiping her hands on a dish towel.

'This is my wife, Mary,' Christie said. 'Mary, these gentlemen are from the police. Investigating the murders,' he added in a studied stage whisper as though his wife were not quite up to speed with the latest events. She darted a nervous look at her husband then gestured the police officers through to the back of the house. 'It's cooler in the dining room,' she said. 'Would you like a cup of tea?'

Without waiting for a reply, Mrs Christie left them to find seats around the table.

'Mr Christie, we just wanted to clear up the matter of the dummy in the boot room,' DS Wilson began. 'We have reason to believe that somebody let Jimmy Greer into Kelvin's grounds that day and that he gained access to the boot room.'

'The journalist who was killed?' Christie's mild manner changed to one of affront.

'Yes. You see, we know he had been inside the boot room.'

'Oh, heavens! Then maybe it was all my fault!' The kitman looked aghast. 'You see, I let Mr Greer into the boot room when he was researching his story.'

'When exactly was this?' Wilson asked.

Christie chewed his lower lip thoughtfully. 'It might have been the day before young Willie found that thing,' he said. 'There were journalists all over the place, every day. Most of them never got past the main door,' he added with a nod to show what his opinion had been of the crowd of reporters.

'But Jimmy Greer did,' DC Cameron suggested quietly.

Christie nodded again. 'He had permission from the gaffer. He was doing a feature on the Ronnie Rankin story.'

'The ghost in the boot room?' Wilson asked with a laugh. 'You don't believe in all that tosh, do you?'

Jim Christie's face grew solemn as he shook his head. 'Don't ever mock the shade of Ronnie Rankin, Mr Wilson.' Then he turned to Niall Cameron who had been staring intently at the kitman. 'I've seen him several times over the years. I didn't doubt that one of the young boys had seen him recently. And I'll tell you this,' he added, wagging an admonitory finger at them both, 'that latest incident was a pure insult to his memory. If that journalist desecrated the boot room then I'm not surprised at what happened to him.'

Wilson and Cameron exchanged a glance. The kitman was absolutely serious.

'And you helped Greer with his . . . research?' Wilson said at last, struggling to keep any vestige of a smile from his face.

Christie nodded. 'I told him everything: all the stories going back over my time at Kelvin and the ones that have been handed down over the generations. I even told him he should write a book about it,' he added, shaking his head as if at his own foolishness.

'So, how was it your fault that Greer had access to the boot room at a later date, Mr Christie?' Cameron asked,

'Oh, that's easy,' Chrtistie said. 'He must have found my spare key.'

'Did you mention this missing key to any of the officers who came to take statements after the boot room had been found all messed up?' Wilson asked.

'Aye, I did. But I didn't think that the reporter might have taken it. No,' he said, with a heavy sigh, 'I didn't think about him at all.'

'Well, that clears up one mystery,' Cameron declared as they drove off from the Christies' home. 'We know Jimmy Greer had easy access to the boot room. He was writing about Rankin's ghost. So he said. And his prints were on that dummy so he must have staged this. But why?'

'A stunt to sell more papers,' Wilson spat out in disgust. 'Greer was a number one chancer but I didn't think he'd go as far as making a threat against Pat Kennedy.'

'D'you think that was him too?' Cameron asked. 'Should we maybe be looking for traces of red paint back at Greer's place to confirm that?'

Alistair Wilson nodded. 'Aye. Then we can wrap up one bit of this case.'

CHAPTER 40

Jimmy Greer had not kept the tidiest of flats. There had been no problem obtaining a warrant to search the place the following morning and now Cameron and Wilson were turning over piles of discarded newspapers and piles of books in an attempt to find what they were looking for. Greer's car had already been searched and there was not a sign of any paint, red or otherwise.

'Nothing,' Wilson said at last. 'Come on, I need some fresh air. The smell in here would choke a horse.'

'Today's Friday,' Cameron said absently as the DS locked Greer's door behind them. 'One more day till Kelvin play Dunfermline.'

'You're going to the game, then?'

'Depends if I'm on duty or not,' Cameron told him with a wry grin. None of the team had been free to enjoy their weekends much recently.

'Maybe I'll go myself,' Wilson nodded. 'Should be a good game.'

'We need a result!' Ron Clark flung his hand in the air, desperate to communicate his enthusiasm to the players. He hadn't given out a team list as yet but Donnie Douglas was back in among the senior squad and listening eagerly to the pre-training pep talk. Clark tried to catch the eye of every man as he looked at them in

293

turn. Baz was grinning back at him, his cheeky face shining with anticipation. He'd be mad to leave the striker out: he had that knack of always being around the goalmouth to toe in a stray ball, a trait that endeared him to the Kelvin fans. Giannitrapani wasn't even a consideration after his recent poor showing. Woods would take his place against the Pars tomorrow, Clark told himself, unless something disastrous happened at today's training. As for his mid-fielders, well, now that Douglas was back he'd take a chance with him, Simon Gaffney was on good form and of course Andy Sweeney, their captain, would find a place on the team sheet.

As Ron Clark gazed at the footballers he wondered how many of them would be here next season. The shock of these murders was enough to make any one of them think about a transfer. Today and tomorrow they might be anxious to be selected for the match against Dunfermline but next week? Next month? Individually footballers were a self-seeking lot, their agents having dinned it into them to look for the best deal, never mind what it might do to their existing club. He'd been around enough Scottish clubs to know that each and every one of them was busy chasing the elusive big money. Mid-season transfers could be a body-blow to a club like theirs as they struggled to regain a position in the Scottish Premier League.

'Okay, same time tomorrow. I'll be reading out the team sheet, so don't go looking for it pinned to the wall until just before the game.'

'Is that in case you change your mind, boss?' Baz Thomson asked, his eyes alight with devilment.

'Aye, maybe so,' Clark replied diffidently. He wasn't going to be drawn on team selection at this stage, no matter how much his mind was already made up.

*

Lorimer stared at the forwarded email in disbelief. ITS YOU NEXT KENNEDY, it said. The Kelvin chairman had done exactly as Strathclyde CID had instructed him to – sending on any scurrilous pieces of mail or any threats. Maybe they'd be able to close in on the sender this time. He looked at the email again and noted the time of receipt. Pat Kennedy had been sent this email at 6.30 a.m. So, anybody inside the club could have been up and about this Friday morning to send it, but it was more than likely that it had come from the same twenty-four-hour internet cafe as before.

The DCI tapped out the code for technical support. Some clever dick might just be able to trace this. Then it would simply be a matter of seeing who had visited Cafe Source early this morning.

'John? DCI Lorimer here. I've got something for you,' he said.

Patrick Kennedy sat staring at the computer screen, Ron Clark by his side.

'You have told the police, I hope,' Ron said.

'Yes, of course I have. First thing I did,' Kennedy snapped back at him.

'What did they say?'

The Kelvin chairman did not take his eyes off the words as he replied, 'They're taking it seriously this time.'

Ron Clark stared at his boss for a long moment. The big man's face was crumpled into a scowl but under that Clark sensed a change; Pat Kennedy was afraid, and Ron could tell that it was an emotion he wasn't enjoying in the slightest.

It wasn't lost on DI Jo Grant that the internet cafe was only fifty yards away from the Uisge Beatha pub. Whoever had written the two anonymous emails might easily stay within walking distance of both of these establishments. Parking round here was a nightmare. Woodlands Road itself had double yellow lines and the areas nearby were either for residents only or had already been taken. In the end she had to double back and find a meter near the Hogshead pub further down the road. Walking along the road she glanced across at the narrow lane running past the bowling green, right across from where the reporter had been gunned down. Lorimer had had the SOCOs scouring every last bit of the area, temporarily closing off the entire road whilst the white-suited figures searched methodically for any trace of the second bullet or of anything that the killer might have left behind.

'DI Grant, Strathclyde Police,' she said, holding up her warrant card for the young woman behind the counter to see.

'Oh, yes, we got a call . . . come on round the back, will you?' The girl looked quickly across at the customers sitting crouched over their computer screens before gesturing for the DI to follow her. It was clear she didn't want to leave the cafe unattended.

'I've been here one my own since six o'clock,' the girl explained. 'There should have been another guy working by now but he hasn't turned up yet.' She frowned, darting glances through the open door as if afraid someone would abscond with the computers. 'So it's me you want to talk to, I suppose,' she added. 'Look, find a seat, sorry, the place is such a shambles but we just took delivery of more stock and I haven't had time to put it away.'

Jo Grant lifted a pile of A4 copy-paper from a seat and dumped it under the table. So long as she could sit down and get some sense out of this lassie she didn't care what the back room looked like. 'You've been here on your own all morning?' Jo asked.

'Oh, except for the customers,' the girl replied.

Grant breathed a sigh of relief. 'We think you might be able to identify a customer who was using one of your machines here at about six-thirty this morning,' the policewoman began.

The girl's face cleared suddenly. 'Oh, that's not a problem. There was only one fellow in then. Didn't want coffee or anything to eat, just wanted to use the computer. That's okay. Lots of them do that. We make enough on the food to pay rent on this place—'

'This customer,' Grant interrupted her. 'Can you describe him to me?'

The girl chewed her lip thoughtfully. 'He was quite old,' she began.

The DI flashed her an appraising look: she was probably not even twenty herself. How old was *quite old* in this young woman's estimation?

'Maybe forty?' the girl suggested. 'He wasn't very tall or anything.'

'Hair colour? Distinguishing features?' Mentally Grant encouraged her to think harder, to recall just who had been there that morning.

'Um, just sort of an ordinary man. Kinda brownish hair, short. Nothing special about him, really.'

'What was he wearing, can you remember?'

The girl heaved a sigh and shook her head. 'No, I can't remember. Sorry. Not anything I'd remember like shorts or a kilt.' She giggled, then seeing Jo's frown, hastily rearranged her features into a semblance of sobriety.

'If I were to bring a photograph of this man to you, could you identify him?'

'Oh, yes.' The girl brightened up immediately. 'I'm good with faces. There was this thing in one of these magazines where you have to identify bits of famous people's faces,' she said eagerly. 'I was good at that, so I was.'

DI Grant tried to smile back but failed. This was a right waste of time. The girl had a cafe to run on her own, was trying to serve coffees and snacks, set up customers at their computers and find time to clear away stock. It was little wonder she'd spent no time staring at their mystery customer.

'If we bring in a photograph,' the DI said, standing up to go, 'can we be sure to find you here?'

'Oh, better give you my mobile number, hadn't I?'

'Actually,' Grant grinned, 'I'd like a wee bit more than that. Like your name and address for a start. Okay?'

'Says she can identify our man,' Grant told Lorimer. She was sitting in her car with the window down, mobile in one hand, cigarette in the other.

'Looks like he's made his first mistake, then. Going back to the same internet cafe,' he replied.

'So what do we do? Take photos of all of Kelvin Football club's staff and players?'

'Can you think of a better idea?' Lorimer asked.

'They'll want to know why.'

Jo Grant could almost hear the wheels of Lorimer's mind turning. To take photographs of them all might alert their killer. And was it worth the risk?

'We don't need players' photographs,' he replied at last. 'For two reasons. One, we've got them all on match-day programmes and two, this girl – what did you say her name was?'

'Wilma Curley.'

'Aye, this Wilma girl says he's an older bloke, about forty, so that cancels out most of the players, doesn't it?'

DI Grant blew out a thin line of smoke before answering. 'Not sure she's even that reliable about ages, but yes, I'd say that probably rules out most of the footballers themselves.'

'Okay, see what you can set up at Kelvin today. There'll be plenty of other officers there anyway for a pre-pitch inspection.'

Jo Grant put down the phone. The actions dealt out this morning had given her a sense that something was happening at last. The other officers had felt it too, she was sure. It just remained to see if her hunch was right and if DCI Lorimer was indeed going to set up a surveillance operation at the football ground.

Solomon Brightman sat, one leg crossed over the other, his foot swinging back and forth as if to some music that only he could hear. His face was intent but Lorimer was gratified to see that the psychologist's customary smile was back in place.

'We can narrow it down to several people,' Lorimer told him, 'both in terms of age and of physique. We must suppose that Pat Kennedy didn't send the email to himself and some of the staff, like Jim Christie, don't fit the girl's description.'

'So, how many middle-aged ordinary men with medium-brown hair are we looking at?' Solomon smiled.

Lorimer shook his head. 'Goodness knows. There are the manager and his deputy, the coach, the club doctor, the groundsman, though I suspect he's probably a good deal older than forty, some of the older players perhaps and a few others who come in and out on a part-time basis.'

'Of course it may be none of these people,' Solomon suggested with a grin. 'It could be the elusive Big Jock that everybody claims to know.'

Lorimer pursed his lips. They'd got no further with tracing the Kelvin Keelie who seemed to be such a fanatical supporter. 'He'll be there tomorrow,' he assured Solly. 'Kennedy says he never misses a home game.'

'The person you're looking for has a degree of organisation to his killing,' Solly reminded him. 'I can't see it being someone as simple minded as this fan is reputed to be. And he knows about firearms. Does anybody fit that description so far?'

Lorimer shook his head. 'No. We've done background checks on most of the players. Nothing has come up so far to suggest a link with guns. But we're still investigating that angle,' he said. For a moment he thought of Rosie and her enthusiasm to root out just what sort of weapon had made away with Norman Cartwright.

Solly lifted a piece of paper from where he'd laid it on Lorimer's desk. 'This looks like the work of an uneducated man to me,' he suggested. 'No comma or apostrophe, for instance.'

'And all block capitals?'

'Ah, he might well use uppercase to emphasise his point. He's not totally illiterate when it comes to using a computer, but I don't think we're looking for anyone who's particularly used to composing letters. And he isn't a professional hitman, doing this on anybody else's behalf. Otherwise why use an internet cafe?'

'Maybe he doesn't own a computer?'

'Or perhaps he doesn't want to risk anything being traced back,' Solly mused. 'Of course, he may deliberately have kept the message simple to throw us off his scent. And another thing,' Solly bent his head to one side, his face suddenly serious. 'He's used the same internet cafe twice which shows that he's gaining in confidence. Maybe your football chairman's more at risk than we imagine.'

'Maybe he is, but he won't cancel the game,' Lorimer said, looking at the psychologist. 'Which means we're going to have our work cut out tomorrow.'

CHAPTER 41

The first rumble of thunder made Chancer rush for cover. Cowering under the overhanging shrubbery, the little cat curled himself into a tight ball, tail tucked neatly beneath him, paws firmly together. Although it was early morning, the usual birdsong was absent from the heavy air. Chancer looked up and sniffed, sensing that rain would come today after those endless weeks of heat that had left dry, cracked patches all over this garden. He had become familiar with every bush and shrub in the Lorimers' overgrown backyard as well as with the signs of life that denoted a full bowl of cat food and a lap to sit upon. As yet there were no humans stirring in the house. At the first twitch of a curtain, the little cat would be up and running, tail erect, ready to greet his new owners, so he kept one eye on the house for any sign of movement while smelling the air around him.

At last there was the sound of a bolt being drawn back and the door to the kitchen was flung open.

'Hello, you.' Maggie Lorimer trailed her fingers through her long untidy mop of curls and regarded the ginger cat standing patiently on her doorstep. Not waiting for an answer, she walked back in, letting the morning air into the room. Chancer stepped over the threshold, gave an inquisitive meow and sat expectantly, waiting for breakfast to appear.

'Still no sign of your owners, boy,' Maggie told him. 'Maybe we're going to get lucky, you and me.' She grinned and bent down to scratch behind his ears. The cat tilted his head and closed his eyes, an ecstatic expression on his face as he lost himself in a paroxysm of purring.

Maggie Lorimer left him to eat his food and flip-flopped through from the kitchen, her sandals making a hollow sound on the tiled surface. It seemed unnaturally loud, and made Maggie glance up. Outside the sky was a deep shade of grey, a streak of burnt orange lightening up the horizon. So, the good spell of sunshine and cloudless days was coming to an end, was it? Well, next week she'd be back in her classroom. They'd had the best summer on record, so nobody was going to complain, least of all the waterboard people who had been issuing dire warnings of shortages. If that sky was anything to go by, there would be a right good rainstorm before the day was out.

Kelvin Park had never looked so good, thought Ron Clark as he stepped out on to the terracing. The pitch was at its best, thanks to Wee Bert's ministrations, and the banners were actually being lifted by a tiny breeze. If the weather forecast was to be believed they should have a dry morning so there was no chance of rain putting off the crowds. He glanced up at the sky. It was dark today and the gathering clouds looked ominous. Clark felt in his trouser pocket. Yes, he hadn't forgotten to put it there. The team sheet with the list of all those who had been picked as players or substitutes was nestled against his right thigh. Big Gudgie was in goal, with Craig Mitchell as the substitute keeper. Woods and Thomson were his final choice of strikers though he expected McKinnery would come off the bench before full-time. Austin Woods was reliable but, like all ageing players, he didn't usually make the full ninety minutes. He'd play Gaffney, Sweeney, McGrory, Douglas and Friedl in mid-field with Rientjes, Lynch and his own nephew, Davie, in defence. Davie's time had come, Ron thought to himself. The wee fella had been football-daft all his days and a Kelvin supporter to boot. Now it was a mark of pride to be able to pick him for his own team, a team that was going to make it back into the Scottish Premier League if their manager had anything to do with it.

Ron Clark straightened his tie and headed back into the clubhouse, rehearsing what he would say to the team once they had assembled in their dressing room.

'Everything's in place,' Lorimer told them. 'We've got cameras covering every entrance and turnstile and the dogs are being brought in to sniff out anyone who has even the faintest trace of firearms or ammunition about them.'

'What about inside the grounds?' someone asked.

'For every one of the usual officers on duty there's a plain clothes policeman. We've got an unmarked van ready to roll into the car park behind the main building. There will be an armed response unit located inside the van and every officer will be in radio communication with that unit at all times. Plus mounted police horses and you lot, of course. *If* you've bought your tickets, that is.' Lorimer's face creased in a sudden grin. At the sight of their worried faces, the DCI produced a bunch of tickets from behind his back. 'Just joking,' he said. 'But a black-and-white scarf or two would help to camouflage you in the crowd.'

All weekend leave had been cancelled due to this massive operation and there had been quite a bit of raised spirits at the prospect of a breakthrough in the case.

'What about Mr Kennedy?' DI Grant asked.

'Don't worry, we've taken care of him,' Lorimer told her. 'But it's up to you all to watch any movement within the ground that seems suspicious. We're on the lookout for anyone who is armed and that may not be as easy to spot as it seems. A pistol and even a sawn-off shotgun can be concealed quite easily.'

'But that would suggest an attack at close range,' DC Cameron said.

'Aye, so anything that looks to you like a sniper's rifle, you don't mess about. You call the unit right away. I'll be in radio contact at all times.'

Pat Kennedy looked down at his stomach in dismay. The Kevlar jacket had cut into folds of flesh and pushed the big man's layers of fat further south, making them jut out above his waistband.

'You'll just have to pull your shirt over it a bit,' the officer told him.

Pat Kennedy glared at the man. Not only did he hate to look slovenly, but this dark blue shirt didn't suit him at all. Still, it would conceal the black bullet-proof vest underneath, but already the chairman could feel trickles of perspiration beneath the heavy material.

'What if he aims for my face?' Kennedy had asked Lorimer the previous day. A specially adapted Kelvin cap had been hastily constructed but Pat Kennedy swore to himself that he would only wear the thing as a last resort. They had a good turn out from their corporate people and Barbara herself would be there by his side. For a wicked moment Patrick Kennedy imagined a sniper's bullet aiming for his chest, missing and hitting his wife instead. His mouth twitched then he shook himself free of such a fantasy, wondering how on earth he was capable of thoughts like that. But he'd had them before, a little voice insisted: ideas of what life might be like if Barbara were suddenly to keel over. Marie McPhail figured in these fantasies, her willing body next to his against some exotic background, far far away.

'All right, sir?' The officer was regarding Kennedy strangely and the chairman realised he had drifted off into a world of his own. Hopefully the policeman would take this for a moment of reflection on life, the universe and some nutter playing silly buggers in an internet cafe.

'Yes,' Kennedy answered. 'Everything's just marvellous.'

Ignoring the sarcasm, the officer patted the vest beneath Patrick Kennedy's shirt, nodding his approval. 'We'll be in constant radio contact, sir. One of our senior officers will be sitting nearby, so no need to worry.'

Kennedy grunted in reply. The last thing he wanted was to appear flustered, especially in front of one of Strathclyde's senior officers.

For years it had been his dream to see inside Kelvin FC's inner sanctum but now that he was actually here, DCI Lorimer felt strangely uncomfortable. A tour of the trophy room had been preceded by drinks in the boardroom and was to be followed by a five-course lunch. Lorimer hung back as the steward described the many trophies on show. Each had its own particular history, some even dating from the late nineteenth century. These were large ornate cups engraved with faded, spidery writing. When he'd been a wee lad just what wouldn't he have given for an experience like this? Now, as the SIO in a serious murder case, Lorimer looked at the people around him much more than at the objects within their glass cases. Most of them carried drinks in one hand and some were chatting amiably to one another as though this was something they did on a regular basis. He recognised Colin

Sharpe and Frank Devine, directors of the club. They'd made their money in a lucrative legal partnership that specialised in commercial property. They were with another of the club's directors, Jeffrey Mellis. Lorimer was not surprised to see them laughing and joking together.

Mellis was a property consultant whose name had figured in the DCI's recent bedtime reading. If Patrick Kennedy and Mellis had their way then Kelvin FC as he knew it would very soon cease to exist. Big plans were afoot to sell the current grounds to a supermarket chain and to relocate the club to a brownfield site in Maryhill. Lorimer had seen the plans, read the figures and thought long and hard about why this had not yet found its way into the public domain. Jimmy Greer and every sports writer in the land would have had copy going to press the minute this was out in the open. But Jimmy was dead and all of the documentation that Lorimer had ferreted out was marked *confidential* in large red letters. Had the *Gazette*'s reporter stumbled across something that was meant to be kept secret? Something that was worth killing for? It didn't make sense. If Kennedy and his cohorts wanted to keep quiet about the development of a new club, could it be for perfectly legitimate reasons? The information disquieted him; could it be one of the missing pieces in this jigsaw, which he was playing round and round in his head?

They had moved away from Kelvin's silverware now and were heading down a long narrow corridor towards the dining room. Lorimer listened to the noise of laughter and people talking to one another as they found their tables. He glanced at his watch. The crowds would be coming into the stadium soon but these corporate guests would not make their way out into the directors' area until just before kick-off. Would anyone be in custody by then? Lorimer hoped so, and knew he wasn't the only one.

Looking over to where Patrick Kennedy stood he could see the red flush spreading across the man's face and guessed at his discomfort.

'Anybody seen ma boots?' Baz Thomson stood in the middle of the Kelvin dressing room, a furious expression on his face.

'Has the wee man no brought them up fae the boot room, then?' John McKinnery replied. 'It's no like him tae forget onything.'

'Mibbe he's seen the ghost,' Davie Clark suggested.

'Wooooo!' Simon Gaffney had lifted up his white shirt and was waving it in the air, making the sleeves dance.

'Cut it out!' Andy Sweeney, the Kelvin captain, hadn't raised his voice much and he had a smile on his face, but the mirth died down as the players noticed a new figure enter the dressing room.

Donnie Douglas looked from one player to another, sensing that he had stepped into the middle of something. He could feel their eyes following his progress as he made his way across to the wall of lockers. Nobody had said anything to him about his absence other than to enquire if he was okay. It was as if they'd been told to leave him alone. In one way it was a relief, but now Donnie felt as if he were an outsider, not one of the team. As he unpacked his kit, the other players resumed their normal banter. It would be fine once they were out on the pitch, Donnie told himself. Clark had warned him that his position might be in jeopardy. Suddenly he thought of Alison and a strange sense of pride made him stand up straight. He had everything to play for now and today he'd show them all just how good he really was.

'Where are you going, son?'

Baz looked at the stranger who had suddenly appeared out of

nowhere. 'What's it tae you?' he asked, his chin jutting out aggressively.

A quick flick of a warrant card changed the expression on the footballer's face. 'Aw, awright, pal. Ah'm jist goin tae get ma boots, see?' Baz looked back at the man then pushed open the door of the boot room. Inside, the airless room was stuffy and redolent of years of sweat and leather. The senior players' boots should have been taken to the dressing room by the apprentice in charge of them this morning, so why this had been forgotten was a mystery. Baz began pulling pairs of football boots out of their dookits to see if any of them had been put back in the wrong place. But there was no sign of his boots. He swore aloud and banged his fist on the wooden cabinet. Just at that moment he spotted something lying in a corner of the room. It was a rolled up Kelvin FC towel, easy enough to miss in that dark shadow. Frowning, he picked it up.

'What the?' he exclaimed as his familiar white boots tumbled out of the towel and fell to the ground with a clatter. Baz scooped them up and turned the boots this way and that. They looked all right to him. And at least they'd been properly cleaned. Stupid laddie had probably been using the towel to wipe off excess polish. Baz threw it back into the corner then froze as the door swung closed and the overhead light began to flicker. For a moment he could feel the hairs rise on the back of his neck and a swish of something cold brushed his bare arms. Baz was out of the boot room like a shot, boots dangling from his hand.

'Everything okay?' the plain clothes policeman's words fell away as Baz Thomson sprinted past him and headed back towards the dressing rooms.

Heart thumping, Baz slowed down. It wasn't true, these things were just daft stories, weren't they? But try as he might, the

Kelvin striker could not help but remember the often-repeated legend about Ronnie Rankin and how his ghost would appear to anyone who threatened his beloved club.

The duty officer turned around as Alistair Wilson entered the tiny room. Perched high above the North stand, this was where the CCTV cameras were housed and where, during every home game, an officer from Strathclyde Police would sit and observe the crowded stadium.

'Everything okay, then?' the officer asked.

'Aye. Nobody's been turned back at any of the gates. And so far the dogs haven't smelled anything suspicious.'

'Wonder they can smell anything for the guff that comes off that lot,' the officer remarked, jutting his thumb towards the hot food vans parked near the entrance. 'Pies 'n' Bovril are one thing, but they just reek of recycled grease.'

'Aye, well.' Wilson moved towards the window that looked out across Kelvin's football pitch. Already the Kelvin panda bear mascot was capering alongside the front rows in time to music blaring from the sound system, much to the delight of the small boys leaning over the barrier. Everywhere he looked there was a mass of black-and-white. Both teams sported these colours, though today Dunfermline would be in their white shorts and striped jerseys with the home team in its familiar black. Wilson wondered what the referee's colours would be. The officials usually kitted out in black had an obligation to stand out from the team players, especially on a day like today when the TV cameras were rolling. They had been in two minds whether to allow them in along with the usual press photographers and sports reporters but Lorimer had decided that everything should appear as normal as possible.

Gazing over the stadium, Wilson couldn't help but feel that nothing out of the ordinary was going to happen. What kind of man would take the risk of bringing a firearm into such a closely policed area, never mind trying to use it? Dr Brightman had talked about someone who felt above such risks, but was he right? Or would the only result they'd have today be the one given as the whistle blew at the end of ninety minutes?

CHAPTER 42

A quick look at his watch, an arm raised and then the referee blew his whistle to signal the kick-off between Dunfermline and Kelvin. A great roar went up as Donnie Douglas scooped up Andy Sweeney's ball and passed it to Baz Thomson. The striker jinked aside two of the Dunfermline players and looked set to take it all the way down the park, but a brief glance up showed him that Austin Woods was onside and in perfect scoring position. Thomson changed his pace and flicked the ball in towards the space that Woods would make in a few paces. The crowd gasped as Woods headed the ball then a collective shout went up as the ball found the back of the net, leaving a bewildered Pars keeper gazing wistfully behind him.

'And it's one-nil to Kelvin in the opening minutes of this match. What a cracker that was! Now let's see if Dunfermline can come back from that early set-back. Kelvin's men look to be in fine form despite all the events of the past weeks. Just goes to show how good management and discipline can lift a team,' the commentator enthused. 'Ron Clark was never going to have it easy, losing two of their key players, but he seems to have fielded a good side today. And just listen to the crowd!'

311

For a few moments the television cameras panned across the ranks of cheering fans, holding aloft their black-and-white scarves, pausing to zoom in on the figure of Patrick Kennedy. Anyone watching the game later might note his corpulent figure clad all in black, a bulky baseball cap thrust down over his brow. But the television screen was immediately filled by the pitch once again and anything untoward about the Kelvin chairman's manner of dress was forgotten in the desire to see the game.

Lorimer touched the earpiece, trying to make out the message coming across but it was useless with this din all around him. He tried to catch the eye of the nearest plain clothes officer standing in the aisle. The man had donned a steward's fluorescent jacket, the collar turned up to hide his wire. A brief nod told Lorimer that all was well and the DCI looked back at the pitch.

A Dunfermline player went into a hard tackle on Donnie Douglas and the Kelvin player rolled away, clutching his ankle as if in agony. Beside him Lorimer heard a sniff of contempt and he turned to see one of the corporate guests shake his head wearily. It was de rigueur these days for a player to fake an injury and have his opposite number penalised if he could, and Lorimer sympathised with the man's cynicism. But, for once, this seemed to be a genuine injury as the team doctor ran on to the pitch and immediately signalled for a stretcher. The stadium lights were on now, the sky having darkened to a deep slate-grey, and thunder rumbled in the distance as the crowd waited for the game to resume.

In minutes Donnie Douglas had been stretchered off and John McKinnery was running on to the pitch, shouting out the instructions that had come from Ron Clark, but with Douglas down, the nature of the game seemed to change. Lorimer had seen it all before. The enthusiasm after being a goal up could vanish like a morning mist. Now the Kelvin players seemed incapable of keep-ing the ball at their feet; their very movements seemed sluggish, as though the oppressive atmosphere was weighing them down.

'And the opposition is coming right back into this game. That's a terrible pass by Rientjes, picked up by Dunfermline's Linley and now the Pars are on the move, deep into Kelvin's half. Ah! Davie Clark's swept right in and the whistle blows for a free kick to Dunfermline. But here's Thomson coming in to argue with the ref and – I can't quite believe what I'm seeing – Thomson has given the referee a shove that's sent him flying! Oh, no mistake now. That's a red card and Baz Thomson is running off the park amidst howls of anger from the fans. What a stupid thing to do! Just when Kelvin is ahead! Well, I'll bet Ron Clark will have some strong words to say to the striker when he comes off. But Thomson is just running down the tunnel, not looking at anyone.'

Lorimer clenched his fists. Stupid, stupid idiot! What had Thomson been playing at? Suddenly he recalled the closing game of last season. It had been the Kelvin striker's temper that had caused his team's relegation, some said. What if . . . ? Lorimer con-sidered the possibility for a moment. No, surely Thomson wouldn't deliberately throw a game. Or had he been in someone's pocket for that very reason? Like Norman Cartwright, could there be an unusually large sum of money squirrelled away in the Kelvin striker's bank account and, if so, who was behind it?

The thunder sounded again, closer this time as the clouds hung like a suffocating blanket over the football stadium. And, despite the clamminess, Lorimer felt himself shiver.

Detective Constable Niall Cameron banged his fist on to the table in frustration. Lorimer had told them to keep in radio contact and yet he wasn't responding to this call. What the heck was going on at the football stadium? He looked back at the piece of paper in his hand, a fever of excitement sweeping over him. This had to be a real breakthrough. The man had seen action in Bosnia, Northern Ireland and the first Gulf War. Who better to have experience of firearms than this? Cameron bit his lip. Lorimer had given him strict instructions to stay at HQ as their base contact, so he had to keep trying to make communication with the SIO. It was all he could do to sit still and redial Lorimer's number, when what he really wanted was to be there himself.

It was as though he were invisible. Nobody could see him because he was part of the place, expected to be there. It gave him a feeling of pride; to be such an indispensable piece of this football club and to have this power, this control. If nobody could see him what great feats might he be able to achieve today? They were all looking towards the pitch where the boys were pitting their skills against each other. He watched for a moment, stopping on the stairs next to a steward – the man's attention so totally taken up with the action that he didn't even nod in his direction. Gaffney was battling for the ball against a Pars defender. The mid-fielder suddenly took the ball away and ran with it for a couple of seconds before passing it across the pitch.

As every pair of eyes followed its progress, he slipped away, still unnoticed, and headed towards the North stand, sports bag slung over his shoulder. Inside it the take-down rifle was hard and solid like the stone steps beneath his boots.

Alistair Wilson passed the man on the steep staircase and nodded. It was fine. Everything was normal, everyone was where they ought to be.

The crackle from his earpiece made him stop suddenly.

'DS Wilson. What's up?'

'Make your way to the main entrance, please. We've appre-hended a suspect,' a disembodied voice told him. Quickening his pace, Wilson hastened down the remaining steps and headed towards the tunnel.

'Better be our man,' he muttered to himself as he entered the corridors of the club.

The place was swarming with uniformed officers when Wilson arrived and he was just in time to see a tall, burly individual being marched into a side room.

'Who is it?' he asked the nearest steward.

'Big Jock. He's Kelvin's resident daft laddie,' the man added with a grin.

'Okay, keep everyone out, will you?' Wilson ordered. His mouth twisted in a grimace of displeasure as he opened the door where moments before the man had been bundled. Big Jock had eluded them so far, though the staff here at Kelvin had assured them he'd be at the game. Was he on Lorimer's mental list of most likely suspects? They'd certainly been advised to nab him on sight, though there was not yet a shred of evidence against the well-known fan. Wilson closed the door behind him and sighed. Maybe this interview would bring the whole thing to an end. Looking at the man who sat staring at him wild-eyed and mouth open in wordless protest, the Detective Sergeant fervently hoped so.

'They've got somebody downstairs,' the voice told Lorimer.

'Right. Keep everyone on alert till half-time. I'll see you there,' he replied, one hand cupping his face so that his words were not overheard.

But Pat Kennedy had turned his way and Lorimer could see the sweat beading the big man's forehead.

Lorimer leaned across to whisper in his ear. 'It's okay. They've got hold of Big Jock. Nothing to worry about.' He met Kennedy's eyes then looked away, pretending an interest in the game that he did not feel. Keeping the chairman safe and secure was what this was all about right now and if they found anything on 'Big' Jock MacInally they could all relax and enjoy the second half.

Climbing to the very top made him feel light-headed and giddy with anticipation. Down below, the figures running about the park looked smaller. Like wee insects. *I could squash them with my thumb.* He smiled at the thought. Three down, one to go, he told himself. Then that would be his mission completed, wouldn't it?

There was only the usual duty-officer inside, staring at the CCTV cameras. The man turned to see who had entered the tiny room, his mouth open in astonishment. But before he could utter a word the rifle butt was smashed across his jaw. He hardly felt the headset being ripped from his ears as he was sent spinning on to the floor. Two more blows and the world fell away into a yawning chasm of black.

The man with the rifle closed the door behind him and slid the bolt. Stepping over the policeman's body with complete indifference, he stood at the window and gazed down on that mass of humanity below him. His eyes drifted to the director's box and, taking his binoculars out of his jacket pocket, he trained them on the rows of people until he found his quarry. Kennedy was sitting next to that detective, Lorimer. For a moment he felt a surge of excitement verging on sheer joy. Perhaps he could take him out too? Letting the glasses fall, he swiftly screwed the three pieces of rifle together with a dexterity that showed his expertise. Then he pushed the window open and held the rifle steady, peering through the sights. One shot and Kennedy would be dead. He could make his way out, leave the gun in its usual place and nobody would ever find him. Two shots and he might lose the advantage of a quick exit. But even as he sought the man wearing the black cap, the temptation to kill DCI Lorimer was growing like a cancer inside him.

'We've lost contact with the CCTV duty officer!' The words in Lorimer's ear made him look up immediately to the glass box perched high above the ranks of seats on the North stand. The open window and the figure standing there seemed to make time stop for a second.

'Get down!' he shouted at Kennedy, pushing him hard on his back then clambering over the several pairs of feet blocking his exit.

'Lorimer to armed unit. All officers to the North stand. Suspect armed,' he roared, careless now of who could hear his words. Looking up again, he saw the open window, but now there was no dark figure, no sniper's rifle pointing his way.

At that moment his radio crackled into life.

'Lorimer,' he answered shortly, his gaze remaining on that square of glass high above the rows of seating. Cameron's lilting voice came over the line, breathless with excitement. Had he been able to see the expression on his SIO's face as he told Lorimer what he had discovered, it would have given Niall Cameron a feeling of immense satisfaction.

'Where is he?' one of the men called out, rifle at the ready. But all the armed response unit could see when they burst into the room was the crumpled shape of the duty officer lying in a pool of his own blood.

Lorimer stood in the open door behind them. He was out of breath after racing up those flights of steps and could barely speak. 'Cover every exit. Don't let him get away,' he ordered, then stood aside as the officers, clad in bulletproof vests and hard helmets, clattered past him. 'Lorimer. Get a medic up here now,' he barked into his radio, staring at the man lying inside. He stepped in, and knelt by his side, feeling for a pulse. It was there, thank God.

The room was suddenly quiet, though he could still hear the crowd's noise like a susurrating wave in the distance as the Kelvin players surged forward. He looked out of the window, not towards the action on the football pitch but to where, only minutes before, he had been sitting beside Patrick Kennedy. It was a perfect angle, he thought. And only an expert marksman who knew this place inside out would have chosen it.

Lorimer nodded to himself. It had to be him. There was nobody else capable of this. Though what had motivated the killer still remained a mystery.

In front of him the bank of cameras still showed differing angles of the park. In a moment he was in the duty officer's chair, scanning each screen for any sight of the man he needed to catch. Impatiently his eyes flicked from one to the next, looking for the familiar figure among the crowded stands. Would he try to slip in with the Keelies? Probably not if he was still armed, Lorimer told himself. Though what havoc he might wreak if he was in the crowd, Lorimer shuddered to think.

Then he saw him, walking slowly along the path towards the clubhouse as though nothing had happened. Lorimer panned in on the grey figure and made the image freeze. Yes! The way he carried the sports bag made it appear weighed down by something substantial. The DCI swore under his breath. He was still armed, then. Barking orders into his radio, Lorimer didn't even give the officer on the floor a glance as he tore out of the room and sped down the stone staircase. Help was on its way, but if he didn't act soon God alone knew how many more would be dead or injured.

There was a flash then another crash of thunder and he felt the air around him tense as the first drops of warm rain began to fall.

He'd been about to pull the trigger when Lorimer had made his move and now it was all about damage limitation. If he could secrete the gun before they found him, there was nothing they could do, was there? Nobody could possibly make out who had been standing, rifle aimed at the directors' box. Not even Lorimer.

The boot room was pitch black when he unlocked the door and he didn't bother to put on the light. He could find his way around here any time, day or night. Above him the rain drummed on to the roof, washing away the months of dirt and dust. The sound made him want to give a shout of exultation. For a moment he hesitated, then, giving a swift glance towards the closed door, he reached into the bag at his feet and drew out the components of the rifle. In less than a minute he had transformed them into a lethal weapon. Reaching up, he felt the place in the wooden ceiling. A firm push and the panel gave way beneath his hands. It was his secret place, a place where he had hidden everything. Feeling in the darkness, his hand brushed the can of red paint. He'd have to shove that aside to make room for the gun . . .

'Stop right there!' A voice made Albert Little whirl around. Blocking most of the daylight was the tall figure of DCI Lorimer. Bert grinned. Well, he'd had it coming.

'Think you can take me down?' Bert sneered. 'Nae chance!'

Lorimer froze as he saw the rifle held in the groundsman's hands, pointing at his chest.

For a moment all he could think about was Maggie and how she would be all alone. He had a sudden image of her laughing, cuddling that wee ginger cat up to her face.

Then he closed his eyes and waited.

The crash of thunder and flash of lightning mingling with a blood-curdling screech made him open them again. And what he saw defied belief. Albert Little had dropped the gun and was on his knees, screaming, hands waving wildly as though someone had him by the throat.

In an instant Lorimer picked up the rifle, but in that moment he felt a wave of cold air pass him by and heard a sigh coming from somewhere deep within the shadows. Or was it the collective intake of breath from a crowd absorbed in the football match that was still going on outside?

Wee Bert was curled up on the ground, hands over his head, whimpering, repeating Ronnie Rankin's name over and over. With shaking hands, Lorimer reached for his radio and pressed the red button, too stunned to speak. Officers would be here in seconds. Then they would finally be able to make sense of the groundsman's killing spree.

Light spilled in from outside the door and the sound of rain falling on to the roof had stopped. Looking around him Lorimer could see no trace of the legendary ghost nor could he feel anything that spoke to him of a supernatural presence. He stepped backwards, still clutching the rifle, desperate for some fresh air.

'All right, sir?' The first of the armed response unit was at his side, taking the rifle from Lorimer's unresisting hands, and he could hear the sounds of boots thudding against tarmac as others came to join him. Lorimer nodded and moved out of the doorway.

There was a rainbow arcing above the stadium, bright against the summer skies. Its bow seemed to end somewhere within the green sward below. The storm had passed. Lorimer took a deep breath, thankful for this sweet moment.

But would he ever know exactly what had taken place in Kelvin's boot room? And had it only been the crazed imagination of a lunatic that had rescued Lorimer from certain death?

CHAPTER 43

Jock MacInally sat grinning at the men by his side. It had been an unbelievable day. First he'd been asked loads of questions, then they'd taken him upstairs where he'd been introduced to some of the club officials. Then, to Jock's astonishment, they'd plied him with anything he wanted to drink, brought him plates of sandwiches and sausage rolls and treated him as though he were visiting royalty. The fact that Kelvin had held the Pars at bay for the whole ninety minutes to gain a vital three points had been the icing on the cake as far as he was concerned. So he hadn't seen much of the game, but what did that matter? They'd given him a free season ticket, told him what an asset he was to Kelvin, and how he was their favourite supporter. Tomorrow the Sunday papers would be full of the stories about the capture of the 'Kelvin Killer' but Jock didn't read the papers and would spend the day regaling anyone who cared to listen with his own tale. Aye, unbelievable so it was, but Jock MacInally would milk the events of this day for all they were worth.

The stadium had cleared eventually and if there was a surfeit of yellow-jacketed men helping around the perimeter of the grounds, nobody seemed to notice. The white van with its Kevlar-clad occupants had slipped away quietly long before full-time, along with an unmarked car which had taken Kelvin's grounds-man away. The rain that had fallen steadily throughout the second half of the match was now abating, leaving muddy puddles on the pitch. A small wind had sprung up too, clearing away the thunder clouds and bringing a freshness to the air that had been missing for weeks. Paper bags and sweet wrappers blew along the empty stands, among the rows and rows of numbered seats with, here and there, a broken polystyrene cup, crushed underfoot by the departing fans.

Staring out from the mouth of the tunnel, Ron Clark heaved a sigh. How long would it be till they left this legendary place and headed up to Kennedy's new dream stadium? The chairman had also disappeared with Lorimer and his team of detectives. Well, Kennedy had some questions to answer too, questions that Ron Clark had been asking ever since his appointment as manager. He looked down as a crisp bag rustled over his feet. Automatically the Kelvin manager bent to pick it up and put it into his pocket. Wee Bert had been a stickler about litter, he thought, a faint smile appearing on his face. It was just a pity his obsessions hadn't stopped there. Ron Clark's smile faded as quickly as it had appeared and he gave a shudder as he thought about the man who had devoted so much of his life to Kelvin FC. Just what had been going on in his mind? And what had driven him to take such desperate measures?

'No, definitely not,' Bert told them firmly.

Lorimer and Alistair Wilson had been with the groundsman now for almost an hour during which time he had been answering questions that related to the shooting of Norman Cartwright, Jason White and Jimmy Greer. Like a good wee boy, Bert had put up his hand for all three of them. But when Lorimer had broached the subject of Nicko Faulkner, the erstwhile groundsman's attitude had changed.

'Nothing to do with me,' he continued with such an expression of effrontery on his face that it made Lorimer want to laugh. 'That slag of a wife did it!' he insisted. 'We'd have had a great season if Nicko had been in the team,' he grumbled.

Lorimer and Wilson exchanged glances. It was as if the man had been discussing the weather, not the killing of three innocent men. This was disquieting territory for the two detectives. In no time at all they would be handing him over to the medics and the last they'd hear of Albert Little would be when he was taken to Carstairs Mental Hospital.

'Tell me again why you killed Norman Cartwright,' Lorimer said.

Bert looked at him sharply. 'Because he was on the fiddle. No self-respecting referee would take bribes like that!' The man's indignation was almost comical.

'And who do you think was behind the bribes?'

Bert grinned and wagged a finger at Lorimer. 'Ah, you don't catch me out like that, Chief Inspector.'

'Let's put it another way, Bert, shall we? You wanted to kill Pat Kennedy today. Can you tell us just why that was?' Lorimer adopted a conversational tone to match that of the groundsman who, as Wilson had suggested to his boss, appeared to be what the boys upstairs referred to as a 'grade-A fruitcake'.

'Mr Kennedy didn't have the club's best interests at heart,' Bert said pompously.

'And you did?' suggested Lorimer.

Bert's eyebrows rose in astonishment. 'Of course! The whole club was going downhill. First he made sure that we were out of the Premier League, then he was going to sell my ground and have a supermarket built on it! He was going to make millions out of that deal. Going to build a pitch of . . .' his voice choked with emotion. 'AstroTurf!' he spat out at last.

Lorimer looked at Wilson, who shook his head and frowned.

'Ach, you don't see it, do you?' Bert continued, glaring at them from across the table. 'He had to come down to Division One, didn't he?'

'But why?' Lorimer asked. 'What was the point of deliberately trying to have his team relegated?'

'The SPL don't allow AstroTurf in their league. So he was going to sell off my ground.' The groundsman's face grew dark with anger. 'My ground!' he cried, thumping a fist on the table between them.

'But it's not your ground, Bert, is it?' Lorimer said gently.

Albert Little stared at him for a moment then his face crumpled and he began to cry like a child, noisy sobs that ended with a wail of despair.

Lorimer looked down at his notes. There was not much scribbled down as everything was recorded on tape, but he had a few memos. Jason White had been gunned down simply for being disloyal to the club and bringing it into disrepute. That was the word Bert had used. Disrepute. And Lorimer had written it down with a large question mark beside it. As if he could scarcely bring himself to believe that a man's life had been blown away for such a slight motive. Jimmy Greer had been involved with the bogus dead body in the boot room. That had been harder to winkle out of the man sitting opposite them. At each mention of the boot room he had clammed up, as if unwilling to relive any aspect of that strange place. But gradually it had all come out: how Greer had suggested the scenario with the dummy and how Bert had later written that threat on the wall with red paint. They had

326

found the paint, of course, along with a cache of firearms that had made Lorimer's eyes widen. Greer had become too close to it all in the end and Bert's only solution was his standard practice: shooting him. He'd even told them in detail how he had fired the first shot to attract the journalist's attention, held up an old hubcap to flash the sun's rays in the man's eyes, then had taken aim and shot him dead. Lorimer had seen the killer's eyes light up then, remembering how clever he'd been.

Lorimer considered his report; there was no doubt the man was psychologically disturbed and he emphasised his opinion that many more deaths would have occurred if Albert Little had not been stopped today. Looking at the man, sobbing into his hands, he wondered what Dr Brightman might have made of him. But Solly was back at the Royal Infirmary at Rosie's side. He'd put in his bit, helped them all to focus on a particular sort of killer and he would no doubt gain satisfaction from seeing his theories justified.

'DCI Lorimer terminating the interview at 6.45 p.m.,' he said aloud. And as he watched the uniformed officers lead Bert Little away to the cells, Lorimer gave a moment's thought to another prisoner. It would not be long until someone informed Janis Faulkner of today's events. And he wondered just how she would react.

CHAPTER 44

It was a typically dreich, wet Glasgow day. All morning the rain clouds had hung over the city, washing the streets into slicks of grey. Yet, to Solly, grinning out of the taxi window, it had never looked more beautiful. Behind them the gloomy chimney that towered over Glasgow Royal Infirmary had disappeared and now they could see the spires of Trinity and the University. They would soon be home. Solly turned his gaze back to Rosie; she was still pale and there were scars that needed more time to heal, but her eyes were bright and she smiled her familiar smile as she took his hand and squeezed it.

'Okay?' she asked him and Solly nodded, too full to speak. Yes, he was okay. He smiled at her word, it was a typical Scottish understatement. He was okay, fine, whatever she wanted him to be. But inside, Solomon Brightman felt like a king.

Maggie Lorimer pulled off her raincoat and rushed to the telephone before it could stop ringing. Maybe it was Solly to tell her that Rosie was safely back home. But it was an unfamiliar voice that met her ears, a stranger who was suddenly asking questions about a little ginger cat.

*

As she slumped down on to a kitchen chair, Chancer came and rubbed himself against her leg. A lump formed in Maggie's throat as she scooped him up and held him to her cheek. Hearing him purr like that was so hard to bear. A few more hours and the house would be silent again, bereft of this little animal that had come into her life and wound his way around her heart. The man on the phone had sounded a decent sort. Well spoken and matter-of-fact about it all. He'd explained how he and his wife had been caring for the cat – whose real name was Monty – while his elderly mother had taken an extended holiday to New Zealand. They'd only had her pet for two days when he had disappeared. Maggie looked at the address the man had given. It was a fair distance away but not too far for a cat who might be trying to find its way home. Could it be that Chancer was really Monty?

With trembling hands, Maggie laid down her notepad. Was it a coincidence that this call had come on the very day that Rosie was released from hospital? She looked out of the window at the rain lashing down from a leaden sky. Had God heard her plea, and was she being asked to sacrifice something dear to her because of the pact that she had made? It wasn't something she did often, and she was assailed by a pang of guilt as she dialled his mobile number, but at that moment Maggie had an overwhelming need for her husband.

Lorimer sat staring out at the rain-washed car park below his office. On his desk there were matters pertaining to serious crimes and he had several important reports to finish before he could head for home. But he needed a moment to think about Maggie and how she must be feeling. Her voice had sounded so desperately unhappy even though she was trying to be brave. Funny how a wee thing like a stray cat could turn your world upside down. If Chancer was gone then he'd find her a wee kitten that needed a good home, he decided. It was the least he could do. His hand reached for the documents in front of him. Matters of life and death were what he dealt with every day but he could empathise with Maggie's loss just as much as he could with the terrible, wrenching grief of the men and women whose loved ones had been torn away by one man's madness.

Albert Little had been committed to an asylum for the mentally insane. Background reports suggested that he might have been suffering from Gulf War syndrome but this had not tallied with his years of capable – nay, outstanding – service to Kelvin FC, Solly had insisted when they'd discussed the man's behaviour. Even Post-Traumatic Stress Disorder was out of the question in someone who had been capable of holding down a demanding full-time job, the psychologist had told Lorimer. If Solly had been able to follow through with this case could he have given them the clues that would have led to apprehending their killer sooner? The question was academic now, but Lorimer found himself wondering at the quirks of fate that had dogged this case, and realised just how much he had missed the psychologist's profiling techniques. This had become another tool for Lorimer over the years, one that he had learned to value.

The veritable arsenal of weapons hidden inside the boot room ceiling – hand guns and rifles, even a Kalashnikov – must have been picked up by Bert during the Bosnian conflict. The ex-army man had left a trail of devastation behind him. Not only were there entire families left bewildered by the man's killing spree, but the football club that he had lived for was now in serious trouble.

Just this week, the administrators had been called in following Barbara Kennedy's decision to sell her shares in the club. She'd make a pretty profit, contrary to the plan that her husband had envisaged. Kennedy had wanted to bring down the club and sell off the place, then buy back the shares for a rock-bottom price. He'd thought everything had been within his control, quite unaware that Wee Bert had discovered some of his schemes. Now the chairman was on bail pending a date on which he would be called for trial. Albert Little's statement had opened up a whole can of worms that included bribery and fraud on a massive scale. Norman Cartwright was not the only person who had been caught up in Kennedy's wheeling and dealing. Baz Thomson's bank accounts also showed discrepancies that had made the striker an integral part of this inquiry. He'd led Weir a merry dance, feigning ignorance of his finances and lying about his accountant being away on holiday. Lorimer had sympathised with their new DC; Weir had taken the matter personally, feeling he should have sussed out the Kelvin player. Only Ron Clark appeared untouched by the scandal. The manager had appeared on television several times stating his belief that Kelvin could again rise from the ashes of its present disgrace. The boys were all behind him, he had claimed, and they were hopeful of fulfilling all of the remaining fixtures of the season, though that was still a decision in the hands of their administrator. Lorimer had watched every news item that related to the football club. A special fund-raising drive had begun, led by Big Jock MacInally, and banners proclaiming 'Save the Keelies' were being unfurled at every match. Whether the club had a future in Scottish football remained to be seen.

A sudden draught blew across his desk, rustling the papers. For a moment Lorimer remembered that small, cold wind that had passed him by as he'd lifted the rifle away from the hands of the man who had tried to kill him. Could a hardened cop like himself ever believe that the spirit of a long-dead footballer had really intervened that day? He shook his head. But maybe the legend of Ronnie Rankin would be powerful enough to save his beloved club from a different sort of destruction.

It was late when Lorimer reached home. The rain had stopped and the grey clouds were scudding across the horizon, bringing a freshening wind whistling through the treetops. Summer was almost over and soon the trees would be turning yellow. But there would be no wee ginger cat to play among the fallen leaves.

'Hi,' he called out, ready to have Maggie throw herself into his arms in a storm of weeping. But when he walked into the kitchen Lorimer was met by the last thing he expected to see.

'He's still here?' he asked, looking down at Chancer, who was busy washing his paws, then at Maggie who was looking smug.

'Yes, and he's ours!' And now she really was in his arms and he was kissing her face, her lips and she was laughing and crying at once.

'His owner's going into a retirement home. Can't take pets,' she burbled between happy kisses. 'And we were asked if we wanted to keep him!'

Lorimer held her tightly, feeling her warmth, sharing in her sheer joy. Then he felt a familiar tap against his trouser leg and he looked down and laughed.

It was Chancer. And their little ginger cat was looking up at them both with an expression on his face that could only be described as a grin.

EPILOGUE

When she opened her eyes it was pitch black. Tonight there would be no moonlight to shine through the thin curtains of her cell. After all these weeks of light-blue skies and rosy sunsets, the nights had become dark and full of shadows. Outside she could hear the wind as it blew a scattering of leaves across the courtyard. Tomorrow might bring more rain and she'd have to wear a warmer jacket.

Janis lay back, staring into the darkness. It would all be over soon. Marion Peters had briefed her well on what to expect. They'd changed her plea to 'guilty' so the odds were that she might be out of there within five years, probably a lot less if tomorrow's judge looked on her case with a modicum of sympathy.

It was strange how she felt a sense of peace now that it was almost over. The weeks of denial had made her tense and brittle, but she had begun to feel a sense of rousing from a bad dream in the wake of Albert Little's confession. How could she have hoped for someone to get away with these murders? That fact alone had given her a gnawing sense of guilt. In retrospect, it hadn't been very likely but so long as the killer was on the loose there would be a doubt in people's minds about Nicko's death, and Janis Faulkner could continue to hope for a full acquittal.

In the end it had been a relief to tell them the truth. At first she had hesitated then it had all come out in a rush, every last detail. How she'd pulled that kitchen knife out and lunged at her husband as he'd come at her again; how she had washed away every trace and thrown her blood-stained clothing into the dark waters of Loch Lomond. She'd told them every bit about that night and about the day that had followed, even about her efforts to find sanctuary in Mull with her grandfather, Lachie.

But she didn't quite tell them everything. Not about the continual nightmares, when he came after her. Nor about his eyes and his laughter mocking her or how she'd woken up sweating and trembling night after night. Once she'd almost told that tall policeman, the one with eyes that reminded her of Grandpa Lachie. But she'd persisted with the lie, telling herself that she'd been punished enough already, protesting her innocence to anyone who would listen, even that journalist Greer. And maybe the judge would agree. Maybe tomorrow would bring some sort of future that was untainted with the memory of Nicko's vicious hands and his voice that had disturbed her sleep for so long now.

It was not yet tomorrow, Janis told herself as she closed her eyes against the darkness. Tomorrow was a new day and might bring a new hope.

She turned on her side, heaved a deep sigh and fell into a dreamless sleep.

ACKNOWLEDGEMENTS

I would like to thank the following people for their help and encouragement.

Dr Marjorie Black for her expertise in forensic pathology; Alistair Paton for his breathtaking knowledge of all things ballistic; Alistair McLachlan, Bryan McAusland, Tommy Docherty, Bob Money of St Mirren FC and Alex Totten of Falkirk FC; Sue Brooks, former Governor of HMI Cornton Vale women's prison, and educational staff Alan Hamilton and Kaye Stewart as well as the prison officers and inmates; Deputy Divisional Commander Brian Lennox and Detective Sergeant Bob Frew of Strathclyde Police; my lovely agent Jenny Brown for her constant support and encouragement, David Shelley and Caroline Hogg my brilliant editors and everyone at Little, Brown for their help and enthusiasm and last, but not least, all those men in strips who put football fans on an emotional rollercoaster for ninety minutes every weekend.